Dear Sir,

You shall taste

my Blistering

FURY.

Dear Sir,
You Shall Taste My
Blistering
Fury

by
Hezekiah Bennetts

(and his idiot brother)

Find Hezekiah online at:
hezekiahbennetts.com
facebook.com/filmhez
youtube.com/hrothmeir

Cover design by Hezekiah Bennetts
Cover art by Hezekiah Bennetts and Felicity Hull

For Dad.
Your departure brought us back together.
I like to think you'd like who I've become.

***

To brotherly love and stupid ideas.

CHAPTER 1
HELL OF A WAY TO START THE DAY

My feet had just stepped onto the grounds of Kelso Amboy Memorial High School when I heard a voice calling my name over the background hubbub of milling students. "Jo! Joanna!" I lurched around, looking for the source; it being Monday morning, my mind wasn't completely up to speed, despite the several-miles walk from home.

The call came again, and I zeroed in on the source: my best friend Agnes, stepping out of her mom's car at the drop off drive thru. She waved at me like a madwoman, matching her outfit of a madwoman: dark faux-leather, layered with incongruous splashes of bright girly color. It was all very Punk, which was good, as that's what her and her erstwhile garage band aspired to be. I returned her wave, then arrested my walk as I awaited her arrival.

I took this respite to glance around the schoolyard and see what my peers were up to. There was a commotion by the school announcement sign; a crowd of students had gathered around the sign and focused their attention at the base. This intense interest piqued my curiosity, so I took a few steps closer to see what the kerfuffle was about.

A steep-banked creek cut through the school's grounds, separating me from the sign. On the opposite bank, where the tree-covered lawn became a schoolyard proper, dozens of half-awake students were engaged in some kind of spirit event. There were cheerleaders dispersed through the crowd, waving pom-poms and leading the gathered throng in the stomping of feet and chanting of chants. Beneath the school sign, two older students capered about, doing just as much as the cheerleaders to whip the crowd into a frenzy.

These two were Cal and Hez, a pair of second-year seniors who didn't so much attend classes at Kelso Amboy as live at the school. Visually, the two were complete opposites. Hez was short, fat, and hairy, while Cal was tall... fat, and hairy. Okay, they were identical, distinguished only by four inches plus or minus on the average height curve. This morning, they were dancing on the concrete base of the sign, wielding posterboards emblazoned with "The End Is Near!" in neon lettering. Hez waved back and forth, yipping and ululating, while Cal bounced up and down in front of the gathered students, leading the first few ranks in a chant of "Four more weeks! Four more weeks!" As the chant spread, I half-heartedly joined in.

Once the chant was self-sustaining, Cal leaped and grabbed onto one of the sign's support beams. "Yes, folks," he crowed, letting go with one hand to make sweeping gestures, "The end is near indeed! Four more weeks is all we have until the Great Amboy Jamboree! Those elect among you have already taken the steps to secure your place in the world to come! But those who tarry, and you, Teri, and those who have waited until darkness falls fear not! Tickets are still available, booths are still open, space remains for all who repent!"

The crowd cheered at this pronouncement.

"And who pay $49.95 for an exhibition booth, or $10.95 for general admission."

There was another cheer, more subdued this time.

Cal let go the beam and dropped back to the base as Hez abandoned his sign. Both fanned out sheaves of fliers to the gathered students.

Speculation had raged on-and-off for the past three years, passed on to my class when we moved up from junior high: just what was up with these two? Though no one saw them in class, they were always the center of attention when it came to pimping out the school via shows like this. Hell, they performed the morning announcements. The going theory as to the source of their influence was that they were the illegitimate children of our assistant principal. While that provided an explanation for their *carte blanche,* it did fail to consider that Kelso Amboy was a memorial high school, not a feudal estate. Another theory was that Cal and Hez simply volunteered for any responsibilities they carried out. No one knew for certain, however, and the consensus was that their origins would remain a mystery...

"Jeez, you'd think they'd realize by now: no one wants to go to this stupid thing."

I flinched away from the grating voice in my ear; Agnes had managed to sneak up on me, standing just uphill from my perch at the edge of the creek embankment.

"Hey, Aggie." I pitched my voice over the roar of the gathered crowd. "What's up with you this fine morning?" The question wasn't mere small talk; I didn't often see her before noon. Besides Agnes getting a ride to school, I usually made my morning hike accompanied by my second-best friend and Freshman lab partner, Edgar. We normally met up as he passed my house on his own school-bound hike, but he was currently on a late bus back from the state capitol for a marching band event. Despite their shared musical pursuits, Edgar and Agnes just didn't get along. Oh, I had forced the issue many a time, but after one birthday party too many ended in tears, I had relented and let them stay segregated. Edgar got custody of me to and from school, while Agnes got me evenings and alternating weekends.

Agnes studied her nails as she answered my question. "Oh, nothing much. Biscuit Filth was supposed to perform a charity gig at the Catholic church, but everyone bailed on me. The hardest part of running a Punk band is that everyone in it is a bunch of punks."

That certainly told me what her weekend had been like, but the bland answer seemed at odds with the excitement she had shown while getting out of the car.

"And..." she ventured, "there is something else I want to talk to

9

you about. It's kind of important." A mischievous grin flitted across her face.

Before I could prod her for more details, there came a tremendous crash from behind me. I flinched, but persevered in conversing. "Oh, yeah? Do tell."

"Do you have any plans for this summer?" Agnes asked. Her laconic affect was gone, and she now positively vibrated with excited energy.

Screams of terror exploded from the direction of the sign. I pivoted away from Agnes, fighting for balance on the uneven creek embankment, and beheld the chaos that had consumed the crowd of chanting students.

"If you *do* have plans," Agnes continued, "cancel them now. *Because I got tickets to Bluker's Creek*!"

I failed to react to what Agnes had said. Perhaps it was the spectacle of Cal crowd surfing on the cheerleader squad. Perhaps it was because Hez's pants had caught fire, and a dozen students were beating him, trying to smother the flames.

"Jo?" Agnes prompted.

The cheerleaders beneath Cal bucked, tossing him into the air. He soared for a good ten feet before coming down atop Hez, quenching the fire. The crowd roared in approval.

"Hello, Earth to Joanna. You in there?"

"Huh?" I looked back up the slope at Agnes. She bounced on the balls of her feet, trembling hands clutched in front of her, eyes wide with excitement barely contained behind her thick glasses. On the whole she was, dare I say it, giddy as a school girl.

"Bluker's Creek!" she repeated, her voice eking out through her vocal cords like a balloon losing the last bit of its helium. "This July, in Chicago! *The* biggest concert of the summer!"

Her enthusiasm kick-started an adrenaline reaction inside my own body. As I comprehended the content of her message, I may have screamed. Scratch that, I *did* scream, though I couldn't compete with the cacophony coming from the sign. Logically, Agnes' pronouncement should have elicited a negative reaction. Here it was, mid-March, and my best friend already had plans for the summer, plans that would eat up at least a week of our precious non-school time. Yet I couldn't help but be excited in the face of Agnes' excitement. Bluker's Creek was, for a fleeting instant, *the* band. According to my mother, every generation had *the* band, one group that managed to shoot to the top of the charts for a few months before disappearing forever. For my mother, *the* band was The Gud-tym Gyz, a generic, poppy boy-band with a hint of Reggae overtones. For my particular blip on the demographic spectrum of "teenage girl," *the* band was Bluker's Creek, a generic, poppy boy-band with a hint of Country overtones. And Agnes was fortunate enough to get tickets...

In that moment, I hated her.

"Oh, my God, Aggie, that's amazing! You're *so* lucky."

Against all basic biology, Agnes' eyes managed to grow even wider, threatening to burst from their sockets. Fortunately, her glasses stood between them and me, so I would be safe from jetting juices. "No, Jo, *tickets*. Sss. Plural. My parents got enough for me to take a friend."

I clamped shut my mouth, lest I jinx what was surely to come, and live out my summer in abject loneliness.

"You're coming with me!"

The flames and chaos roiling behind me were thrust from my mind, forgotten along with the Gud-tym Gyz in the annals of popular memory. I lunged forward and grasped Agnes' hands, entwining her fingers in my own as we jumped and spun. My summer was set: Bluker's Creek, this July, in Chicago. I could die happy.

We made it three rotations before Agnes' heavy boots caught in an arched root, and both of us went tumbling down to the creek. End over end we fell before jarring to a stop at the bottom of the ravine, our feet resting in ankle-deep water.

I checked over my body, taking stock that nothing warm and sticky leaked from my skin. Nothing did, though my jeans were coated in thin mud, and one sleeve of my turtleneck had ripped.

Next I checked over Agnes. Her hair stuck up around her scratched face, clotted with mud and twigs. Her glasses were nowhere to be seen.

"Hell of a way to start the day," I said.

11

"Amen," answered a deeper voice from across the creek. Hez sat in the middle of the creek bed, the water up to his waist and his pants steaming. Behind him, Cal crouched just out of the water, stacking stones into a primitive dam along the creek's edge.

"We, uh," I began, my vision twitching as my fall-addled brain ran to catch up with my unmoving body. "We should probably get to class."

"Amen," answered Agnes, her voice unsteady.

Turning our back on the creek, we began our laborious climb back up the embankment, going slow to avoid accidentally crushing Agnes' glasses.

CHAPTER 2
SCIENCE--A MOST DISAPPOINTING EXPERIMENT

My first instinct had been to go to the restroom and use an entire forest's worth of paper towels to daub myself clean. Something in me disparaged the idea, though, and so I let the mud remain. In the end, this was the right choice. The mud, already more a solid than a liquid as it came from the higher portions of the embankment, dried quickly and flaked off my clothes. By the time I changed back following third-period gym, all it took was a whip-crack shake of my garments to coat the dressing room in a layer of fine dun dust.

The fact that Clarice, the head cheerleader, happened to be plunged into a fit of coughing and sneezes as I cleansed my clothes, was a happy coincidence. I was nerd-girl getting revenge on the cheerleader elite. Score one for the downtrodden.

It was with clean clothes and a glad heart that I continued onto the last pre-lunch class of the day: Freshman Science. As with my other classes this year--Freshman Math, Freshman Literature, Freshman History--this would be my final science class that not only had the word "Science" in the name, but also taught a generalized overview of the subject at hand. Next year, I would be moving on to bigger, more specific studies: Geometry, Modern Classics, American History, Biology. And while Freshman Science was taught in a downright obtuse manner, I savored the knowledge that I was being taught a subject which I fully understood and might actually apply to life outside these hallowed halls.

Inside the science room, things were as they always were in the minutes before our instructor arrived. The slackers sat in the back of the room, cracking jokes and passing time. Two cheerleaders were practicing a routine near the teacher's desk, oblivious to the bottles of carcinogenic chemicals within reach of their whipping ponytails. And at the lab bench where I sat was--no one. I pumped my fist in the air; everything was going my way today. The innermost stool, warmed by a beam of light from the window, stood open, un-sat-in by my erstwhile lab partner, Edgar.

As I bent to place my book bag beneath the seat claimed by Edgar whenever he arrived from his class across the hall, I sensed a presence behind me. Straightening, I whirled on my interloper, afraid it may be Edgar, returned to reclaim his usual spot.

Instead, I found the perfect, clear-faced blondness of Clarice, dressed in her navy-and-gold cheer skirt. "Um, Joanna, do you think you could possibly, please, just be a little more aware of your surroundings before shaking dust off your clothes?" she asked in an affected Valley Girl accent, though we lived thousands of miles from the Valley, and California, and that entire side of the nation.

"Yeah, sure, whatever," I replied. Why was she hassling me like this? So the flapping of my clothes in her general direction had caused her a bit of discomfort; the flapping of *her* clothes in *my* general direction had caused me discomfort all year.

"Thank you *so* much for considering the matter," she said with mock sincerity, before joining her fellow cheerleaders for a few more minutes of inappropriately placed practice.

I returned to arranging my bag, and was just easing onto the coveted window-stool when a voice called out, "Don't even think about sitting there."

I winced, my thighs already pressed against the sun-warmed faux-leather, and grudgingly stepped away from the magical stool. Slipping my foot inside the strap of my book bag, I dragged my supplies with me as I slunk the few feet to my usual abode.

There was a ruffling and a shuffling and a desperate wheeze for

14

breath as Edgar edged in behind me. His narrow face and shoulder-length black hair dripped with sweat, and his sunken eyes were lost behind the swollen lids of an insomniac.

"Dear God, Ed, what side of hell did you crawl from this morning?"

"I, uh, I just woke up when the bus got back." He upended his backpack, raining down splintered pencils and crinkled loose-leaf paper over the lab bench.

"I had kind of hoped you wouldn't make it back before lunch."

"Yeah, well, the marching band director didn't want to stay in Columbus any longer than necessary."

"I take it things didn't turn out well."

"We lost." He folded his arms across the bench top and flopped his head down over them. "Those bastards at Zwick Technical Academy beat us again, just like they do every year."

I didn't point out that this was Edgar's first year with the marching band, and thus Zwick had not in fact beaten him like they do every year.

"I just don't know how. Their marching was mediocre at best, but their music, dear God, their music. It was like an angel choir. It's a wonder none of their students had recording contracts already."

I patted Edgar on the shoulder, doing my best to minimize our actual touching. The level of sweat oozing from his body implied that the bus had pulled up mere minutes before.

Edgar slumped and began a subdued snoring, his back relaxing and his body spreading amoeba-like across the top of the bench.

It was then that our much loved and utterly whimsical teacher, Mrs. Yogmier, flounced into the room, her long, tight curls bouncing like springs and her tie-died floor-length dress swirling around her ankles. Though not much older than forty, she had the "cool old lady" vibe nailed, complete with flower-patterned shawl and bifocals hung on a chain around her neck. In another class--*any* other class--this ensemble and her quirky attitude would have made her an instant favorite. Unfortunately, her loose, flowing clothes rather undermined her speeches about lab safety and made her, in my considered opinion, a hypocrite. Perhaps that's why I phased out whenever she spoke for extended periods...

"Good morning class!" she crooned once she had reached her desk.

"Good morning, Mrs. Yogmier," we responded as one. Nearly one; Edgar was still sleeping by my side.

"Please, call me The Yog," she demurred.

We did. We *always* called her The Yog, the exception being this brief morning ritual of calling her by her full name. As with many of our school traditions, no one quite knew why.

"Before we begin," The Yog began, "I'd just like to remind you all of the impending Jamboree. I've been instructed to inform you that it's not too late to purchase tickets, and that admission is not limited to Kelso Amboy staff and students. Bring your parents. Bring your friends. Bring your older siblings, your younger siblings, even outside students. We need the revenue, people!" She smiled, tilting her head and bundling deeper into her shawl. "But above all, remember that there will be a science fair running concurrently with the bake sale."

As almost one, the class perked up at the words "bake sale."

"Not many of you have signed up for the science fair, and I'd like to encourage each and every one of you to step up and enter a project. The winning team gets not only a trophy, but their picture featured on the school blog."

As almost one, the class slumped back in its seats; with no further information on homemade goodies, there was no further reason to visibly pay attention. I went a bit overboard in slumping; I almost fell from my stool. It was only through a grab onto Edgar's soaking shirt that I arrested my fall. The shirt grab jerked his collar up into Edgar's throat, rocketing him awake. He peeled off the table, eyes becoming visible as they widened in alarm.

At the front of the room--possibly the back, as it was farthest away from the door--The Yog noticed Edgar's break into consciousness and turned her smile upon him. "Ah, Mr. Latterndale; so glad you could finally join us. Tell me, how fared the Kelso Amboy Potoos this weekend?"

"Second place," Edgar said on the tail end of a weary sigh. "Beaten out once again by Zwick Technical."

"Those bastards!" The Yog punched her open palm and adopted a look of outrage for an instant before returning to her usual subdued demeanor. "I believe that concludes the announcement portion of our lesson; now we begin the lesson portion of our lesson. Book time!"

As one--truly one now, with Edgar tuned in--the class groaned.

"Please turn with me to page four hundred and twenty, as we begin our study on pharmacology and how chemicals affect the human body."

The sound of thirty hands rifling through thirty books filled the room, sounding like a roost of pigeons bursting into flight, though with considerably less guano. Once the sound died away, The Yog began elucidating on the points spelled out so succinctly in the books. It was interesting material, to be sure, and I swear to God I started out following along, but before five minutes had passed, I was engrossed in doodling on my notepad. And though the space-out seemed to last only a few minutes, when I came out of my daze and looked up at the class clock, forty minutes had slipped away. I had missed everything The Yog said. I refocused, determined to catch the last of the lesson.

"--be on the test. Probably a good quarter of the overall content, so God help you if you weren't paying attention today."

As was often the case, The Yog's words reassured me and filled my heart with joy.

"Now, one last thing before the bell rings and you all go scurrying off to lunch," she said. "I've got last week's test graded and ready to pass back, along with your semester grade thus far."

As one, the class groaned, though my groan was half-hearted: I had a pretty good idea that I had done well on this test.

"Ah, come on, it's not that bad," The Yog said with the hint of a pout. "Grades were up across the board. More than half of you got perfect scores, and almost everyone's riding A's or B's."

Now there was excited chattering, students postulating that they had been among that more than half who aced the test. The Yog made her way down the aisle between the lab benches, passing out the tests. The chatter grew more excited in her wake as those up front discovered just how well they had done.

As The Yog approached my bench, I held out my hand, eager and confident. She leaned across me, however, and slid Edgar's paper face-down across the bench top before turning towards me, her face a mask of solemnity. Without comment, she laid my test face-down upon the table; I didn't need to see the circled number at the top of the page to know the score would be abysmal. The Yog graced me with a lingering look of dismay and returned to disseminating papers to the rest of the class. My hand was still outstretched, waiting for the test to be placed within; I lowered the offending limb.

"Alright!" Edgar enthused from beside me. "Perfect score. And I didn't even study for this one."

I flipped my paper over. At first, I mistook the circle of red ink in the header as a bold rendition of the letter "O." Upon further inspection, the "O" resolved itself into a zero, the numeric grade, circled in a hasty loop. Next to the grade was the semester score-- 29%--and a note: "See me after class." I gulped.

"What'd you get, Jo?" Edgar asked, failing to detect the stink of fear I exuded.

"I--" I should tell him, shouldn't I? If I passed the result off as a better grade, my crumpling the test into a ball and sitting on it until class ended would put the lie to my words.

"Didn't do good, huh?"

"*Well*, Ed, I didn't do *well*."

"That's great, but this is Science, not English, so how'd you do?"

I crumpled the test into a ball and threw it at him. It stuck to his hair for a moment before tumbling onto the bench. He uncrumpled the page. "Wow, you really bombed it, didn't you?"

I sobbed, once, high-pitched and almost laugh like, and flopped forward onto the bench.

"I mean, a bad grade is one thing, but you've really got to *try* for a zero."

Though I'm sure he thought differently, Ed's commentary wasn't helping me feel any better.

"*And* you're failing the class. Damn."

I wracked my brain to figure out why--*how*--I had gotten a solid "F" in science. There were the lab reports from the first six weeks of class; I was still coming down off winter break, and might have forgotten to do them. Then there was the frog dissection; yes there was a virtual alternative, but the school's network had been down that day, and I had forgotten to do it that weekend... The more I thought about it, the more I realized the assignments I had forgotten outweighed those I had remembered to do.

The bell rang, and I slid from the stool as the room exploded with the sounds of thirty bored teenagers desperate to for lunch.

"What do you think she's going to talk to you about?" Edgar asked as he shoveled stationary into his backpack.

I rolled my eyes and shook my head, sprinkling dried mud from the ends of my hair. "Gee, Ed, maybe the fact that I'm failing?"

"Well, yeah, obviously. I mean, like, specifically. Maybe she'll give you some kind of ultimatum involving summer school."

I retorted with a derisive laugh. Agnes would have been proud at the speed with which I plastered a sneer across my face.

Edgar answered with a mock salute. "Have fun with The Yog," he said as he slunk off to lunch.

Heading to the front--back?--place where The Yog sat, I fought my way through the steady stream of lunch-bound students, flailing like a salmon swimming upstream to breed and--more accurately for the metaphor--to die. Clarice laughed as she passed me, and I spared her a death glare before breaking free of my classmates and stopping before the altar of the Almighty Yog. "You wanted to talk, Mrs. Yogmier?" I asked, bulging my puppy-dog eyes in an effort to elicit illicit sympathy.

She smiled, her thin glasses riding up her face to disappear in her tangle of frizzy hair. "Please, Ms. Matheson, call me The Yog. It sounds so much cooler."

I wanted to snap that she should call me Joanna, or Jo, or anything other than a formal last name, but I held back any retorts that might further damage my standing in her eyes.

"I hate to say it, Ms. Matheson, but you're cruising with an 'F'. Even if you pass everything from here to the final with a perfect score, you'll be just short of a 'D'." She leaned forward and flashed me a conspiratorial grin. "And let's be honest here: that's not going to happen. You got a zero on this test. You've got to outright *try* for a zero. In other words, it looks like you'll be repeating this course in summer school."

My stomach lurched, and I felt as though I were rolling down a steep embankment for the second time that day. Summer school was bad at the best of times; this summer, out of all my summers past and all my summers yet to come, *could not* have school in it.

"Isn't there another way?!" I blurted, squelching my face into as cute an expression as I could muster, hoping I had gone up to wounded Chihuahua, but not past it to Shar-pei. "Can't you hold me back, repeat this year all over again?"

She shook her head. "This isn't kindergarten; you don't repeat a year all-or-nothing. You have individual classes, and you failed one. To keep your graduation on track, you'll need to repeat it this summer." She paused, building the suspense. "Unless..."

My stomach lurched again, and I clung to that "unless." "Unless?"

"Unless you enter the science fair."

I blinked at the statement and stepped back a pace from the desk.

"Look, I don't usually give extra credit for this kind of thing, but I'm willing to make an exception for you. Your work, when you bother to do it, *is* good, this last test aside. I spoke with your other teachers, and they all agree: you're a smart kid, and you know your stuff. In this class, you just aren't making an effort. So, should you make an effort with the science fair, show off what you've learned this semester, *and* get better-than-average scores on the remainder of the course work, I'll bump you up to a 'D', and you can pass." She leaned back in her chair, the ancient coils squeaking, and a curl dropped down into her eye. She puffed her cheeks and blew it away. "Deal?"

Practical projects aren't my forte. That I hadn't already signed up for the science fair with its promise of a trophy and middling nerd-fame spoke to my all-consuming interest in participating. Still, Bluker's Creek was on the line, and Agnes would never forgive me if I didn't put forth every effort to go. Worse yet, I would never forgive myself. "Deal." I stuck out my hand as I had done when The Yog was passing back the tests.

And as she had done when passing back the tests, The Yog ignored my hand. Instead, she hunched over her desk and rifled through a collection of hand-written notes. "You will of course need a partner for this..." she said.

Damn it! More so than practical projects, group projects existed in a realm outside of my area of expertise. Why couldn't teachers just leave me alone to sink or swim on the merits of my own work? I was about to voice this opinion when I remembered that I was already sinking on my own merits. If I ever hoped to swim--specifically in the cool refreshing waters of Bluker's Creek--I would need a lifeguard to carry me back to shore. And someone from the English department to tell me when I was taking metaphors too far. As it happened, though, I knew the perfect person to work with me on this project.

CHAPTER 3
SHE BLINDSIDED ME WITH SCIENCE

I found Edgar outside when I exited the building at the end of the day. He stood at the edge of the driveway, glaring enviously at the cars speeding by. I sent some envious glares of my own-- one more year, and I too would enter the glorious ranks of those who terrorized the front drive--then descended the stairs, two at a time, plunging headlong towards Edgar. I body checked him, running at full tilt, my slim frame bouncing off his slightly bulkier form. I imparted enough momentum that he stumbled forward, one foot coming close to slipping off the curb.

"Ow," he said, rubbing at the spot on his rib cage I had rammed.

Reaching into my repertoire of expressions, I pulled out the sneer used to such great effect earlier in the day. "Oh please, that didn't hurt."

Edgar noted the positioning of his foremost foot and shuffled back onto the sidewalk. "No, but you could have run me into a car."

"Oh, like that would have hurt."

To illustrate my point, a BMW with a vanity plate reading "ROJI V" went screaming past, doing fifty in a fifteen.

"So what did the Yog want to talk with you about back there?" Edgar asked.

I stepped off the curb and began to cross the driveway. "Come, walk and talk."

Edgar did as asked; he lived a scant few blocks past my house. As he stepped off the curb after me, there was a honk and the screech of tires.

I explained that Agnes had gotten me tickets to the Creek, appropriately enough, while we were crossing the creek. Edgar had some choice words to deliver about my summer plans. "Bluker's Creek? Really? Isn't there a more worthwhile concert you could go to? Like... I don't know, two toddlers and a frying pan?"

"Please. Like you wouldn't go to an amazing concert given the chance?"

"An amazing concert, sure, but not this crap. I'd rather live through a nuclear apocalypse than go to Bluker's Creek."

"Well, you're not going; I am."

"Thank God."

Leaving the schoolyard, we entered the endless tangle of suburbia between school and home. "Can I finish now?"

I told him about the doom The Yog had placed over my head, the great threat to my perfect summer. I then laid out the salvation the Yog had so graciously extended unto me. Then I took the final plunge, hoping to sell Edgar on giving up his free time for the next few weeks so I could abandon him this summer and enjoy his least favorite band with his least favorite person.

"...so, I don't really have a choice but to do it," I said, finishing the backstory and winding up for the pitch. "Unfortunately, it has to be a group project, so I need a partner...?" I added a piteous whine at the end of the sentence, angling to make him feel guilty for entertaining the possibility of saying "no."

He sighed, stretching out a single lungful to express volumes of long-suffering annoyance and disdain. It wasn't a disgusted sigh though; it went on far too long for that. It was a sigh of defeat, the last sound a dying animal makes as it collapses, utterly exhausted, at the hunter's feet.

Still, I retained a modicum of doubt, in case Edgar got a second wind, or a scavenger swooped in and took my kill, or I carried the hunted animal metaphor too far. I pressed in harder, determined to trap Edgar beyond any hope of escape.

"Pwease, Edgaw," I said, bulging my puppy-dog eyes and jutting my lower lip in a glorious pout. "Pwease, wiw you go to da science faiw wiff me?" I fluttered my eyelids: blink blink, blink blink.

Edgar closed his eyes--he seemed to close his whole face, drawing a blind that shut out the world--and produced another long-suffering sigh, bordering on a groan. "You'll just keep nagging me until I say 'yes,' won't you?"

"Until your death and beyond, even if you live for three hundred years."

"Eh... You have to do the actual work on this thing though, alright? And don't expect me to put any money towards this thing. I'm already out of pocket for my uniform and the Columbus trip."

I nodded vigorously, not caring about the restrictions he placed upon our working relationship; I was simply overjoyed that he had taken up my burden and freed me to have a kick-ass summer.

"Any ideas for what you want the project to be on?"

My feet stuttered on the strip of grass running beside the uncurbed road. Seconds into the science fair, and Edgar had already put more thought into the project than I had. "No idea. I can ask my mom; I'm sure she'll have some ideas."

Edgar diverted what was no doubt a nasty chuckle into a snort. "Isn't it ironic that a virologist's daughter is failing science class?"

"It's like rain on your wedding day."

Now it was his turn to stutter on the grass. "I thought it was just Science you were failing."

I took a swing at his arm; my fist connected with a solid thump. "It was a quotation, dammit." I don't think he heard me. He was too busy alternating a hearty laugh with a hiss of pain as he rubbed his arm.

We walked along in silence for some ways before Edgar said, "You know, I think I've got a damn fine idea for what the project should be." He rubbed his chin as he spoke, as though he had a beard to stroke.

"Shoot."

"Okay, so we go to the pet store, right?" He was excited for this idea, whatever it was; he walked faster, his voice pitching up to combat the traffic that wouldn't be there for another hour or so. Holding his hands before him, outlining the shape of an imaginary box, he continued, "We get us some of those feeder mice--they're cheap--and we test the effectiveness of different rat poisons on them."

The compassionate, humane person buried beneath my prickly exterior met up with the rational person who abhors touching dead rodents, sat down for coffee, chatted amicably for a few minutes, and borrowed my face to deliver a withering death glare to Edgar.

The practical person who, at age eight had gone at one of my loose teeth with a flathead screwdriver, frowned in admiration and nodded her head. My family had suffered a rodent problem in our attic for about six months now, and not even professional extermination helped. Edgar and I could start over, build a better mousetrap as it were, and purge my house once and for all. Unfortunately, the practical person had failed to stay current on her expression payments, and was unable to convince compassionate humaneness and rationality to give her a few minutes on the face.

"Holy crap," Edgar said, his face split by a mad grin, "you actually took that seriously?!" He tossed his head back and laughed, his lank hair wriggling down his neck like worms. Rationality approved of that metaphor no more than she had of Edgar's suggestion. "You should see your face, Jo; you look like I had suggested barbecuing puppies!" His laughter faded, and silence reigned once more. "Actually..."

I walked stiff-kneed past him, unwilling to let him see the trembles of my own barely-contained laughter. "It's not too late to find another science fair partner, you know!" I called back once the threat of levity had passed.

Edgar's hair shifted as his ears perked up, doglike. "Promise?"

I refused to dignify that with a response.

***

A mile and a half isn't a long distance. In a car, one would be looking at maybe a five-minute trip, depending on road conditions.

A mile and a half is a trip to the nearest grocery store and back; you don't even need to jump on the freeway. "Oh," one might ask, "you're going out? How far?" "Mile and a half," another might answer. "Oh, see you in five minutes then."

Still, when one has no car, such as when one is underage and has no driver's license, and when one is tired following a long day of school, a mile and a half can seem to drag on forever. It did so for me as Edgar and I trudged up my driveway and through the front door of my home.

I tossed my book bag onto a chair, startling the cat and sending her speeding upstairs. "Hello? Anyone home?" I called to the seemingly empty house.

"In here!" my mother answered from the kitchen.

Turning to Edgar, silhouetted in the doorway, I beckoned him enter. "She's in there," I said, jerking my head towards the kitchen.

Edgar tossed his backpack onto the chair next to mine; I half expected a second cat to spring forth and follow our one and only pet up the stairs. Alas, the gods of humorous repetition did not smile down upon this fortuitous event, and so we slunk away.

My mother was in the kitchen, as advertised, mincing an onion and filling the air with stinging juices.

"Hey, mom," I said. "Edgar's here."

Mom looked up, still pistoning her knife with one hand and pushing the onion forward with the other, sliding her fingers ever closer towards doom. "Hey, Ed," she said. "What brings you here?"

I spoke over Edgar's answer, diverting mom's attention back to what she was doing with her hands. "Oh, you know, he's just here. And speaking of here, you're home awfully early. And why are you cooking? Tonight's dad's night."

"Didn't go in today," she said, arresting the knife's mincing movement and sliding the onion bits into a frying pan. "The night crew had a containment breach, so the whole place was on lockdown today. Since I'm already home, I can cook."

Edgar's ears perked up at the mention of "containment breach," and had I been looking at his butt--which I most certainly was not doing--I wouldn't have been surprised to see it wagging like a dog's

26

tail. "What happened?" he asked. "Is there, like, some kind of massive plague outbreak or something?"

"On a different scale," mom answered as she tossed bloody strips of steak into the pan. "All of the active cultures on my level are contaminated. There will be purges, billions dead--but it's all bacteria and a bit of slime mold."

"So the virus was airborne or something?"

Mom smiled; her work never got this level of attention from me. "I've got at least seventeen NDA's that prevent me from answering that."

Edgar stepped back, held out his arms, and flicked his fingers down and up as if to say, "look at me; I'm just some dumb kid." "Come on, Mrs. M, do I really look like a corporate spy?"

A hiss of steam obscured mom's face as she turned on the stovetop, but I'm sure her smile remained. "Alright, but no blogging about this, or sharing it on Instachat, or whatever it is you kids do nowadays."

"Direct brain uploads."

"Right, that. Okay, well, lately I've been studying a culture of *e. coli* that's been infected with a modified..."

As mom spoke, I tuned out. I often tuned out whenever mom started talking science. And not just science--a fair bit of her harangues and sermons fell on deaf ears. Most of it I had heard before, or wasn't interested in hearing the first time, and her dialogue fell by the wayside as I narrated things in my head. Could this tendency to tune out mom's lectures be the reason for my failing science grade? I had no problem with listening to teachers dissemble --my other grades proved that--but perhaps I had subconsciously created a logic chain that prevented me from paying attention to science talk. Mom grouses at me for not taking the trash out, and I don't listen--> mom talks about sciency-things and I don't listen--> The Yog talks about sciency-things and I don't listen. The theory seemed to fit the evidence at hand... no, sorry, the *hypothesis* seemed to fit the evidence at hand; I knew enough about both science and English to distinguish those two concepts. All I needed now was an experiment to test the hypothesis. Perhaps mother could elucidate on sundry topics while I checked for a corresponding dip in productivity at school? I doubted The Yog would accept my findings as a suitable project.

Speaking of The Yog's project: it was time to ask mom for ideas on how to redeem my summer. I refocused and waited for mom's words to filter into my range of hearing.

"...potentially tailor-encode to a target's gene sequence, thus ensuring only one specific death for any given dispersal."

"That is friggin' sweet!" Edgar enthused. He was leaning on the kitchen island, mouth agape and eyes focused beyond the horizon, like he saw a possibility for mom's work that he dare not share with the world.

"That was--wow, that was some pretty cool stuff, mom," I said, trying to hide the fact that I hadn't been listening. "Hey, that reminds me, Ed and I were thinking about signing up for the school science fair..."

"Oh, at the Jamboree?" There was another hiss of steam as mom squirted half a plastic lemon's worth of real lemon's juice into the pan. "You father was thinking of setting up a booth for the junior college, and was dickering with Thumbs over some kind of discount."

I shuddered at the thought of my parents having *any* kind of contact--professional or otherwise--with our principal, Mr. Thumbs. There were some personages best left at school. "Yeah, it's... it's for the Jamboree. Anyway, we were thinking about signing up, but honestly, we can't think of a good idea for what to do a project on. Do you have anything off the top of your head?"

Mom considered me through a curtain of steam and just a little bit of smoke, and I tried the eyelid trick that had been so effective with Edgar. Blink blink, blink blink.

"Let me think about that." She lifted the frying pan from the stove and shook it, sending its contents spiraling into the air. "Well, you could make it practical. We've got that rodent problem going on, and I was talking with some of the other parents at the last PTA meeting; it seems the whole town's got rats bad this year. Maybe you could do a comparative study of rat poisons, using different colonies as testing grounds."

I closed my eyes, needing a few seconds to prepare myself for

Edgar's sure to be smug grin. I opened my eyes a slit, cheeks still scrunched up beneath my eye sockets, ready to clamp down if the force of Edgar's smugness proved too powerful to endure. This time, his butt really was wagging, and his face was pulled back from lips, forming a surprised "O." The phrase "I told you so" went unsaid, but the sound of it echoed through the kitchen. Had mom not been there, and had the island not separated us, I might have punched Edgar.

Seconds passed in silence, interrupted by the sound of steak and onions stir-frying. They exuded an aroma that both burned and soothed. Finally, mom said, "I mean, well, if you've got the stomach for it; not everybody does. Killing mass quantities of rats might be seen as a little unethical, especially for a school project."

Once more I closed my eyes, letting the aroma of impending dinner waft me away to a calmer state. "No, no, it's okay." I cracked open one lid and glanced at Edgar. His arms were folded over his chest, bouncing as he held in silent laughter. "It's a good idea; wish we had thought of it ourselves."

Mom smiled at me, oblivious to the tension dominating the room. "No problem at all, Jo. Just remember to credit me as a contributor if this thing gets picked up by journals."

"Will do, mom." I wanted to get out of there, but any exit strategy would involve being alone with Edgar and his cackling "I told you so" smugness. "Well, it has been a blast, but we really should get started on the project. These rats won't kill themselves!" I clapped my hands in a show of forced excitement. "Actually, I guess they will. Kind of the point."

Mom replaced the frying pan and scraped a spatula through it, creating a sound like crumpling paper. "Be ready to drop everything at a moment's notice; tonight we eat when your father gets home. Ed, you staying for dinner?"

"I'll call home and check, Mrs. M."

I grabbed Edgar by one arm and frog-marched him out of the kitchen and up the stairs.

In my room, I shooed the cat off my bed and flopped down in the middle of the faded purple comforter. I scrabbled with one hand at the bedside table, trying to snag the spiral notebook and pen I kept stashed there. Ed watched me for maybe a minute before huffing in disgust and lunging forward, snagging the writing implements for himself. He pulled my rolling chair from under my desk and dropped into it.

Cheap cardboard squealed against wire rings as Edgar flipped open the notebook. "Alright, what are we doing?"

I stared at the ceiling, pondering Edgar's question and considering the science fair ideas accumulated throughout the day. Since my options were "kill rats," "barbecue puppies," and "find out *why* I'm failing science," the process didn't take long. "Okay, if we're really going to go through with my mom's idea--"

"*My* idea."

"If we're going through with the *rat killing* idea, we're going to need to test a bunch of poisons." I paused as Edgar dirtied my spiral with his chicken scratch. "Maybe get some different flavors of cheese, taint each with a different poison, then see who's got what in their stomachs?"

Edgar grimaced and made a mock gagging sound. "Jeez, Jo, you're taking to this a little *too* well. I don't think we're up for dissections."

I paused again, giving the illusion of considering his critique before accepting it with a nod. I had planned to have *him* do the dissections, so his blanket refusal didn't much affect me.

"And we have to use the same cheese each time," he continued, "otherwise the extra variable could give us false positives. The best cheese will kill the most rats. We'll have to do this sequentially; maybe give a week to each poison."

It was time for me to demonstrate that science-knowledge The Yog assumed I possessed. "Performing sequential poisonings would give us a fluctuating population, which would further skew our results. If one poison starts killing off a lot at the beginning, there will be fewer... *subjects*... to die later, thus making any late-test poisons appear less effective. What we need are different populations for different poisons."

As Edgar scratched away at the spiral, he frowned and inclined his head towards me. "Okay, then we find other people with rat problems. Like your mom said, shouldn't be hard." His eyebrows rose as a light bulb materialized above his head. "Better yet, we get some other people to do our work for us. Call a bunch of exterminators, find out what they use, pull in their results as further experimental evidence."

"Groovy." I rolled to the side of the bed and sat up. "Okay, tonight you start calling exterminators, and I'll call some neighbors to find out who's got rats."

"Copy that." Edgar kicked off a wheel strut, spinning to face my desk. He deposited the spiral then, giggling to himself, kicked off the strut again and spun.

I chucked a decorative pillow at Edgar; it hit the back of his head, sending his curtain of hair flying.

"Ow."

"Quit playing around, Ed. I'm not doing all this work myself."

CHAPTER 4
A PLETHORA OF PAIN

A week had gone by, and Agnes had no idea that our plans for the summer were jeopardized. If all went according to plan, Agnes would never have to find out the truth. As far as she was concerned, I just wanted to win a trophy and a photo on the school blog, a publication read by tens of parents every academic year as they checked for snow cancellations.

Fortunately, the project was going smoothly. "Stage one: research the problem," had been an unmitigated success. Ed had found three vermin exterminators willing to share data on colony sizes in the area, what poisons they used, and how many rats they culled in a typical house call. Fact: Rat colonies average between fifty and one hundred members. In especially accommodating locales, that number can jump into the several hundreds. As we lived in a small Midwest suburb of a slightly larger Midwest suburb, we decided to cap our experimental estimates at fifty rats per household.

Meanwhile, I was able to elicit the help of several neighbors. When first I put about that we eager young scientists were in need of experimental colonies, a great many neighbors rushed to take part in the project. I was going to pick the ten nearest houses, but Edgar presented a pertinent caveat: if we grouped our subjects too close together, we risked cross-contamination. It would be disastrous if, for instance, a rat from colony A snuck next door to colony B, was poisoned by brand X, and returned home to die in the presence of brand Y.

Our solution: pull up a map of the neighborhood and plot out all the willing households, as well as my own. From there, we mapped distribution patterns and planned gaps between experiment houses, ensuring that no two colonies shared yards, common fences, direct power lines, or street facings. Of the twenty-two initial colonies, we came away with seven isolated locations, ripe for poisoning and harvesting. The neighbors gave permission to plant poison and root about their attics, and in exchange, I would kill and collect as many rats as I--or more specifically Edgar--could ever want.

Stage two was placing poisons. The plan was to bait all eight locations this afternoon, and then wait two days before repeating the experiment twice more, collecting any bodies we might find. Once cause of death was determined, we'd dispose of the corpses; we didn't want electrocuted/pecked to death/just plain old rats polluting our data pool. And by this time next week, a data pool we would have. We would test four different brands of rat poison, giving two colonies to each. Assuming colony size was well distributed, we would know beyond any doubt which poison did the most killing.

In stage three of our project, done the week before the Kelso Amboy All-School Jamboree and Swap-Meet, we'd collate our results with some hopefully grade-A bullshit into a report, plop in some graphs and a preserved corpse or two, and deliver the whole thing on a trifold board unto the great and powerful Yog.

Well, that was the plan, anyway.

"How's that research write-up coming?" I asked from my place on the bed, staring at the ceiling and pondering the many mistakes that brought me to this impasse. It was Friday night, and I was at home, doing homework.

From my desk came the clattering of computer keys depressed in rapid succession. Some seconds after my query, the clattering ceased and my desk chair whined as Edgar turned to look at me. "Got it just up to the point about hashing out experimental locations, and now I'm going to explain this weeks' protocol."

"Excellent! Carry on, then, Ed. Write your little heart out, for then we shall begin our true work!"

Edgar answered with an a-grammatical grunt before turning back to my computer. The clatter resumed for a scant few minutes before falling silent once more. "And done," Edgar announced, rolling away from the desk and standing. "We've got two pages of background material, double spaced."

"Groovy." I crouched on hands and knees, a predator ready to pounce. "And so now we begin at last our great work! To the garage, my minion!"

As I crawled from the bed, Edgar lowered into a crouch, drooping his shoulders and letting his left arm dangle lifeless. "Yesh, mashtuh!" he cried in a garbled Eastern European accent. "Yesh, garassshhhh!" He shuffled to the door, dragging his equally lifeless left leg across the bare floorboards and making a terrific racket.

There was an echoing thump from below as someone pounded on the other side of the floor. "What are you two doing up there?" my mom called, her voice muffled.

"Science, Mother!" I called back. "You wouldn't understand!"

This was followed by a litany of *soto voche* swears.

Edgar and I descended downstairs and thence to the garage. Lying on the concrete floor was a plastic bag brimming with poisons of all variety, deposited by my father the previous night. Thanks to oppressive local legislature enacted by reactionary politicians angling for undeserved reelection, minors were forbidden from purchasing potentially fatal ingestible substances on their own.

While I sorted the brightly colored poison boxes according to brand, Edgar mounted a stepstool in the middle of the room and flailed at the cord dangling from the folded attic ladder. "Eh, cannot reach, mashtuh!" he wailed. "Too high, too high!" He was still posed in his awkward Igor stance, leaving his arms about six inches too short to operate the ladder-pull.

"Screw you," I said. "You're too high."

He straightened, the end of the cord now brushing the top of his head. "I wish. Have you *seen* what they're charging for weed these days? It's positively criminal." He leapt from the stepladder and stumbled a few steps before stopping beside me. He ducked into a bow, more formal than his Igor pose, and made a sweeping gesture towards the stepladder. "After you."

I blushed at his absolute cheek. "What, you expect me to go up there?"

"Let's see..." He held up a fist and flipped out his index finger. "There are two major components of this project. The first is the essay," he shook the extended finger in my face, "the second is the experiment." He extended his middle finger and shook it as well. "I've already written the essay, barring results and conclusions, which I *will* write, rest assured. So that leaves it to *you*--" He folded back his middle finger and pointed his remaining finger my way, "to do the actual experimental portion. It's fair division of labor. Plus, it's *your* grade on the line; I don't think I'm guaranteed any benefit from helping out."

I glared at him with hatred intense enough to kill a goat. He answered with a nonchalant vacancy that absorbed and neutralized my death-glare, like an acid poured into a base. With Edgar proving obdurate to my silent fury, I retrieved the plastic bag. "Fine; I'll poison them. But you have to muck out the bodies at the end of the week."

"Meh." He shrugged.

I stuffed the bag into his chest, eliciting an "Oof!" as he stumbled backwards and I mounted the stepstool. Being several inches shorter than Edgar, I really did have to jump to reach the dangling cord. I snagged it on my third try, then tumbled from the stool as fifty pounds of warped wood and metal swung down at me. The ancient springs stretched and twanged, producing an unholy shriek that sounded like the hinges on the gates of Hell grinding open.

Ignoring muffled laughter from out Edgar way, I again mounted the stepstool and continued up, transitioning from molded plastic and tubular metal to a skeletal construct, all splinters and rust. It looked ready to snap at any moment, either folding back and crushing me or collapsing and dumping me to the floor. I didn't weigh much, but the attic ladder sagged and groaned as I climbed. I peeked over the edge of the attic floor, the light from the garage below negating any visuals of the wider space beyond. Perhaps the gates of Hell was not that hyperbolic a description for the sounds the ladder made as it opened; the eternal darkness beyond my rectangle of light was hot and musty, easily ninety degrees, despite the mild outside weather.

With great trepidation and gnashing of teeth, I took one hand from the safety rail and thrust it behind me. "Okay, pass me the poison." I waited, arm outstretched, core taut as I fought for balance on the ramshackle ladder. The slat beneath my feet felt *way* too thin to support me... "Seriously, dude, the freaking bag!" The reassuring slickness of plastic pressed into my hand. "*Thank you.*"

Poison in hand, I continued upwards, the ladder springs contracting with a final groaning twang as my weight came off. Around me was the framework of the house, glowing red in the light from below; beyond that was darkness. I took a deep breath through my mouth, the air burning in my lungs, bringing with it vague odors that wormed into my nose. There was the citrus and beef smell of last weeks' fajitas... a touch of mold, maybe a little bit of damp rot... and, laying over everything like a shroud, the smell of rodent waste.

I eased myself forward on hands and knees, wanting to stay as close to the safety of the trapdoor as possible. Just beyond the door, the attic floor, such as it was, gave way to exposed joists, a foot apart from each other, filled in between with ragged, dust-tinged insulation.

I ventured onto the first joist, careful to keep my hands out of the rotted insulation, and coughed as another deep breath sent a good quart of dust into my lungs. I was maybe five feet away from the trapdoor when I heard an animal squeak. My hand slipped from the joist and into the insulation, sending up a cloud of carcinogenic dust. Coughing and wheezing, I set myself back on course and continued into the unknown.

I soon came to a wall that angled up into the roof above my head. As I reached it, I stopped to retrieve a poison canister from the bag. It was then I realized how important planning was to the success of this project, and concluded that we may not have done enough planning before rushing on to the fun stuff. The poison was still in its original packaging; as it was poison, it was not meant to come out of said packaging without a fair bit of effort. You know, for safety reasons. I was perched over a drywall ceiling that would collapse should I slip off the joists, wrestling with an adamantine clamshell package in near darkness, hyperventilating in the close air, and choking on fluff. You know, for safety reasons.

Jamming the package onto a nail jutting through the roof, I made myself a decent entry hole. I pried and twisted at the hole, easing the plastic apart. I was at the stage where one good pull would separate the clamshell when I heard another squeak, followed by low chittering and the sound of claws scrabbling across wood.

I gasped and half-stood, whacking my head against the roof, just managing to avoid a protruding nail.

"Jo?" Ed's voice drifted from the magical land of light and ventilation and happiness some million miles away.

My voice quavered as I spoke; it may have been from the strands of insulation coating my throat or it may have been from raw terror. "I think there's a rat in here..."

"That's kinda the point, Jo," Edgar said. "That's why we're doing this."

There was another squeak, then a rustle as insulation began moving all on its own, forming a hump that rose and elongated and--*Something touched me! Something friggin' brushed my friggin' hand!*

Abandoning the half-opened rat poison, I scuttled backwards to the door, collecting splinters that jabbed through my jeans and into my knees. Ahead of me, where the *thing* had touched me, I could see eyes, glowing yellow in the garage light. One foot suddenly dangled over cool open air, and I thrust that leg down, scrabbling to find the top rung of the ladder. Instead, with dimming light and a reverberating echo of over-taxed springs, the ladder found me. I screamed, a primal sound of terror and just a little bit of honest pissed-offedness. "Ed!"

"It's okay, Jo!" he shouted over the heaving of the springs, "I'm just closing the door; don't want any rats to get out."

"*Ed!*"

The spring's groan rose in pitch and the upward pressure disappeared as the door returned to its open state.

"Okay, jeez; I was only joking." Against any semblance of human decency, he sounded hurt.

"I'm coming down!" I bellowed.

"Alright," he said. "I'll just call up Agnes so you can explain to her why you won't be going to see Bluker's Creek."

Low blow, Ed, low blow... I stopped, one foot resting on the top step, my body half in and half out of the attic.

"I'm willing to help you," Ed continued, "but this is still your project. I'll deal with bodies, but you have to deal the death."

Damn Edgar and his damnable logic and damnably fair conditions. Why did I keep him as a friend? I mean, seriously. "Fine, I'm going back in... but I won't forget this."

"Meh."

As I pulled myself once more into the darkness, I questioned the logic of eschewing a flashlight. In theory--excuse me, *hypothesis*--I was just going to the outer edges of the light to deliver the poison; there was no need for a flashlight. Still, I should have insisted on having one.

Once more engulfed in darkness, I crept to where I had abandoned the poison. I was surprised to discover that my panic-induced jerks had ripped the clamshell asunder, and the container of poison lay in one half. I pulled it out, popped the lid, and slid the whole sorry mess down a crack between the farthest-out joist and the wall. The package said the poison was self-baiting; at this point, I wasn't willing to investigate the matter further.

Returning to the trapdoor, I followed another pair of joists into the unknown. I shuffled along until the light failed, opened a package on a roofing nail, and deposited the poison down into the ceiling for all the good little rats to nibble on. Once completed, I returned to the hole and began again, working clockwise around the attic, trying to cover the entirety of the kitchen and garage. Starting at twelve o'clock, I moved to two o'clock, then four, then six.

I was at eight o'clock when the bag got stuck. I pulled it towards me, but the sucker refused to budge. There was just enough pale light to see that the bag was hooked on a nail; something like an eighth of an inch of cheap plastic kept me from completing my job. I yanked again, harder this time, but the bag would not move. Additional pulling succeeded in doing exactly squat, and I wondered why it was that the less something was stuck on an outcropping, the harder it was to pull that thing free.

Taking a firmer grip on the bag, I surged forward mightily, putting all my momentum into yanking the damn thing. The bag remained in place a moment longer, suspending me over a pool of insulation just long enough to realize this was a bad idea. Then the bag ripped and I hurtled forward, tumbling head-over-heels into the insulation and--wonder of wonders, miracle of miracles--over the joist beyond that, into the outer darkness.

There was a moment of absolute stillness as I lay in the soft embrace of the insulation dust, cocooned in darkness. Then I sat up, feeling movement beneath me and hearing the creak of straining drywall. I flailed for a joist, the spumes of dust tearing at my lungs and burning my eyes. I stumbled away, coming to the next joist in the worst manner possible. It rose up from the darkness, just high enough to trip me. Again, I went plunging headfirst, but this time I ran into *something.* I couldn't see what it was, but there was a decrepit smell of old organic matter, the creak of ancient things moving in the dark, sudden sharp points biting into my flesh. I screamed and hopped backwards, ignoring the bowing of the ceiling beneath me, concerned only with reaching the rectangle of light made vague by the dust clogging my vision.

"Ed!" I cried, my voice registering an octave or two higher in panic. "Ed! Emergency! I need help!"

There was no answer.

As I scrabbled for freedom, the *something* behind me scrabbled in hot pursuit. There was a gestalt form of brown, made of a thousand-thousand spheroid bodies, all rattling and hissing behind me, a thousand-thousand razor-sharp points bearing down upon me. A quick glance back was all it took to convince me to pour on the speed as I saw what could only be an entire colony of angry rats swarming after me.

Despite my increased speed, they were faster.

Two feet from the edge, two feet from safety and life everlasting, I was subsumed in the terrifying, sharply pointed swarm of death. Teeth and claws dug into me, ripped at my skin, sent my blood spraying out over the insulation, and then I was over the edge, grappling with the ramshackle ladder in an effort to arrest my fall.

Something did arrest my fall. A slab of concrete--scratch that, an entire *planet*--caught me, jettisoning the air from my lungs and stranding me beneath the aperture as the swarm continued to pour down, following me lemming-style to the ground, impaling me on their hideous claws.

This was it; this was death. God, I hurt all over.

Above the sound of chittering rats and falling bodies, I heard running feet clattering across the garage floor. "Jo!" Mom ran towards me, her face a rictus of fear. She dropped to her knees and slid across the floor, lifting my head and cradling it to her chest. Then I saw Edgar, clutching a broom, swatting at the things that continued to pour from the attic. As the flow of spiny brown forms slowed and stopped, he turned the broom on me and swept me clean.

It was then, surrounded by friends, family, and precious electric light, that I got my first solid look at what had chased me from the attic. At first, I refused to believe they could be what they actually were, but as adrenaline and pain faded, I made a firm identification. My cheeks flushed with rage and more than a little embarrassment. I pulled away from my mother and scowled at her. "Why do we have so many pinecones?!"

She folded her hands in her lap and shrugged, the fear on her face giving way to lip-biting sheepishness. "They were decorative! We used to have them everywhere before you were born, but we packed them away because we thought they would be too dangerous."

"*Really?*"

Sheepishness transformed into guilt. "It won't happen again;

we're downsizing."

That assurance was profoundly reassuring. With a groan, I rolled over and struggled to me feet. Balancing was difficult as my muscles shivered from the pain of my ordeal. Sending one last resentful scowl mother's way, I began to pick out the pinecone-- what, petals?--that pierced my flesh.

Mom stood with me and took in the garage floor and the hundreds of shattered pinecone bits covering it. "Well...we have... first aid upstairs," she said in staccato bursts. She surveyed the carnage for a minute or so more before nodding and returning to the kitchen. I was thankful for having such an effusively nurturing mother to look out for my well being.

Ed stepped closer, twirling the broom like the world's worst oscillating fan and whistling in admiration of the blood tricking down my limbs. "Damn, Jo, but you make science look hardcore. You must have fallen a good eight feet."

I wrestled the broom from his hands and hurled it across the field of shattered pinecone. "Where the hell were you?" I bellowed. Some of the words came out hollow as my voice pitched up into a reedy shriek. "For all you knew, I was being eaten alive by rats! I was yelling for help and--and--and where the hell were you?!" There was more to my argument than just his absence as I was grubbing about in the nether hells, but I was beyond the ability to articulate said argument.

He looked down at his feet and nudged at a pinecone. "Sorry; I've been out of the garage for a while."

"Well, you had better have been on a friggin' shit break, because if not, there was no reason you should have left me alone up there!"

"I was taking a phone call, okay, if that's really so important to you. I was going to tell you when you got down; I need to leave early tonight."

"*What*?" My fingers slipped from a deeply lodged petal in response to Edgar's answer. My hands came away bloody. As I stared at my precious life fluids leaking from my body, I couldn't help but feel betrayed that he was off having a social life. "You're taking phone calls and making alternate plans while I'm up in the cloud forest risking my ass? The hell, Ed? We're supposed to be working on this science fair project together!"

He gave a mighty kick that sent the pinecone ricocheting off the rollaway door. His head came up, his eyes burning with cold fury. "You know what? We're *not* working on this project 'together.'" He put finger quotation marks around the last word. "In case you've forgotten, this is *your* project, working to fix *your* crappy grade, to preserve *your* summer. I'm helping you in my free time, out of the goodness of my heart, but it no way is this *my* project. Remember that next time you plan on dumping the work on my shoulders, all right?" His eyes softened. "Now, are you alright?"

I stared at him, gape mouthed. Just who the hell did he think he was? In case *he* had forgotten, *he* had agreed to be my *partner,* on *our* science fair project.

Before I could articulate *that* argument, he gestured into the kitchen. "Look, maybe you should just go in and get patched up. I've really got to go; the marching band director called, and something big has come up."

I was still too enraged to articulate a quality response, so instead I fell back to the basics. "But what about the rats?"

"Forget the rats, at least for tonight. You're bleeding and covered in Chewbacca's almighty drain clog. Get yourself cleaned up, and I'll try to get back tomorrow to help out, okay? I won't do everything, by I'll still help."

I mouthed something, but was too apoplectic to produce any sounds. Edgar took my lack of response for a lack of disagreement and hurried from the garage, leaving me all alone to lick my wounds and regroup.

CHAPTER 5
PUTTING THEM ALL IN ONE BASKET

Edgar didn't return the next day, nor the day after that. For the second time in two weeks, he failed to walk to school with me Monday morning. I didn't see Edgar again until Science class, where I found him sitting in his usual spot by the window, fresh-faced and bushy-tailed.

Perhaps I should have expected him to flake out on me. Though we had been friends for half our lives, he had abandoned me in my hour of greatest need, that hour being the one spent in the attic, chased by rabid pinecones. If a so-called friend can take a call through that, why should that so-called friend bother to show up when that so-called friend promised to do so?

I slammed my book bag down on the lab bench with enough force to send beakers skittering away. The surreal sound of glassware warbling on faux-marble pulled Edgar from his distracted window-gazing, and he turned towards me, his head seeming to float, held aloft by the mellow smile perched on his lips.

"Thanks so much for all that help on Saturday," I sneered. "With your generous contribution, I was unable to finish poisoning my own home, nor start on any others. Now I'm half a week behind, with a severely diminished data pool. Truly, this project is shaping up to be Nobel level work."

My fusillade of harsh words failed to breach his good mood. "Oh, Jo," he intoned, his cheeks glowing with inner light, "this weekend was amazing."

Yanking open the zipper on my bag, I dug in and pulled out my textbook. I slammed it down on the table, doing my best to jar Edgar from his pleased stupor.

He was having none of it. "I came to school Friday night; the whole marching band was here. Coach Z lined us all up in the gym, and then talked about how disappointing last week's defeat at state had been; about how he had been sure we were the best the high school marching band had to offer, all that jazz. Well, all that Sousa; the jazz band wasn't invited, save for the brass section. Then he talked a little about how Zwick Technical Academy had managed to field a superior team, and proceed to hand our asses to us on a silver platter, disgracing us before all of Ohio and our ancestors, yea, back even a thousand generations--"

I snapped my fingers in Edgar's face, and a bit of the dreamy quality faded. "Hey. You said you had a good weekend; this sounds terrible." Despite my loathing for the damnable Judas sitting across from me, I was compelled by his words, and wanted him to get to the point already.

"Right, yes, anyway, after setting up that backstory and coating us with a thick layer of shame--"

"That's what she said!" a voice crowed from behind us.

Edgar looked lackadaisically over his shoulder to the next bench back. Sitting there was Camacho, self-professed class-clown and general annoyance. "Listening in, Macho Man?" Edgar asked.

"Nah," Camacho answered, flicking a dismissive hand in our direction, "just saw an in and took it. Carry on, and think no more upon my interruption."

"Will do, buddy," Edgar said, turning back to me. I shuddered; Camacho was creepy, and the less I had to do with him the better.

"Where was I?"

I shot my gaze back to Camacho, ascertaining that he was distracted. "Coach was covering you in shame."

"Right, so anyway, he got us all worked up, and then revealed

Zwick Tech had been disqualified from going to nationals." Edgar thrust both arms into the air, outstretched fingers on each hand making the "V" for victory. "The Kelso Amboy Potoos are now officially state champions by default!"

"What?" His bar must be set pretty low for this news to make his weekend, quote, "amazing."

Edgar dropped his arms and leaned forward. "You remember last week, when I came in from the bus? I said they played so well, it was a wonder they didn't already have recording contracts? Turns out, one of them *did*, and her album debuted this week, number one in instrumental woodwinds. Anyway, the state marching band board--and yes, we have one of those--decided to look into it, to see if that violated any rules, looking to maybe disqualify that one student. From this simple investigation, they uncovered a tangled web of scandal and deceit, going back *years*."

The bone I wished to pick with Edgar was placed by the wayside; this sudden twist in Ed's story intrigued me enough that I settled onto my stool to listen.

"It turns out that about five years ago--the same time Zwick's program turned around and they started beating us every year--they started using ringers. It was a play to try and boost their prestige and exposure. They would find talented but not-quite-good-enough-to-make-it students who dropped out of Julliard, and pay them to be in their band. Then they'd generate false student records and suddenly *bam!*" he clapped his hands in front of me and I jerked back, gasping. "--they'd have a high school marching band that sounded just as good as a classically-trained college band. When the board looked into the student's contract, they found that while she was using her Zwick Tech name, she was routing all the money through her real identity, and all it took was some web searching to find she had done a couple semesters Julliard. They searched other students, and found that their records only went back as far as their Freshman year at Zwick. And thus with a pull on that one string, a mighty dynasty is unraveled, and Zwick's reign of terror is no more!" Again he thrust up the victorious "V"s.

"Holy crap, Ed, that's wonderful," I said, unable to stay angry with him in light of this news. Though I was inconvenienced, his nemesis had been slain. Good for him.

"And since Zwick is no longer in the running," Edgar continued, "next month we go to Washington!"

"What?" A dark cloud crept over the moment's sunshine.

"Yeah, for nationals. That's why I was gone all weekend. Coach says we need to raise a couple thousand dollars for the trip and do a couple thousand rehearsals until then. Oh!" His smile dropped away, replaced by a sickly grin. "That reminds me. I'm sorry to have to tell you, but I'm going to need to pull out of the project. Sorry."

"What." Now there was no more light; from horizon to horizon, all was storm clouds.

"Yeah, again, sorry. Kind of a dick move, I know, but the band needs me, and as a member of said band, I'm kind of already involved in this."

I couldn't believe I was on the verge of making nice with him. He abandoned me in my hour of need, he abandoned me this weekend, and he was abandoning me now. Though I didn't voice these sentiments, the grinding of my teeth clued Edgar into the gist of my thoughts.

"I'm not--I am *not* abandoning you. I just have prior commitments."

"Prior commitments that just so happen to have come up *after* my commitment."

Guilt tempered by exasperation played across his features. "Marching band was a pre-existing condition of this relationship, and you knew that! So I'm sorry, but I simply *will not* have the time to help on this project anymore!"

"If I don't get this project done, I can't go see the Creek!" I wailed.

"Pre-existing condition; you should have been not failing science!" he shot back.

"That statement doesn't even make sense!" I rejoindered.

A sharp rapping echoed through the room, and we fell silent. The Yog stood beside the white board, one gnarled knuckle tapping against its pearlescent surface. "Gnarled" was an exaggeration, but I wasn't well disposed towards The Yog at this moment.

"You two good now?" Her eyebrows rode above the rims of her spectacles. "I can delay class; I'm sure no one else would mind a few extra minutes on their phones."

It was an offer The Yog had extended to students through the years; I had been the subject of that offer twice before. According to school folklore--a credible source in such matters--a promising young student had taken The Yog up on the offer during her second year of teaching; he had not been seen since.

I turned to my lab partner and offered him a nostril flare of disgust before slumping across the lab bench.

The Yog twitched her head to the side, sending her curls bouncing. "Excellent! Then let us start the class, shall we?" She crossed to a colossal machine that I had failed to notice hulking beside her desk. It was made of contoured grey metal, as long as a person, crouching on thick, wheeled legs. At waist height was a glass-sided tray strewn with hay. Orange lights shone into the tray from an upper portion, surrounded by another glass wall, giving the machine the appearance of the world's worst salad bar. "Now, before we start with today's lesson, I've got some really exciting news for everyone. There is an opportunity for a bit of extra credit to roll out your way."

I perked up as a faint ray of sunshine sliced its way through the clouds.

"Not a lot of extra credit, though," The Yog clarified, "just enough to give one a bump if one were borderline. Like, really borderline. We're talking one final point here."

I slumped again as the clouds shifted to cover the errant sunbeam.

"Now, how many of you know Roger Eland, that damned filthy hippie farmer who brings those delicious organic eggs to the farmer's market?" Her question was answered by a dull roar of non-committal answers. "Well, it seems security on his farm wasn't everything he'd hoped it would be, and though a fox didn't get into the henhouse, a rooster did, resulting in an entire month's product line being knocked-up. Due to our community's general squeamishness towards finding partially-formed fetuses in their breakfasts, Farmer Eland has graciously donated the despoiled eggs to the school!

"And," her excited tone dropped away as a hard edge entered her voice, "after extensive negotiation with the cafeteria staff, I've managed to acquire some of the eggs for the science department."

A jag of something like stomach flu ripped through my guts; I made a solemn vow to limit the number of meals purchased from the cafeteria.

After this instant of melancholy, The Yog continued, "Anyway, last night I dusted off the old incubator," here she patted the sneeze-guard of the world's worst salad bar, "and we will now be raising chicks of our very own!" She smiled at us, radiating the wonder of learning. Unfortunately, we were inert matter, reflecting none of the Yog's excitement back towards her.

Her throat jerked with a pained swallow. The expression on her face was that of a woman regretting fifteen years spent going down a career path that offered little pay and no benefits, and which had no light at the end of the tunnel. Following a long silence she spoke. "Screw it. Everyone pair off and get an egg from the incubator. Valerie, Skyler, you two; Camacho, Jesus, yes; Ed, Jo, c'mon. Everyone grab an egg, grab a marker, and enjoy the miracle of life."

"That's what she said!" Camacho barked out.

Despite The Yog's instructions, I alone approached the incubator. I could feel Edgar's gaze on the back of my head, glaring with a ferocity left over from our argument. I queued up behind Camacho at the incubator, and when it was my turn, I reached in and selected an egg at random. It was a brown egg, a "turd egg" as my grandmother used to call them. Bending under the sneeze guard, I saw the others were all pristine and white. Lucky me: even if the marker rubbed off, it would be easy enough to identify my--excuse me, *our*-- egg. I uncapped a marker and quickly scribbled my name around the pointed end of the egg: "jo," with a little heart over the "j" just for fun. I wrote Edgar's name on the underside and returned the egg to its artificial chicken butt, placing Edgar face down in the fresh hay via proxy.

"Hopefully you won't bail on this group project," I muttered when I slid back onto my stool. "Don't think I could stand to see our little chicken die 'cause daddy abandoned him."

Edgar opened his mouth to spit out a venomous reply, but The Yog preempted him. "Alright, class, now that the chicks are all snuggled up and cozy—"

"That's what she said!" Camacho brayed once more.

"That doesn't even make sense, Camacho," The Yog said, her words buried in the tail end of a weary sigh. "That gets you a detention."

"Yes, ma'am..."

"Anyway, we have things to go over, and only thirty-five minutes left to cover them. Everyone open your text-books..."

Her voice became at once more muffled and less loud--which I'm about ninety percent sure is an improper phrasing of the sentiment-- as I tuned her out. The fate of my summer was on my mind, and it was exponentially more important to me than today's lesson. Unless I got a new partner, the project was dead; I didn't have enough time to get a sizable data pool from which to pull meaningful conclusions. Aside from a lack of time to place poison and wait for results, there was no way I was going to collect dead rats by my lonesome.

I toyed with the idea of asking Agnes for help, but... I didn't want her to know how precarious our summer was, not yet at any rate. I'd just have to come up with some fix to this predicament on my lonesome...

***

By the time I tuned back in, The Yog had finished lecturing and was staring at the big analog clock common to all classrooms. "Okay, everybody, wait for it..." she muttered with the tense determination of one who was indeed waiting for it. "Wait for it..."

The room exploded with the cacophony of an analog bell ringing, the spring-powered clapper slamming repeatedly against the metal dome of the bell. Beneath the clangor, stools scraped over linoleum with a synchronicity we never could have achieved consciously.

49

"See you all tomorrow!" The Yog called in a voice more imagined through the hubbub than actually heard.

Edgar brushed past me, snorting as he did so. I stared after him, shocked that he possessed the audacity to be mad at me; *I* was the one who had been betrayed, *I* was the one who should be seething. Inhaling a shuddering breath, I tried to ignore Edgar and settle myself for what was to come. I had one chance to save my summer, and I needed to be calm as I laid out my logical points to The Yog. Excess emotion would sink any chance for a reprieve.

Holding that last shuddering breath, I crossed the classroom, approaching my doom. The Yog was turned away from me, leaning over her desk and shuffling papers. I was still five feet away from here when she said, "Yes, Jo?" without looking up.

My shoes squeaked as I came up short. My heart hammered away within me, driving out every vestige of calmness. "Ihadaquestionabouttheextra-creditprojectyouassignedme," I blurted.

The Yog placed her papers on the desk, then straightened and faced me. "Well, I hope it's not an important question; it's a bit late to be asking for deep systemic clarification. I assume you haven't been waiting until now to start...?" By making the statement a question, she implied at once that of course I wouldn't be stupid enough to lose a whole week on the project, but also that she had been teaching a long time, and her student's propensity for compete bone-headedness never ceased to amaze her.

I prefaced my answer with what I hoped was a relaxed chuckle. "Oh, no, I've got a project underway--started the very day you assigned it. The problem is, my partner kind of flaked out on me, and I'm doubting my ability to finish this on my lonesome." The plan was to present my predicament as a problem with no solution, one I had already considered from every angle. The Yog would then swoop in with a solution I couldn't have used on my own initiative, even had I considered it. "Well, you kept to your end of the bargain to the best of your ability, so I guess I'll go ahead and credit your effort," was the preferred response. "Well, maybe this project idea isn't working out. Here, do these worksheets instead," was another amenable compromise.

Unfortunately, The Yog failed to pick up on the results of my problem and was enamored of the cause. "Ed, flakey? We are talking about the same kid here, right?" That was the part I hoped she would ignore, hence the reference to "partner," rather than proper nouns. While not the best student in the class, Edgar was up there, and The Yog had a soft spot for him. Now that she was focused on him rather than my problem, I could expect zero sympathy.

Time to give Ed the benefit of the doubt, and make myself appear as the victim of circumstance. "Well, he got word that the Potoos are back in contention, and he's had to drop out of the project to help out his team. Band. Band-team."

The Yog nodded sagely. "It's good to see he's got his priorities sorted out. The question is, do you? Have you asked any other student to be your new partner?"

I had not, but that fact wasn't going to stop me. "It's like you said; it's too late in the project to just be starting out. There's no way I could get a new partner up to speed with the experimental protocol in the time allotted."

"And yet you have to explain said protocol in less than two pages of essay... *double* spaced."

Damn you, The Yog, damn you...

She furrowed her brow as she thought. "Tell you what, you stay here a few minutes; let me check on a couple of things. I'll get back to you with a solution to your problem." She turned back to her desk and resumed rifling through her pages.

I stood there dumbly for a moment, wondering if she were actually going to offer a solution, or if this were the end of the dream. How had I talked myself into thinking she'd see me partner-less and alone and just let me off the hook for effort thus far? Right. No, in five minutes' time, she was going to say, "Sucks to be you; have fun in summer-school!" and that would be the end of Bluker's Creek.

I couldn't stand here any longer. I needed to get back to my desk, where I could relax and think and begin to breathe again. Turning to the classroom at large, I jumped and nearly screamed as I found Camacho standing behind me, sis face split in a manic grin.

"Hola," he said in Spanish.

"Heyyy, Camacho," I said once my heart had resumed its usual rhythm. "You waiting to talk to The Yog?" As I spoke, I slid past him and continued to my stool. Overlapping the staccato *click!* of my own small feet was the *clack!* of much larger shoes.

"Actually," Camacho said from an uncomfortably close distance behind me, "I wanted to talk with you."

"Oh, really?" I grimaced and climbed onto my stool.

Camacho leaned against the lab bench, elbow propped up at a rakish angle. "I couldn't help but overhear that you and Edgar are having some problems. You know, it's really a shame that some guys just can't see where there priorities should lie. If you need some help Jo, I want you to know that I am up for *anything* you may need. I know me my science, and I am *always* willing to make time for you." He waggled his eyebrows suggestively.

Dear sweet baby Jesus in a manger, was he hitting on me? Worse yet, did he really think that Ed and I were... a couple? I stretched a smile across my face, trying to match the intensity of Camacho's own. "That's really sweet of you, Macho, but completely unnecessary. Thank you all the same."

"Hey, come on, no time to get humble now. Or proud, I guess... Anyway, I saw your graded paper when you left it behind. I can help; I can be there for you when you need some sweet, sweet, extra credit, baby. Macho Man can take care of you."

I had not left the graded paper behind; I had thrown it away. "Yeah, that's, that's great, Camacho, but really, I'm good. I'm working it out with The Yog right now."

He brushed a strand of hair out of my face, sending my skin into paroxysms of gooseflesh. "Why you got to get her involved, baby, when you got me? I can be the only partner you ever need."

I brushed his hand away. "Okay, look, you're not taking the hint, so here it is: you're creepy, okay? I'm sorry, but that's the truth." His smile remained manic as before, but there was tightening around his nose and eyes. "If you were anyone else, I might, *maybe*, accept your offer. And I really do thank you for it; I meant what I said about it being sweet. But dude... you're freaking creepy. Please, just take my no as no, okay?"

52

His smile melted, but he managed to transition seamlessly into a new expression of casual disregard. "Nah, I get it; it's cool. You don't want to pick up what the Macho Man is putting down; I can respect that." He pushed away from the bench. "You just remember: it's still down there. Anytime you need it, you can pick it up. You know I'll always be right behind you."

I braced to shudder at this last comment when I noticed that he was pointing. The line of his finger led back to his bench, which was, as implied, behind me. Oh. And then he was gone, leaving me alone with the dreaded Yog.

"Good news!" she said after a few more minutes passed.

A million contradictory thoughts, hopes and fears sped through my mind at those words, but I blocked them out and focused on locomoting to her desk.

When I was within arm's reach, she continued, "I double-checked the science fair rules, and it turns out that you only need a partner if you're competing for a prize. If you're just showing, you can do a solo project. All you have to do is finish, set up a booth, and meet with my approval, then you're home free for the summer!" If she expected a show of thankfulness, she would be disappointed. Why hadn't she told me this in the first place? Had I known I could do a solo project, I never would have picked Edgar, never would have picked the rats, and never would have been in this thrice-damned situation! Completely misinterpreting the look of multi-layered unease rippling across my face, The Yog asked, "Do you think you can finish it by yourself?"

I lifted my chin in a show of subdued dignity. "I don't suppose I have a choice."

Her lips parted in a toothy smile, displaying creepiness far stronger than anything Camacho could ever hope to muster. "Oh, Jo, you always have a choice."

I swallowed, unnerved by this sinister display. "Well, thank you for checking into that. I guess... I guess I'll just have to work extra hard to get it done on time."

She brought her lips back together, lessening the horror-factor of her smile, and I got the hell out of there.

CHAPTER 6
SOMETHING WORSE THAN PINECONES

I stood once more on the step stool in my garage, staring up at the attic's trapdoor. I had to finish with the full round of planned poison. Once I did, I could move on to another house and poison there, and maybe, just to get *some* kind of objective result, poison a third house. The resultant data pool would be shallow, but at least it would be *something*.

Many factors held me back from unleashing the ladder, though. First, I didn't want to go into that dark void; I never had, but knowing someone was below watching out for me had done a great deal to alleviate the raw terror last Friday. Second, I just didn't feel like doing this anymore. I was frazzled from supporting my fragile summer plans with one hand, building up a good hate-on directed at Edgar with another, and living in fear of disappointing Agnes with a third hand, which I didn't have, forcing me to juggle. The third and most important reason for my reticence was that there were now going to be a fair number of dead rats, assuming the brand planted above worked as advertised. No one liked dead rats, except maybe rat terriers. Okay, definitely rat terriers, but not me.

"Jo?" my father called from somewhere in the house.

"In the garage!" I called back.

His ruddy face poked through the kitchen door, cheeks bulging and bottlebrush mustache dripping with sweat. "Jo? You okay? You've been standing there for almost an hour."

"Mmhmm, yeah, just getting my nerve up."

"Oh, well... At least there are no pinecones up there this time."

After dignifying his witticism with a thin smile, I grabbed the dangling cord and relaxed, letting my weight pull the ladder, popping and groaning, into the lighted world. The ladder bowed and creaked beneath me as I took a tentative step onto the first rung before scampering the rest of the way up into hell.

"Be sure to wash your hands before dinner, honey!" dad called after me.

I swung a chunky metal flashlight up over the ceiling's edge. My last journey had taught me something, unlike science class. I shone the flashlight around; the attic remained a void of impenetrable darkness, only now there were starkly lit joists and supports cutting through the black. Settling tufts of insulation filled and defined the cone of the flashlight's beam. It was little wonder we had a rat problem; the insulation, though toxic to humans, provided a perfect nesting ground for the wee red lumps of baby rats. The nut-bearing trees that overhang our roof further provided the little darlings with a consistent food supply. Our attic was a little ratty wonderland; it was past time to change that.

I swung my other arm over the ceiling's edge, bringing with it the plastic bag of rat poison. Besides "bring a flashlight, dummy," another lesson learned was, "always unpack clamshell items before you need them." This bag was significantly less bulky than the bag carried up Friday. Both these important lessons would be included in the "What We Learned" section of my final presentation.

I clambered over the ceiling's edge and journeyed once more into the void. After only a few feet, I stumbled across the first dead rat, "stumbled across" being an apt description. I was on my knees, one hand holding the flashlight, the other entangled in the plastic bag, when I overbalanced and tumbled forward, coming down in the inter-joist insulation. Dropping the flashlight, I arrested my fall on a hard lump buried in the fluff. The flashlight landed in such a way as to light up my hand and the lump, and when the swinging plastic bag's wake pushed aside the insulatory fluff, I saw it, exposed in garish relief. The rat must have been an early adopter of Friday's self-baiting poison; it was many days dead, and though I was neither forensic expert nor rodentologist, this specimen appeared in good health, aside from, you know... the whole being dead thing. The moisture in the body had wicked into the surrounding insulation, leaving the body dry and partially mummified. Yet it retained a certain juiciness, with puss and other wet matter dripping from its eyes and mouth.

This clinical observation of the body belied my far less dignified response to nearly touching a dead rat: I screamed. It wasn't much of a scream; it was more a simultaneous inhalation/exhalation crossed with a gurgle and a retching sound. Not a scream, yet... that's the best word to describe it. Yanking my hand from the soggy bits of insulation surrounding the body, I stumbled backwards, screaming again and again as chunks of disturbed insulation touched my exposed flesh, convincing me with every tickle that another dead rat was touching me.

In that moment, the project died. Had Edgar performed the first round of rat touching, I could have stomached the rest. In the light of the garage, I could have tagged 'em and bagged 'em, possibly sliced open a few to display at the Science Fair. Without Edgar, I couldn't do that. Without Edgar, there would be no collection of specimens, and without collection of specimens, there was no use in setting poison, and without setting poison, there was no experiment, no extra credit, no passing grade, no summer, no Bluker's Creek. I may have indirectly killed this rat, but this already dead rat directly killed my summer vacation.

I scooped up the rat corpse in the plastic bag--I would not leave here empty-handed--and snagged the flashlight. Then I was out of there, swinging my legs over the edge of the ceiling, and returning to *terra firma*. I gave a protracted shove to the attic ladder and its tired springs gratefully sprung close, snapping the trapdoor shut. Tossing the bag with its containers of poison and other less savory contents into one shadowed corner, I ran like the dickens into the house.

"How's it going, honey?" dad asked as I sprinted through the kitchen.

"Hngleugh!" I said, or words to that effect. I stumbled into the den and collapsed headfirst onto the couch. In the stygian blackness of the cushion that enclosed my head, I could still see the body, stiff and brown against the pink and blue insulation. I could still smell the overpowering sweetness of the decaying corpse underscored by the bitterness of liquefying organs and an entire intestinal tract's worth of--

I freed my head from the cushion and the cloying closeness of my own breath. I gulped greedily at the fresh air, alternatively snorting through my nose to get another smell--*any* smell--to come in and overwhelm my mind. Dad was cooking in the kitchen, the boiling asparagus and slowly roasting roast letting off pungent swirls of--God, I could still smell the rat. Gagging and fighting back the urge to vomit, I prayed time would deaden the smell that stalked me from the attic.

As time passed, the smell of--hngleugh--the smell began to dissipate, and I sat up on the couch. Desiring to distract myself from--hngleugh--distract myself, I switched on the television and flipped to a teen-oriented network. Though it was in the middle of a commercial, I settled in to watch, hoping against hope that my mind would drift from--hngleugh--drift.

The current commercial faded, and a new one began. I focused on it, taking in every moment, letting it become my whole world. It depicted an animated man, his head twice the size of his body and glowing beet red. His teeth were clenched and a vein pulsed on his forehead, giving him the appearance of either being in great pain, or realizing that yes, teaching freshman science would be the height of his career. The man remained still as the background cut without transition: first he was in an office, then at a party, then on a train, and finally in line at a store. The background cut to white as the man swallowed some pills before running off screen. There was the sound of grunting, and a tidal wave of blue water exploded from where the man had run. As the torrent subsided, the words "Gelfelax: It Makes You Poop ®" appeared on the white screen, and a cheery voice crowed, "Call now to get your free sample!" before the screen faded to black.

Suddenly, the melodious stylings of Bluker's Creek singing "Baby, I'm Noodlin' For You" streamed from the speakers, mixed with the prerecorded screams of a thousand-thousand wound up fans. I added a moan to the uproar as I realized this product was now beyond my grasp. Snippets of video appeared, showing the band bedecked in overalls and Stetsons, standing on a dark stage as purple lasers burned through the haze around them. The band dissolved into sweeping shots of fans, all standing, all throwing their hands in the air and pulsing to the music, their thousand-thousand faces lit by roving spotlights. The music faded, and a baritone announcer cut in, listing the Creek's credentials--two platinum albums, a sold-out world tour, fifteen weeks on the billboard top 40--and their upcoming tour itinerary. When he mentioned Chicago, I nearly cried. The commercial seemed to last forever, with "Baby, I'm Noodlin' For You" dissolving into "Tractor License For Two" before ending with a final fade to black.

I was on the verge of changing channels, desperate for meaningless distraction from--hngleugh--meaningless distraction, when the high-energy tones of a news broadcast sprang into life, followed by a puppet floating above stock footage of a busy newsroom. The legend "The Evening Report With Lentils The Wonder Dog" ran across the bottom of the screen. I sat up straighter, wiping the illusory tears that were not streaming down my dry cheeks. I liked this show; it was funny, it would distract.

The raggedy puppet--a one-eyed dog wrapped in a pale green sweater--jerked around the screen, its ears flailing. "And in other news," Lentils reported in a sing-song tone, "Los Angeles police found three bodies in the trunk of an abandoned car in Laurel Canyon today. The bodies were identified as college students reported missing last week from--"

My gorge rose once more. I could imagine those bodies, trapped for days in a hot trunk, drying out and--hngleugh. I scrambled for the remote, doing my damndest to ignore anything else Lentils said. I shut off the TV, and after a few minutes spent with my head buried in a cushion, the image of... of what I had seen in the attic, along with... with the smell... faded away to nothing more than a pained memory.

What hadn't faded was the realization that it was over. I had no further cards to play; summer school was my fate, my doom, my one recourse. The only thing left was to roll over and tell Agnes. She had the right to know I wouldn't be joining her in Chicago; call it my two weeks' notice on our friendship.

***

Agnes answered after only two knocks, despite the late hour. She peered suspiciously from behind her front door, then peered even more suspiciously when she recognized me and questioned why I had shown up without first calling. "Hey, Jo, what's up?"

I produced an inarticulate whine, and she opened the door wide enough for me to push inside. I stood in her foyer, trying to look pathetic, staring at Agnes with big puppy-dog eyes and shivering as water dripped from my clothes. It hadn't been raining on my walk over, but I passed under the community center's sprinklers to achieve the maximum level of destitute pathetic-ness. "Please, Aggie, I need your help."

"Oh, Jo." Her glasses slid down her nose as her suspicion softened into amused pity. Draping an arm over my shoulder, she led me upstairs to her room. "Are you having boy trouble?"

I sniffled and nodded, sending a fat drip of water off the tip of my nose. "That I am, Ag, that I am."

"Aw."

She sat me down on the edge of her bed and lowered herself into her desk chair. She rotated to face me, overshot, and scrabbled at the carpet to get back into position. "Tell me all about it."

So I did, blubbering all the while, starting with a tear-and-sprinkler soaked apology about not telling her sooner, transitioning into a stark explanation that I would have to cancel our plans for Bluker's creek, then explaining the project, Edgar's part in it, his subsequent betrayal, and my final attempt to make it work. "And I just can't go on with it!" I concluded, sniffling and rubbing at my nose. "Camacho offered to help, but he was just too damn creepy, and besides, he'd be worse than useless; he's just barely passing!"

"Oh, Jo, oh, oh, oh," she clucked, rising from the chair and joining me on the bed. "You should have told me sooner, Jo. I could have done something to help; *would* have done something to help."

Her words filled me with hope and gave me the courage for one last desperate gamble. "Oh, Ag, maybe it's not too late. You can still help me. Take up the mantle of the scientist, help me in solving the greatest mysteries the universe can offer, and become a far, far better friend than Edgar ever was."

"No."

I bulged out my puppy-dog eyes, waiting on tenterhooks for an answer. After some time with no reply from Agnes, I tried again. "Help me, Agnes, you're my only--"

"No."

Classic Agnes, playing hard to get. If I tried long and hard enough, she'd buckle and give in to my wheedling. "I'm not asking for much, just a few days of helping me collect--"

"Seriously, no." With a sigh, she placed her hands on my shoulders then, feeling just how wet I had gotten, pulled away and dried her hands on her shirt. "Look, I can appreciate your plight, really I can, and I really, *really* want you to come to Bluker's with me, but our friendship isn't worth picking up dead rats over. I mean Ed, he deserves it; it was his idea. But I'm not picking up dead rats for his sake. Sorry. You either have to find another partner, or another project I can help on, and I don't know if I can put in much time, anyway."

I moaned and collapsed onto the bed. As my clothes pressed up against me, I had a realization: I was completely soaked. What the hell? I had stood beneath the sprinklers for no more than a minute, yet it felt as though I had jumped in a swimming pool... "I can't think of anything, Ag," I wheedled. I put in as much petulance as I could muster, trying one last time to sway her. "I'm out of ideas for another project. I didn't even have any ideas in the first place; it was all Edgar! I've been failing science all this time; how am I supposed to suddenly pull genius out of my ass?" I stuck out my bottom lip and pouted.

"Yeah, still not going to reconsider."

I slammed my fists against the bed. "God! The whole summer's shot! What the hell should I do?"

Agnes tilted her head, her brows furrowed, and stared into the distance for several long moments. "Revenge," she hissed.

A chill pass through me: her air conditioner had clicked on with a choking groan. My clothes felt like they would freeze solid. Besides that, excitement coursed through my veins at the thought of punishing Edgar for ruining my summer. "What did you have in mind?"

Agnes continued staring into the distance. She stood and paced the room, tapping her chin all the while, before returning to her desk. There, she pondered her carpet, then kind of kicked at the floor, then began slowly rotate in the chair. After the chair made a revolution and a half, she wheeled back to face me and shrugged. "No clue. I just think revenge sounds cool. You have any ideas?"

"I'm not exactly queen of idea land. I kind of ran out after the whole rat thing."

"I thought that was Ed's idea."

"Shut up." Now it was my turn to stare thoughtfully into the distance, to tap my chin, and to kind of kick at the floor. "Well, I'll think of something horrifyingly appropriate. In the meantime, though, we can at least screw with his head."

"How?" The lamp on her bedside table cast a glare over her glasses, obscuring her eyes behind a white haze. I was glad for that; her tone implied a predatory intensity that I wasn't comfortable gazing into.

A survey of Agnes' room produced a spiral notebook and a collection of glitter pens. I surged from the bed, flipped open the notebook, and began writing in my best girly-script, switching pens for every letter, dotting every 'i' with a little heart, letting the madness of the moment guide my hands. When I was done with the short missive, I laid the notebook down on Agnes' desk and stepped back to admire my handiwork.

Agnes leaned around me to gaze at the dire warning I had penned. "Dear sir," she read aloud, "you shall taste my blistering fury." She remained motionless for a long moment, the silence broken only by the background roar of the air-conditioning, and then offered a slow nod of approval. "This'll freak him right the hell out."

I mirrored the nod. "Get him paranoid. Then, when he least expects it..."

"Revenge," we said in unison.

CHAPTER 7
A DISH BEST SERVED COLD

Against all odds and the words delivered to Agnes the previous night, I concocted a most ingenious means of revenge upon my return home. Tuesday at noon was when I planned to strike, after some prep work in the band's storage closet that morning. To that end, I decided to slip my note into Ed's locker. With luck, he would find it as he dropped off his books before lunch, and be none the wiser about my involvement until it was too late.

So there I was in the gap between gym and science, trying to slide a sheet of folded paper through the vent of Edgar's locker. The paper was halfway through when it stuck, and I wasted precious moments reversing it, waggling it, and invariably shredding it. I should have given Edgar the note outright.

Footsteps clattered up the near-empty hall behind me, and someone asked, "What're you doing at my locker, Jo?"

I yelped and spun to find Edgar standing behind me. He looked much as he had upon his return from Columbus: eyes sunken behind bags of purple flesh, hair hanging lank and greasy past his ears. "Good God, what happened to you?" I asked.

"Band practice. In case you haven't noticed, we're going to state." He squinted at me. "I ask again, Jo: what are you doing?"

"Oh! This!" I took my hands off the dangling paper and pointed at it, then tried to jerk it loose. When it failed to disengage from the vent, I resorted to pointing at it again. "This! I was walking by just now and saw someone stuffing it into your locker!" I fluttered my eyelids, aware that every word and gesture exuded nervous guilt.

"Who'd you see?"

"Hez!"

To answer my declarative statement, three short beeps issued from the intercom system, followed by Hez's voice, transmitted from the office on the clear other side of the building. "Attention, a white BMW, license plate 'ROJI V,' your lights are on."

Ed raised an eyebrow, daring me to stick to my lie.

"It might have been Cal. You know they both look alike."

There were three more clicks, and now Cal's reedier voice spoke. "And it appears you're illegally parked in a handicapped spot."

My smile remained, but my eyes betrayed its confidence.

"Uh-huh." Ed reached out and tugged the note; it came free easily. He unfolded it and read the dire warning within. "Jo, this is your handwriting. What the hell?"

"Um..." My brain joined my eyes in the betrayal. My body was now in a state of complete rebellion. Thank God, my bowels had remained in the loyalist faction. "Science class. Now. I need go." I pointed down the hall, considered my finger's orientation, pointed the other way, and smiled.

"We sit next to each other," Edgar reminded me.

I swear to you, short-term memory, once the revolt is crushed, you will be the first one against the wall. Assuming I remember this.

Class had just begun when Ed and I rushed in, him looking as though he would fall asleep on his feet, me drenched in a flop-sweat.

"Ah, Ed and Jo," the Yog said as we entered, "causing a commotion for us, as always." She produced a strained smile that didn't quite convey the sense of whimsy for which it was intended; odds were good that within five years she'd be broken. We took our seats, and she returned to the lesson in progress. "Alright, everyone, pass your homework to your partner and pull out your red pens..."

A hand raised and frantically waved.

"No, Camacho, if you did the homework in red pen, you should have it graded in blue."

The hand lowered.

Edgar pulled two sheets of paper from his binder and passed one to me. The other he reread again and again, half-smiling through the haze of sleep covering his face. "Really, Jo, this is hilarious."

A fold obscured my view of the multi-colored letters so the page read "Dea-- Taste my bl-- Fu--"

"I mean, what do you expect to convey with this, huh? Is this supposed to be a threat? Or the most passive-aggressive social challenge in the history of mankind?"

Ignore him, Joanna, all you can do is ignore him. I did, thinking instead of what I planned for the lunch period while in the here-and-now The Yog read the answers to the homework I had neglected the previous night.

Edgar's amusement transmuted into annoyance as he continued rereading the note. "Dear God, you're immature," he hissed as The Yog listed off solutions to the matching problems. "I tried to help you, out of the goodness of my heart, on a project that I had *no stake in whatsoever*, and now you're threatening me because a major scholarly activity required my time?"

I couldn't let this last assertion go unanswered. "Band is not a scholarly activity!"

"It is scientifically proven to increase my math comprehension!"

"That may be true," The Yog interrupted, "but right now we're talking about astrophysics, not neurology."

Edgar and I hung our heads and pretended to focus on correcting each other's homework. Ed had a bit of a harder time, having no homework to grade, but I wasn't having much of a better time either: out of twenty questions, I had heard the answers to three.

"Okay then," The Yog muttered.

As I struggled to listen to the remaining answers, as well as look around to see if I could catch answers from other people's papers, I thought about what Edgar said. Yeah, to some extent, he was right. I *shouldn't* really be mad at him for sticking to his guns and helping out the band. What I *should* be mad about, though, is that he agreed to help me, even though he knew he might not be able to carry through. Revenge was still on the table; I just needed him to relax enough that said revenge would get to him. Time to play nice.

"So, uh... how's the whole band thing coming?" I whispered.

No answer.

"Ed..."

He looked up at me. "We've been practicing a lot, and I think we're pretty good, sound-wise. We still need a crap-ton of money to get us there, though, so we're doing a bake sale at the Jamboree."

"Is a bake sale really enough to raise everything you need?"

"Band director's selling blood on the weekends, and all the teachers are pitching in as much as they can."

"Well that's... that's good."

He nodded tentatively, unsure if he actually trusted me to bury the hatchet.

I smiled at him, assuring him that, yes, things were better for the moment, and he looked down to my non-existent homework.

***

As today was a balmy seventy-eight degrees, the school's management was magnanimous enough to let us eat outside. Doors were flung wide, and students streamed from the building. Most students streamed to the stream, partaking of benches shaded by the yard's copse of trees, but I had another destination in mind. Before heading to said mystery destination, however, I sought out my erstwhile partner in crime.

I found Agnes in line in the cafeteria. "We eatin' down by the riverside?" she asked after I wove between the deserted tables to reach her side.

"Nah; football field."

"Football field?" She took a step forward, and a cafeteria attendant plopped something at once wet and crusty onto her tray. "Why? The football team practicing?" It is said a picture is worth a thousand words; if true, Agnes' waggling eyebrows contained the English language's entire supply of innuendo. She took another step forward, and something solid yet dripping with slime plopped down.

I made the mistake of breathing through my nose, and was assaulted by the stink of cabbage, intercut with the sharp tang of smoke and just a hint of bitter rot. I gagged; *this* was why I always brought my own lunches. "No," I managed between coughing fits, "no, the marching band is practicing."

Her eyebrows dropped flat. "Eh, the flautists are the only ones who do anything for me." Something that I'm marginally sure were green beans squelched onto her plate. Her jaw dropped, then pulled back up into a sly grin. "You want to see Edgar, don't you? See his muscles bulge and strain under that big, heavy tuba."

I rolled my eyes. "No! I mean, yes, I do want to see Edgar, and it involves the tuba."

Agnes stared back at me blankly and took another step forward.

"The letter," I prodded.

"Oh, oh, yeah, that." The sly smile again. "*Revenge*."

I shushed her, not wanting to be found out before the plan went into motion. She paid for her food, and we hurried across campus to the football field before the band began practice and we missed the fireworks. Well, not literal fireworks--*that* kind of revenge would land me before a judge.

We climbed the bleachers and found a good seat overlooking the football field. Below us, the marching band milled about, tuning their instruments, prepping their gear, and doing a thousand tedious tasks that served only to delay my gratification.

Seeing the contents of her tray exposed in the naked daylight, Agnes' face gave way to horror. She gagged and placed the tray aside. "So... what's the plan here? What grand sweeping act of revenge have you concocted?"

I shook my head. "Nothing grand and sweeping. Not yet. This is merely the appetizer, a taste of the fiery retribution to come."

Agnes' glasses glinted in the sun as she grinned a wicked grin. With any luck, my eyes glinted just as wickedly as hers. "If Ed can't come to the science project, then the science project will come to Ed."

A senior in a ridiculous four-foot tall furred hat strode onto the field, brandishing a baton striped with the school colors. He whipped the baton through the air and ordered up his band. The flautists, the cymbalists, the French horn players--all easily grabbed up their instruments and formed into neat rows. The drummers, the sousaphonists, the tuba players--Ed among them-- stopped their back-of-the-group conversations and hoisted up *their* instruments, grumbling all the while. The four-foot column of faux-fur swayed as the bandleader tapped his foot.

I took a bite of my sandwich--it was the only thing keeping me from megalomaniacal laughter as I anticipated what was to come. Truly, I had devised a most heinous revenge. The tension was so thick I could taste it... Something squirmed in my mouth. No, that was the mayonnaise I tasted, not the tension. The mayonnaise had turned. I'd need to discourage my parents from bulk buying. As delicately as I could, I spit the morsel out. The spit was *too* delicate: my bit of sandwich dangled in mid-air at the end of a strand of spit.

"Gross," Agnes scoffed.

I snorted, and the bite of sandwich disconnected, disappearing into the darkness below. If the regurgitation my lunch was too much for Agnes' tender sensibilities, she wouldn't enjoy what was coming next.

Three sharp whistles brought my attention back up--no, wait, down--to the field, to see the band marching in place while the music started. Their playing was rough--apparently, they *hadn't* been using their down time to tune their instruments. I zeroed in on Edgar. He was blowing with all his might, cheeks ballooning and face glowing beet red under the strain of playing the tuba. Even to my untrained ear, it was obvious no sound came from him.

The bandleader whistled again and gestured with his staff of limitless power. The music petered out and the heavy lifters lowered their instruments. Other tuba players gathered around

Edgar, chattering excitedly. I couldn't make out any words from the babble. That was the downside to this particular method of revenge: I wouldn't be close enough to hear the reactions. Ed looked over his tuba, then reached inside the bell and--

From this distance, they all looked like railroad miniatures. Little people-shaped blobs gathered around a shiny blob, picked it up, and examined it. One little blob reached inside and jerked back, pulling a little brown blob with it. The brown blob went flying, catching the air and gliding a remarkable distance thanks to its flat, rigid body.

A moment later, the sound hit us: screams, shouted words, an entire marching band suddenly moving far faster than it was supposed to.

"Holy crap!" Agnes spluttered, laughing and coughing and wiping at her eyes. "Was that a rat?"

"Yep," I answered, beaming with triumph. "I managed to get *one* body down from the attic before I realized there was no way I could get more. Then I figured, 'hey, why not share the excitement of learning with Edgar?'"

Edgar stumbled about the field, gesticulating and uttering oaths most foul. My concerns proved groundless; despite the distance, I could hear Edgar perfectly.

"Not a duck, Edgar," I said, wiping mirth from my eyes, "A rat."

Agnes stopped laughing and looked at me oddly. "He didn't say 'duck.' That's not even remotely what he--"

"It sounded like 'duck,' okay?"

"I guess, but he said fu--"

"*I* didn't want to say that, okay?" I sighed, feeling some of my joy slip away. I loved Ag, really I did, but she could kill a moment like no one else.

That was when Edgar spotted us. He pointed and shouted my name.

Ice water flushed through my bowels. "Oh crap!" I lurched forward, sliding from my seat. "Hide!" I pulled Agnes down beside me, and we both slid under the bench. We shuffled backwards until we hung above the void, then we dropped the remaining few feet to the ground. We rolled in the wilted grass, Agnes losing her glasses and me picking up the chunk of sandwich I had so soundly rejected. Through it all, we laughed.

"I will end you!" Edgar bellowed from beyond the bleachers. I could just see him, cut up into bars of light and shadow, running to where we had been. "Do you hear me? End! *You*!"

I handed Agnes her glasses before we ran from under the bleachers and back towards the main school building, not daring to look back, laughing the whole way.

CHAPTER 8
HOLDING IT IN

Before lunch ended, the marching band had swarmed back into the main building, filled with stories of a great gooey flying disk of horror that zoomed over the field, blasted from a tuba by the force of Edgar's breath. The story grew in the telling. Seeing as Ed had followed the clues to the discovery of my involvement, it wasn't long before *everyone* knew of my involvement, and once they knew, they had to let me know they knew.

Camacho spent one passing period leaned against my locker, telling me how cool my act of revenge was, and how much he wished he had actually been there, and that I could shove a rat in *his* tuba anytime. I told him he was creepy, but my words failed to dissuade him.

Clarice, the head cheerleader, passed by me later and visibly sniffed. "Don't you think that was just a little cruel, Jo?" she asked judgmentally. "I can understand the need to kill pest animals when they directly interfere with one's own survival or livelihood, but weren't there more humane ways to deal with your infestation?" I had ruffled her feathers and scored one against the cheerleading elite; that served to make my revenge all the sweeter.

The Yog accosted me in the hall after sixth hour and said, without any trace of humor, "I expect wind conditions to be factored into any aerodynamics conclusions before you present your results." It was only then that I truly appreciated her as a teacher.

The absolute highlight of the day came when the principal--Thumbs himself, not Cal or Hez--announced over the loudspeaker: "I'd like to assure everyone that news of flying rodents attacking the band have been greatly exaggerated. Though the field house has a history of bat infestations, today's events are unrelated. Furthermore, though the creature was later found and identified as a rat, it should be noted that it was already dead and was flung like a non-specifically branded flying disk, rather than flying under its own power." He sighed, releasing a rush of fetid wind that carried decades of pain and disillusionment. "So please, tell your parents to stop calling me, complaining of rat-bird attacks. It's really not funny." His words were broken up at the end, and the intercom cut off, though not before transmitting the sounds of an old man beginning to cry.

The first phase of my revenge had been a success.

The glow of that success dimmed as I walked home. Edgar still walked with me, mirroring my progress on the far side of the street, trudging along in sullen silence.

"Hey," I called after a mile with no conversation. "I cleaned the little critter as best I could, but you might want to sanitize your tuba."

I waited for some kind of acknowledgment, the merest hint of a smile. Nothing.

"You know, if Camacho were here, he'd have something to say about that."

He clomped his heavy shoes over the dry earth, brooding all the while.

"'That's what she said?'" I prompted.

Tough audience. It was tempting--nay, only natural--to be angry with Edgar in light of this silent treatment. Upon further reflection, I realized I did kind of deserve it. Justified as my revenge was, it had been horrifying, and Ed was more than a little freaked out. Touching a dead rat was no fun under the best circumstances; being surprised by the feel of its bristly dead body down a tube you had just had your lips on was sure to be traumatizing. In a show of magnanimity, I decided to give him another day of this childish sulking; two days, tops. In that time, he should have calmed down and apologized for bungling this whole thing. He might even buckle down and give the project one last push, so as to avoid further reprisal.

That was Plan A. If after two days he proved unwilling to put the past behind him and grow up, well then, I'd just have to get downright vindictive, wouldn't I? He would taste my blistering fury, of that there was no doubt.

We parted as we neared my house, Edgar continuing the final few blocks to his home, me making my way to mine. On a better day, I would have invited him in for a snack or a glass of water, but it seemed unlikely that he'd accept my offer.

I tossed my book bag onto a chair, once more producing a cat from the aether, then stopped dead in my tracks as an unpleasant aroma assaulted my nose. It was a thick odor, redolent with spices and the sickly smell of methane. It suffused every cubic meter of air in the living room; even breathing through my mouth, I could smell it. I thought there might be a gas leak, and that I should relight a pilot light somewhere. The recollection that we had an electric furnace slowed me as I headed to the garage, and a sound like rubber rubbing on rubber froze me, alerting me that while there *was* a gas leak, it was unlikely fatal in the short-term.

Flicking on the overhead lights exposed my father, asleep on his favorite recliner. A look of deep existential pain contorted a face already swollen, red, and sweaty. His tie hung loose around his neck, and farther down, I noticed his pants were unbuttoned.

His eyelids fluttered open moments later, and he shielded his eyes with one beefy palm. There was another one of those rubber-on-rubber sounds, and the smell grew somehow worse.

"Oh, God, Dad, that's foul! Warn someone next time!"

He peered at me from through slitted eyelids. "Sorry...." As he leaned over to unlatch the reclining mechanism, he produced a plethora of sounds and smells before righting himself and gasping in shallow wheezes.

I crept closer to him. "Are you okay?" Dad wasn't what one

might call fit, but today he looked positively ghastly.

A burbling deep in his gut delayed his response. "No, no not really," he said after the intestinal temblor. To underscore this assertion, a high-pitched squeak escaped him, followed by another waft of foul perfume. "Sorry. I...I haven't had a bowel movement in four days."

That was more information than I ever wanted to know.

"I had an entire head of broccoli this morning, but all it's doing is backing up--" He was cut off by a massive fart. The house rattled, and a decorative plate over the fireplace fell flat on the mantel.

I gagged. "You need a doctor!" I yelled, putting my vast scientific knowledge at his disposal.

"Yeah, well...." There came a wet burble, followed by a tenor squeak. "I can't really take time off work..."

"Where's Mom?"

"She should--ahhh!" He held his gut as more abortive bowel movements rocked his body. "She should be home soon."

"Yeah, okay. Um, is... is there anything I can do?" I prayed the answer would be "no."

"No, I'm... I'll survive."

Despite his welcome refusal of service, I lingered near him, feeling at a loss of what to do. I toyed with telling him about the excitement at school, but realized A) as an academician himself, he would hear the more interesting exaggerations to bloom in the coming weeks, and B) he wouldn't look kindly upon my part in things. Instead, I settled on catching some old *SpongeBob* reruns before mom came home.

She got in an hour later, curtly acknowledging my existence before crossing the living room to dad. "Jeez, Curt, are you doing any better?"

"Does it smell like I am?" he asked amidst a concert of muted trumpets.

Mom righted the plate on the mantel. "Look, I can understand why you don't want to go to the doctor; colonic irrigation is rarely enjoyable, even under the best of circumstances. But you already have him checking your prostate--"

I turned up the television, not trusting my normal filtering ability for when mom talked science.

"JO!"

I turned the volume back down to a manageable level. Though it hadn't been my intention, the sudden blaring of the TV might distract my parents from their... discussion.

"Alright, Curt," mom said once words other than, "*I'm ready, I'm ready, I'm ready...*" were audible, "I'll do it, but if you don't see improvement in twenty-four hours, you have to promise me you'll get the irrigation done, okay?"

I gradually increased the volume, missing my dad's answer.

"Jo?"

I lowered the volume and looked over the side of the couch to where mom stood.

"You have much homework tonight?"

I shrugged. "Not really."

A mixed expression of relief and hope crossed her face. "You want to go with me to get your father some laxatives?"

I grimaced and began priming puppy dog eyes. "Oooh, sounds fun, but I am absolutely swamped with homework tonight."

She responded with a *look*.

I tried responding with a counter look of purity and innocence, a look in desperate need of not being grounded. A muffled fart ruined the mood and I contorted my face into something that should be locked away on principle. Fortunately, mom pulled that exact same face at that exact same moment, so my comments regarding homework passed to the wayside.

"Please...." dad wheezed, his voice little more than a whisper, "I beg of you. Just go to the thrice-damned store...."

My resolve was shaken under this fusillade of pitiful moaning. Dad needed something, *anything* to take care of what ailed him, and if I were being honest with myself, there wasn't that much homework to do, though I actually needed to do it, in contrast to last night's assignment. On the other hand, mom had no pressing need for me to accompany her... I sat unmoving on the couch, crippled by indecision and caught between selflessness and selfishness.

"I'll let you drive on the way home," mom offered.

Sold.

We set out at once, unwilling to spend more time in dad's noxious presence. Once away from the reek of the house, my mind fell back into the last week's constant routine: thinking about my thrice-damned science fair project. Now that it was blown, I put all my effort into thinking of ways to get back at Edgar. Unfortunately, I had used up my one good idea with the rat. Perhaps I could pick traditional practical jokes and record how much rage each generated, and convert the results into a usable report. Did a bucket of water over a door cause as much swearing as a whoopee cushion, say, or did ketchup packets on the underside of a toilet seat cause one to punch a wall harder than getting black eye-rings off of binoculars? What I needed was just one good idea, and everything *might*, maybe, just possibly, work. Unfortunately, Edgar was the idea guy.

"Whatcha thinking about?" mom asked as we pulled out of our neighborhood and onto a main road.

"Oh, you know...sciency things."

"How's that rat thing of yours going? I thought you were going to work on it this weekend."

A moan worked itself up from the core of my being and I slumped into my seat. "Oh, well, you know, I'm thinking now maybe it isn't really worth the effort to finish it," I said around a mouthful of seatbelt.

"Sorry to hear that," mom said as she swerved through a left turn on a yellow light. "Well, at least it was just extra credit and not an important assignment, right?"

The seatbelt chafed my nose as I nodded. "Yup. Just a little bit of extra credit. No big loss."

We drove along in silence for two blocks. At last mom said, "You know, Jo, I don't appreciate it when you lie to me."

I pushed myself back upright, unsure of what she meant, but wanting to match her on more-or-less equal footing when she let the accusations fly. "I'm afraid you've caught me at a disadvantage, here," I said, stalling for time.

"The Yog sent us a letter two weeks ago, when your grades

really started dipping. Did you think we wouldn't know?"

Dear God, was everybody just going behind my back, plotting around me and hoping I would fail? I managed to put logically coherent words into a serviceable order and came out with, "You knew all this time, but didn't say anything?" I tried underscoring my outrage with a shocked expression, but it was lost on mom's driving focus.

"I figured it would be a good learning experience for you," she said. "Ms. Yogmeir told us about the alternative she had given you, and I saw how eagerly you were approaching the project. I figured, 'Hey, you're handling this on your own, so why not just let you handle this on your own?' If--*when*--you were all finished with it and had passed, we'd sit you down and have a good family discussion about it."

"All of this sounds more like *you* lying to *me*," I retorted before realizing I had just prodded the proverbial sleeping bear with the proverbial pointed stick.

"If you were having problems getting your project done and were going to fail, you should have talked to us," mom said. "Because this isn't just some extra credit project. This is your whole GPA on the line."

I crossed my arms over my chest, jamming my hands deep into my armpits to find some measure of warmth amidst the sudden chill. "I've got it covered; just give the benefit of the doubt here, all right?"

"We already gave you the benefit of the doubt. We believed you could do your assignments as assigned and work out a passing grade in class. But you didn't, Jo. We trusted you with science class, and then we trusted you with fixing science class, and now you've lost our trust."

I leaned my forehead against the window, hoping to find some measure of coolness to sooth the burning behind my forehead. "I just can't deal with the rats anymore, you know? It's... nasty. Just give me another chance; all I need is another idea for a project, and I can fix this, I can get out of summer school, and I can spare you the shame of being a scientist whose daughter failed science."

Mom sighed, fogging the window so there was nothing outside

save for patches of colored light. "Your father and I are very proud that you took steps to correct your grade. We *are* concerned that you let it fall that far, though. Seriously, what happened? Have we failed as parents?"

I produced a sigh of my own. "No, Mom."

"Are your friends affecting you? What about drugs? Did someone talk you into drugs?"

"No, Mom," I said, slipping a note of exasperation into my voice.

"What about Agnes? Is she distracting you from your schoolwork?"

"Mom!"

She shrugged. "I'm sorry, I just don't trust her. I've seen her so-called band. Bunch of juvenile punks is more like."

"Well, yeah, obviously."

"I don't mean that musically, and you know it. She's a wild child, Jo. Your father has feelers all throughout the school system, and the buzz he's getting is that your so-called friend Agnes has *zero* plans for college."

"Is that really such a bad thing?"

Mom looked away from the road and faced me with an expression of horrified incredulity. "How's she going to get anywhere in life without a college degree?"

"Everyone has a college degree now; they're useless."

"Extrapolating that logic backwards then, she's tantamount to a high school dropout, and I'd appreciate it if you didn't hang out with her anymore. The friends you have in high school are so important."

My first several responses to this assertion would only escalate matters. Taking a calming breath, I composed the following argument: "Agnes has not had a detrimental effect on my scholastic career. In fact, her inviting me to the concert this summer served as the primary motivator in my buckling down to do this extra credit project."

Mom also took a calming breath before responding. "Oh, well... that's good, then. Just so long as you're not on drugs."

"I'm not."

We pulled into the parking lot of a mom & pop pharmacy that happened to be a wholly owned subsidiary of a major chain outfit, though no signs announced this fact. Mom and I climbed from our warm car and into the cold, creepy, overly fluorescent hell-world that was the drug store. Our faces turned green from the store's inner glow as the automatic doors churned and groaned. When they finally deigned to open, mom made a beeline straight to the checkout counter. The somnambulist manning the till barely glanced up from a laminated sales circular as mom approached.

"Hi!" she said in a misguided attempt at politeness. "Where do you keep laxatives?" A moment of silence passed between them. "They're not for me. They're for my husband."

The cashier cranked his neck to a nominally alert position and just stood there, considering mom from under heavy eyelids.

"Please, I need some laxatives," she reiterated. "I'm kind of in a hurry." She shared another moment of silence with the cashier. "But they're not for me."

Standing behind a rack of magazines, I should have been detached from this tableau, but I still cringed at their interplay. Could this trip get any more embarrassing?

Without taking his eyes from my mother, the cashier raised a limp arm and pointed in the direction of the rest of the store.

"Thank you," mom said icily. "You've been very helpful." She half-turned, as if to leave, then saw me hiding behind the magazines. "Oh, Jo, while we're here, do you need any more tampons?"

In response to my earlier question: Yes, this trip could indeed get more embarrassing.

I scurried away from mother, going in the direction the cashier had indicated. After going down five wrong aisles and skirting a wet floor sign, I at last found that which we sought. Before me were row upon row of laxatives in bright boxes proclaiming in polite and convoluted language that yes, they would make you poop good.

Footsteps clicked on the faded tile as mom approached me, her eyes wide and face pale. "Dear God, how will we figure out what to get?"

Having no answer to that, I began to browse. First up was Gelfelax, the most forward of the bunch. A little red-faced man squatted on the front of the box, with the logo and motto contained in a speech-bubble issuing from his mouth: "Gelfelax: It Makes You Poop!" Next to that was a green box showing a middle-aged woman caressing her belly. Floating beside her in a looping serif font was: "Nature's Way: An All Natural Relaxing Agent." And beyond that, in a zebra striped magenta and blue box was: "Chewable Regglies! They Keep You Kool and Regular!"

Mom began rifling through the boxes, flipping them over and considering the drug facts printed on the reverse side. "Why can't they just have a box marked 'Laxatives'?" she asked around a lopsided grin.

I refrained from pointing out the hypocrisy of her question; she worked in the kind of lab that churned out endless patent-defying variants of the same simple drugs. Instead, I held out a box to her. "Here you go."

Mom ignored my offering. "Oh, that's store brand, honey; too sketchy." If anyone would know, I guessed she would. She returned to perusing the poop pills, her shoulders slumping and the wrinkles on her forehead deepening. "I can't decide which one is best," she said in an exaggerated deadpan. "They all say they're the best, but only one can be the best! I need to call Grover up at the lab; he was on the team that helped develop Gelfelax. I just can't decide..."

As my non-science grades proved, I was a smart kid; I could take a hint when it was given. "Look, I'll take care of this, okay? Why don't you go get a magazine or something?" I took the laxatives from mom's hands and tried to pat her back. The gesture was awkward with the boxes wedged betwixt my fingers, but I made it work.

"Thanks, honey, I think I will at that." Her lopsided grin grew more lopsided, and she winked. "I'm sure you'll come up with an ingenious laxative-picking protocol." So saying, she drifted back to the front of the store.

Alone now, I stared down at the little boxes. The conversation about my grades--or lack thereof--was by no means over, but I had been granted a reprieve, and maybe, just maybe, another shot at a summer. Staring into the confusing mass of fecal marketing before me, my perspective shifted, and I saw what it was that I truly held in my hands: redemption.

Held within each box was the solution to my problems...

CHAPTER 9
LETTING IT OUT

After weeks of anticipation, the big day finally arrived: The Great Kelso Amboy All-School Jamboree and Swap Meet. A venerable and ancient tradition that dated back... ooh, five years, to when the previous superintendent was discovered embezzling funds and the district budget came up short. Since then, the Jamboree had become *the* social event of the school year.

Though the tradition started out as--and ostensibly still *was*--a blatant cash-grab, the Jamboree had become a place where everyone in the school showed off what they did best for the edification of the student body. And yes, begged a little more funding their way. The drama department had pimped out the auditorium with as much glam and glitz as they could muster, and now it played host to the most talentless talent show ever conceived. The cheerleaders were there, doing their thing, as was the school marching band, the venerable Kelso Amboy Potoos, performing small musical sets throughout the night.

Above the auditorium and slightly to the left was the science fair, packed to bursting with the fruits of Kelso Amboy's best and brightest's labor. And just beyond that was the English Department, sharing out esoteric poetry and hosting a wine tasting that did *not*, they *swear*, get passed down to the children in any way, shape, or form. And just beyond *that* was the third-floor janitorial supply closet, which housed an illegal off-the-books casino. The less said about that, the better.

But the main event, the reason parents let their kids drag them from the safety of their homes, was the bake sale. The gym was packed with tables and booths laden with yeast and carbohydrates as far as the eye could see. While every event that night would be tacitly begging for spare change, the back sale wouldn't just be demanding money, it would be earning it. This is where parents came to lose money, and where departments and organizations and so-called charities came to find their budgets: everyone from the destitute Potoos all the way down to the Friends of the Second World Club, desperate to fund their annual trip to Transnistria.

Though this was my first year attending the Kelso Amboy school, it wasn't my first year attending the Kelso Amboy Jamboree. As Dean of Admissions for Telethepee Junior College, my dad hovered around the college's yearly recruitment booth, bolstering his school's numbers with those Kelso Amboy students who lacked the drive to do anything special with their lives. As a local virologist, my mom hovered around the science fair, trying to function as a living recruitment poster for The Yog as our teacher tried ushering kids into the STEM fields. It rarely worked out.

In years past, Edgar had come with us. This year he was already at the school, setting up the Potoos' bake sale booth and warily tuning his tuba, reticent to touch it to his lips. Thanks to his absence, Agnes was able to carpool with my parents and me.

Our aging principal, Mr. Thumbs, greeted us as we neared the front steps of the school. Per tradition, he served as the first school representative anyone saw coming to the Jamboree, likely as a way to pressure better donations from the visiting adults. His jowly bald head glistened in the moonlight as he approached, arms outstretched and welcoming. "Ah, girls!" he exclaimed, voice raspy and hollow, perpetually on the verge of a coughing fit. "How nice of you to come."

"Hi, Mr. Thumbs," Agnes and I said in unsettling unison.

A line of sweat broke out across his forehead. "Please, this is after hours! We're all friends here! Call me Rick!" His face drooped down around either side of a wide smile. Though his intent was clearly "jovial," the expression made him look unwell.

Some teachers could pull off the hip, laid-back thing. Example: The Yog. Mr. Thumbs, no matter how hard he tried, could not do it. His failure was caused by a combination of always looking pissed whenever one talked to him, and simply trying too hard to be liked: he once spent a month signing off announcements by reminding us that, "out of principle, I'm your princi-*pal*!" Poor man; no one much liked him.

Dad stepped forward to grip Mr. Thumb's outstretched hand, giving it a hearty shake. "How ya doing, Rick?"

Thumbs winced at said hearty shake. "Good, good. Yourself?"

An expression of proud pain crossed dad's face as he opened his mouth to speak, but mom cut in before he could share his recent colonic troubles with the principal. "So, you have a big turn-out this year?"

Mr. Thumbs shrugged, sending his jacket up around his ears like a snail retreating into its shell. "Could be worse, could be worse. I notice that you brought Agnes along with you tonight; shame her parent's couldn't make it. Did you happen to bring her parent's money as well?"

My parents stared at him wide-eyed, too shocked to answer.

He broke out into maniacal laughter, a sound that said, "I was totally serious with the question, but since you're offended, then it was a joke! It was *always* meant as a joke! Stupid!" My parents kind of chuckled, having heard the principal's unspoken words, and wanting to agree to his pact so they could pretend their daughter's school wasn't run by a creep. Have I mentioned Mr. Thumbs was appointed by our previous superintendent?

He wiped his eyes, pretending to be crying from laughing so hard, then his smile disappeared and any trace of levity, false or genuine, fled from his face. "I'm serious, though. We're way behind on the budget."

Aggie and I shared a look that screamed, "Run!"

So we did.

Once away from my parents and in the vestibule of the school, we found a sea of wonder and excitement. No, wait, scratch that. We found fifteen bored teenagers and three ramshackle carnival games. The only game getting any attention was a booth lined with coconuts, manned by Cal and Hez wearing red-and-white striped hoodies.

"Step right up!" Cal called in his best carnival barker voice. "Try your aim, win a coconut!"

"Don't be shy, try the coconut shy!" Hez amended.

A girl from my French class, Genevieve I think she called herself there, was next in line. As Cal and Hez shouted their wares to a saturated marketplace, Genevieve exchanged a dollar for a softball. She hunkered into position and began the wind-up.

"*Oh, I've got a lovely bunch of coconuts...*" Hez began singing. He was off-key.

"*Deedle-dee-dee,*" Cal added as counterpoint. He was little better than his brother.

"*Tais-toi,gros nez,*" Genevieve muttered before letting fly with a tremendous pitch that bounced off a coconut and hit Hez in the nose. Blood sprayed across the furry fruit.

"Nice try, nice try, at the coconut shy!" Cal intoned, taking Genevieve by the shoulders and steering her away.

"*Merde…*" she grumbled.

"A dollar gets you a ball, a ball gets you a chance to hit, a hit gets you a coconut!" Cal called over his shoulder to the other students in line.

"No fair!" Genevieve yelled in a terrible French accent. "Zat coconut vas nailed to ze booth!"

Cal and Hez looked to each other, eyes wide, and swallowed. I looked to Agnes. We both knew this: if ever a carny should acknowledge their game was rigged, no matter how passing that acknowledgment, it was time to get out of there.

We slipped from the vestibule and into the school proper, where this time there really was a sea of humanity, made up of students, parents, and community members with nothing better to do on a Saturday night. We milled through booths for the library, the chamber of commerce, the parks department, the junior college, *et cetera, et cetera,* collecting bookmarks and fun-sized candy and pencils and all manner of crap that would sit on our bedroom floors until the end of the school year before being dumped in the garbage, unmissed and unmourned.

"So, what do you want to do?" Agnes shouted over the hubbub.

I shrugged, a gesture audible despite the din. "Well, I have to get up to the science fair to protect our concert."

"Count me out."

"Okay, well, I'll go, and then after that, maybe we could take in the bake sale? Play some carnival games?"

She nodded along to my suggestions. "Sounds good!"

"Great. Break now and see you in, say, half an hour?"

"Sure!" She continued nodding, then headed down the hall in the direction of... damn it, the bake sale. The sheer noise of this place must have prevented me from getting across that I wanted to peruse sketchy homemade confections *with* Agnes. Hopefully, she would still have the stamina to stay with me when I cruised the bake sale later...

But I couldn't focus on our miscommunication now. The time had come for the moment I had been dreading: the hour of dread that would decide my year and make or break my social life at least up until college. The time of the Science Fair drew nigh!

I edged out of the crowd and made my way upstairs. With every step I grew farther from the fun and frivolity below, surrounded by fewer and fewer people. At last I was alone in the dark, headed towards a modicum of light trickling from an ajar door. Inside was The Yog, her classroom, and...

Wow, not much else.

I had been in after school yesterday to set up my display. At the time, there were two other projects set up. I assumed that I was one of the first to get there, a go-getter if you will. In years past, the science fair had been grand, fully encompassing three lab-classrooms and partially filling a fourth. Parents flitted freely between the rooms, looking in on the best projects, grudgingly acknowledging to themselves that their kid wasn't the most pungent rag in the chloroform bottle, and deciding that maybe community college wouldn't be so bad for their little darlings. Though science was mom's bag, dad enjoyed the fair more than she: this was where he hit his semester's recruitment quota.

It turned out that I was not a go-getter, or that if I was, everyone else was died-in-the-wool procrastinators of the worst kind. Spread thin across the lab benches before me were five projects, mine included. Each trifold display and papier-mâché model got its own table and then some; one multi-part display had colonized an entire row of benches. Nine faces peered at me from the puddle of craft store paper goods as I entered the room: eight students competing for prizes, and The Yog, there to pass unholy judgment.

"Jo, glad you could make it!" The Yog said. "I know it must have been a close battle, fighting your way into our little sanctuary of inquiring thought."

"What happened?" I asked. "Where are all the other projects?"

The Yog floated out from behind a trifold entitled "Juggle Your Way To Health-Fact or Fiction." "There are none other. No one participated." She brushed the tips of her fingers against a faux-gold trophy on the front table. "It seems the treasure of knowledge is not enough for some people. Those who wanted more, who sought to seek their fortunes, are at the bake sale, trading academic prestige for brownie money." She gazed into the distance. "Damn this obese nation and its insatiable lust for chocolate!"

She then focused on me. "Enough about that! Let's see if you put in enough effort to avoid the dreaded summer school!"

I led the way to my trifold, refusing to comment on the speech The Yog had delivered. On the few occasions that I had actually hunkered down and listened, I found her to be just plain weird.

The other students remained by their own projects, as though they feared that leaving their trifolds invited a swarm of corporate saboteurs who would forthwith scrabble up marketable material and leave the displays in shambles. Nine sets of eyes watched from the shadows of trifolded cardboard as I stood beside my display and launched into my spiel.

"For a pharmaceutical product to make it to market," I began, using my best English class dissembling tone, "it must go through innumerable stages of product testing. Does the product perform the way its formulators intended? Are there any legally actionable side effects? Does the product work well in conjunction with other drugs? All of these tests are vital to ensure that what the consumer--you--puts into his or her body is both safe and functional. However, none of these tests help you--the consumer--decide which pharmaceutical to purchase for a given situation. The product works as advertised, certainly, but how well does it work compared to that of another brand? Recently, I found myself asking just such questions when purchasing laxatives."

The trifolds exploded with a flurry of titters.

"They were for my dad."

The titters were not letting up.

"Really." God, high schoolers could be immature.

"Anyway," The Yog prompted.

"Yes, anyway, I found myself asking just such questions when purchasing laxatives--*for my father*--and thought to devise an experiment testing the relative worth of a variety of laxative brands. Parameters tested for include release time, rate, and severity of intestinal cramping. Any product that caused bleeding was dinged on all accounts. Please see my board for more details, or feel free to ask questions."

My eight competitors--no, wait, I wasn't competing--*compatriots* muttered and retreated behind their trifolds to guard their displays against imagined hordes of plagiarizers. The Yog remained with me, peering at my board and folding back pages of the *Conclusions* report.

"So," she asked as she shifted her attention to a page of colorful pie charts, "where did you find test-subjects for this?"

"Oh, you know, around. I put an ad online, seeking middle-aged men with impacted bowels. I got... a lot of responses. A lot of... *weird* responses." I fell silent, thinking back over the emails I had received in the last week. I shuddered.

The Yog stepped away from my trifold and considered me, lips pursed and eyes thoughtful. "Honestly, this project represents about the smallest amount of effort you could have put in."

My shoulders slumped. After all that work, after all those weird men wanting to tell me about their bowel-movements, I was going to fail and miss the concert with Agnes; she would never forgive me, just as I would never forgive The Yog, nor myself.

"However."

I perked up; a 'however' was a good sign.

"When you first picked Edgar as your partner for this project, I was concerned. *He's* a good student, *he* actually turns stuff in. I figured between the two of you, he'd do all the work, and you'd mostly be along for the ride. But since he dropped out, you stepped up, picked a new project, and did it. Like I said, you didn't put *much* effort into it, but you identified a problem, created an experiment to test solutions, and came to a reasonable conclusion. That's the scientific method; that proves you at least get the basic gist of what this class is all about. That boils down to this: you got the extra credit. So long as you turn in the rest of your assignments, I guarantee you a passing grade."

Something left me, moving in a warm liquid wave. I was concerned that I had peed myself from excitement, or that the constant contact with laxatives over the past two weeks had somehow given me contact squirts. But when no one else reacted in derision or disgust, I realized the warm, wet feeling was anxiety flowing from my body. After a month of constant worrying, and rat touching, and keeping secrets from my best friend, and more rat touching, and weird strangers telling me about their bowel movements, it was all over.

I took a tremulous breath and released a tirade of exhilaration. "Thank you, Ms. Yogmier."

"Please, Joanna, call me The Yog." She smiled and let out a light chuckle. "It sounds so much cooler."

That it did.

She turned away and clapped her hands twice in quick succession. "Okay, now that the charity case is out of the way, let's get the real science fair going!" She pointed to a lumpy brown cone. "Gene and Tina, you made a volcano; you're out. You other three, play rock-paper-scissors amongst yourselves to determine your trophy."

The six remaining entrants glanced between themselves, glad they hadn't been eliminated in such a desultory manner, yet miffed that their hard work would be rewarded by chance, not merit.

Meanwhile, The Yog scurried for the door, a mischievous

twinkle in her eye. "While y'all do that, *I'm* going to the bake sale."

***

There must have been a thousand people crushed into the cavernous gym: parents, students, the lazy scientists who had so thoughtfully lowered The Yog's expectations and allowed me to pass with flying colors. Speaking of passing... Had I passed Agnes in the hall and not noticed? I scanned the gym, desperate for a glimpse of her; I needed to let her in on the good news ASAP.

"How'd it go?"

I flinched away from the horrible, squeaky voice shrieking in my ear. Even with a thousand other voices mumbling and grumbling, Agnes could cut through a crowd like an ice pick into my ear. I was on the verge of answering her when I ran back through that last metaphor. It was...eww. Mental note: use less violent metaphors. Similes. Metaphors. Mental note: study English notes before the final. I was better at English than Science, but I wouldn't rely on skating by anymore.

"Hey, Ag," I demurred, allowing the suspense to build before answering her question. "Where were you? I thought you were going to scope this joint out." No, it had definitely been a simile; it used "like."

Agnes shrugged and gazed around at the buzzing bake sale. "Clarice offered me a free blandie if I helped her carry some stuff down from the cafeteria."

But a simile was just a type of metaphor, wasn't it? "Clarice? The cheerleader?"

She nodded.

"How was the blandie?"

"Bland. And strawberry flavored."

"Knowing Clarice, probably poisoned. Maybe you should go and bulimia that up in the nearest toilet. That's what Clarice would do if she actually bothered to eat anything.

Agnes brayed out a laugh. "Good one, Jo, I'll have to include that in my cheerleader protest song." She straightened her glasses. "Anyway, though, after the blandie, I scoped out the cafeteria a little. There's still a crapton of stuff to come down." My deferral registered with her then, and she began bobbing up and down, like she had to pee. "So, how'd it go with The Yog?"

I heaved a melodramatic sigh and slumped my shoulders as if I were nothing more than a half-melted candle in a stormy window. "Well, I tried my best, but..."

Agnes whimpered. Shock and profound disappointment clouded her face.

This was amusing at first, but now it bordered on cruel. I smeared a manic grin across my face and stood straighter. "I did it!" I bellowed over the noise of the packed gymnasium. "I passed!" I threw my arms wide and swooped in for a hug. "We're going to see Bluker's Creek!"

We embraced and squealed with joy, ignoring the confused stares from those around us.

When we parted, I clapped my hands together and surveyed the smorgasbord. "So! We gots us some celebratin' to do! Let's get us some food!"

We wound our way through the crowd, stopping here and there to shell out copious amounts of money for minuscule amounts of homemade food, sampling wares that were probably not up to conventional hygiene standards, but good enough.

Despite my earlier mockery, one of our first stops was Clarice's booth, where we partook of her blandies. As advertised, they were bland. And strawberry flavored.

Next we came to Camacho, who sold pudding cups from a tray, without the extravagance of a dedicated booth. When I say pudding cups, I don't mean cups of pudding, I mean straight-up, fresh-from-the-store-with-the-wrappers-pulled-off pudding cups. Still, they were cheap, so Agnes and I each got one.

"Mmm, this tastes really good," I said, choking down the bitter, chocolate-like chemical.

"That's what she said," Camacho replied, nodding slowly and winking.

We turned away and discreetly regurgitated what we had eaten back into the cups, sure that Camacho meant well, but not trusting him in any way, shape, or form.

Fifteen minutes and seven deserts later, we arrived at a flotilla of interconnected booths belonging to the Kelso Amboy Potoos All-School Marching Band. These booths took up the back wall of the gym, and seemed to be turning a brisk trade. Teams of third-chair students made never-ending cafeteria runs, bringing fresh goodies, while an off-key subset of the band played to draw in a steady stream of customers. When the crowd around the booth thinned, Agnes and I squeezed in next to an abandoned table.

"Dang, looks like they might be able to pay for their trip after all," I said to no one in particular as I scanned the crowd for my parents.

"Yup," Agnes answered, scanning the crowd for her own inscrutable purposes.

"I wonder where Ed is in all this?"

There was movement behind the table. "Can I help you ladies with anything?" asked a familiar voice.

Edgar rose above the table, chef hat blooming from his head and oven mitts ballooning over his hands. It was all I could do to keep from laughing. "Ah, Ed," I said, "so glad to see you, toiling away with your... what exactly are you serving here?"

"Brownies."

"Ah, brownies." I sniffed and tossed my hair. "How plebeian. Business good, I take it?"

He shrugged. "We've got enough to get to Washington, but not enough to get back. Still, night's young."

"So sorry to see you cooped up in a booth like this. You could have been in the science fair, you know, basking in the adoration of those who value you for your mind, and not your," I gestured at the booth *en mass*, "brownies."

He grunted. "I thought you'd given up on that."

"Oh, please, Ed, it takes more than the duplicity of others to keep me from my goals. I found another project, a *better* project, and I'm sure you'll be glad to know it got rave reviews from The Yog."

"Surprised you didn't push through with *our* project. You didn't seem too shy about touching dead rats a couple weeks ago."

I flashed him a smile that a hypothetical outside observer might be forgiven for misinterpreting as a sneer.

"Well," he said, "I'm glad that's over with. Maybe now you can give up on that revenge nonsense and we can get back to being friends?" He looked me up and down imploringly, his eyes having the air of a wet-nurse who had been vomited on one too many times.

I flashed him a smile that no one could possibly misinterpret: a cold smile, an evil smile, a smile that said, "Hold on, I'm about to burp, and it *will* be wet." "Oh, Ed," I said, "the revenge nonsense has only just begun."

Edgar sighed and rubbed his face with the oven mitts--a deed I'm 100% sure was unsanitary--and gave me a look both weary and wary. A long, taut moment stretched between us, predator and prey, as I reveled in my eventual victory and he trembled at the prospect of defeat.

That's when Ages interrupted. "Um, can I get a brownie?"

I gripped her arm and spoke, never once taking my eyes off Edgar. "We'll take nothing from this booth, especially none of these accursed brownies. Edgar wouldn't help us get to Bluker's Creek? We shall offer him no assistance in getting to Nationals."

"Back from Nationals."

"Whatever." I dragged my one *true* friend away from my erstwhile one, taking pride at this little victory. It was spoiled by Agnes mouthing, "Sorry!" back at my nemesis, but I suppose you can't have everything in this life.

That was when we ran smack-dab into my parents. Clarification: they ran smack-dab into *us*.

"Ope, sorry there, Jo," dad said as I brushed brownie crumbs from my hair. "Didn't really see you in all the hubbub."

"Are you still good on money?" mom asked, helping Agnes to her feet.

"Yeah, you? Did Thumbs suck you dry?"

Dad chuckled a sad and weary chuckle. "Very nearly, very nearly. No, though, we got away when some kid with a BMW drove by." He concluded his pronouncement with a hearty belch. I flinched away and gagged. "Hey, you got any more of that Gelfelax left?"

My eyes widened, Agnes grimaced, and mom lowered her head into her hands, sighing in exasperation. "No, sorry, used it all."

Dad looked crestfallen. "Ah, well, it's not that I need it, mind you, just a... precaution." He held up what remained of the brownie he had dumped on my head. "Had three of these so far. Your buddy Edgar's quite the cook! Glad it's going to a good cause."

"Yes," mom added, eyeing Agnes, "It's so nice seeing kids involved in extra-curricular activities. A shame he couldn't finish the project. Too bad you didn't have any *other* friends who could help..."

"Fortunately, *someone* inspired me with an idea for another project," I said, taking the heat off Agnes.

Dad's mustache trembled with anticipation. "Oh, that reminds me! The science fair! How did that--" A tremendous fart, audible over the noise of the gym, cut him off.

Mom gasped, "Curt!" and back-handed his belly, eliciting a small squeak.

"Sorry, sorry. Just the brownies talking."

I surveyed the crowd to find an escape route. Perhaps if we backtracked to the coconut shy, no one could trace dad's stench to us...

"Anyway, as I was saying, how did the science--" Dad stopped, seemingly of his own accord this time. There was no sound. As we waited for him to continue, surrounded by an overwhelming *mélange* of fresh bread and cinnamon and baked chocolate, a smell hit us, a cabbage-y, raw sewer stench. Dad's eyes grew monstrously wide, the irises becoming like accretion disks around twin black holes. "Where's the bathroom?"

Mom wrinkled her eyebrows--and nose--at dad. "Curt?"

"Where's the damn bathroom, woman?" He leaned close and clutched my shoulders. "Where is it?!" he all but screamed in my face, his own burning with inner fire.

"Curt!"

Dad trembled a moment longer, then ran stiff-legged from the gymnasium, stringing a procession of dropped food and angry shouts in his wake.

Mom huffed and puffed and made unpleasant expressions at

dad, then shot us an apologetic/apoplectic look. "Girls. I'm sorry you had to see that. Please, please can we not talk about this moment ever again?"

Neither Agnes nor I answered. As we stared after dad, we noticed a most curious phenomenon. Starting at dad's path and radiating outwards, a calm descended on the gym. People who had been milling, or talking, or swaying to the half-heard band stood stark upright, not moving, not talking. The music became clear and loud, then, instrument by instrument, fell silent.

The entire gym held its breath...

A clear, chime-like voice rang out: "Where's the bathroom?!" It was like a starter's pistol.

The now running crowd split into two groups making a mass exodus from the gym. One headed to the double-doors leading into the school proper; the other funneled into the convolution of hallways emptying into the locker rooms.

Amidst the sudden chaos, Agnes and mother and I held hands and tried to remain a together as the stampeding crowd parted around us. Through the writhing confluence of arms and legs, I caught a glimpse of Edgar, hat flying, as he struggled to remove his oven mitts and claw a few body-lengths closer to the door.

A pained gasp brought my attention to mom, who let go of Agnes and pawed at her stomach. Her mouth stretched in a rictus of pain and horror. She tore her other hand from my grasp, then took off after the crowd. She made it a dozen steps before she stumbled to a stop, shuddered, and groaned.

The smell--the one that had so recently forced itself from my father's bowels--hit me again, fresh and moist. A few feet away, mom relaxed, wrapped her arms around her belly, and settled to her knees on the gymnasium floor.

The stampede was still in full swing--several hundred panicked people couldn't exit a space this large in an orderly manner--but people were slowing, stopping, shuddering just as mom had done. All around, the smell grew thicker, clouding my mind and distorting my vision.

As people stopped moving and shoes stopped squeaking on polished wood, I heard the sound. It was something like squeezing the last bit of ketchup from the bottle, something like pouring cranberry sauce from a can, something like scraping baby food from a jar. No matter the simile, it was the sound of something not-quite liquid exiting a vessel. Quite a lot if something not-quite liquid.

"Look!" Agnes yelled as she pawed at my shoulder. I looked. A multicolored mixture of hundreds of dollars of homemade baked goods, chewed, eaten, and not quite digested, oozed towards us. In this primal sludge were enough brownies to send a high-school band to Washington, D.C., an innumerable supply of strawberry blandies, and at least half a gross of store-bought pudding, all swallowed and swirled and spewed from the right end of the human digestive track at the very wrongest time.

Looking at the carnage surrounding us, at the horror too great for my mind to fully comprehend, I felt a rumbling deep within me, and the nascent push of gas ready to be expressed. I clenched up tight, not trusting that fart, no sir, not one bit.

"Holy crap, Jo..." Agnes breathed.

Other sounds registered then: grunting, straining, sobbing, open weeping. A rustling rose up soon after as a thousand mortified people began trudging to the parking lot, wondering just how they would make it home without ruining the upholstery.

Maybe fifty people remained upright, including Agnes and me. Each of us survivors, us blessed few, made eye contact and wordlessly transmitted a single question: What the hell just happened?

I looked down and skipped back a few feet. How was I going to get out past all of this... *this?* These shoes, and probably these low-hemmed jeans, were going into the firepit in the back yard.

Mom was still crouched a few feet ahead of me. A few feet past her was Edgar, eyes wide and chef's hat held tightly against his backside. He must have felt my gaze upon him, for he turned back and scowled, as if this were somehow my fault.

And that was the end of the great Kelso Amboy All-School Jamboree and Swap Meet.

CHAPTER 10
THE BELL TOLLS FOR ME

Classes at Kelso Amboy Memorial High School did not resume until the following Wednesday. Though victim's clothing took the brunt of the, shall we say, "water damage," quite a bit of... *material* was left on the gymnasium floor, dragged into the halls, and spread across the school. It took all weekend and most of the following week to muck out the building. The smell remained, however, and the gym was closed until new flooring could be installed over the summer.

Following the mass attack of diarrhea, area hospitals were inundated with hundreds of cases of extreme dehydration, as well as dozens of bacterial infections. A citywide dysentery scare ensued, and the rumor mill produced such jewels of journalistic insight as an Ebola outbreak, a hyper-flu, alien parasites, and even the Black Death. Each of these culprits was summarily poo-pooed by sensible minds, but the fact remained that there were four hundred and eighty-seven casualties, all occurring within ten minutes of each other. Fortunately, there were no fatalities.

Once it became clear that the events of the Jamboree weren't caused by bacterial contamination or naturally occurring illness, blame for the destruction of the bake sale fell to a terrorist cabal which had poisoned the food, and a demi-mythical "Mad Crapper" was dreamed up to take the blame. As this was much harder to disprove than *E. coli,* it was the supposition that the community held to most dearly. However, the police assured us they would investigate any and all leads.

I was thankful for the time off school; in those last few minutes at the Jamboree, I had seen far, far too much of my friends and classmates. Yet my suffering paled in comparison to that of my parents. Mom was able to towel herself off and leave with Agnes and me, but dad was in the hospital for two days, undergoing rehydration. He lost fifteen pounds. Over the following days we didn't talk, barely looked at each other. Mostly we sat in the den, staring at the powerless TV, contemplating life and its fragile nature. I'm willing to hazard that life was much the same for the others who had gone through what by Tuesday was known as "The Crappening."

The mood was somber as students trudged into the school Wednesday morning, six hundred teenagers with eyes wide and empty. Another two hundred students were absent; it was doubtful they would ever return.

Throughout the building, the smell remained.

In first hour came the daily announcements. Cal and Hez read the cafeteria menu before one of them intoned, "Please stand by for an address from Principal Thumbs."

There was a squeal of static followed by, "Good morning, students," said with a voice even more strained than usual. "You may notice visitors through the building today. These are detectives from the police department. Please do not let them distract you from your studies. However, should they ask you any questions, please be courteous and cooperative. Thank you, and have a good day."

The day dragged by. Teachers read directly from textbooks, didn't make noise, didn't ask any questions. Students sat motionless, didn't make noise, didn't answer questions.

I was leaving French and going to the auditorium for so-called gym class when I caught sight of Edgar. He was speaking to a tall man with a business suit and a thin mustache, probably one of the detectives...

Something--perhaps a sound I made, or the way I walked, or maybe the pressure of my gaze--caused Edgar to look up. He said something I couldn't make out to the detective, and then the two were gone. I continued on to gym--now little more than a study hour--then on to Science.

To my eternal relief, Edgar wasn't at our bench; with the way things had been left between us, it was for the best that I didn't see him. It seemed that I wasn't the only one who didn't see him; I made inquiries of my classmates, and no one had seen Edgar for two periods. Rumor had it he was still talking with the detectives. Could he have insider knowledge of the Crappening? I didn't think so. Despite my problems with him, I had to concede Edgar was a fundamentally good guy. The detectives were probably interviewing every food vendor from that night.

At the front of the classroom, The Yog cleared her throat, and class began. "Yes, hello," she said in a monotone. "I hope you all had a good weekend, though I'm sure you didn't. I would like to take a moment to touch on the results of this year's science fair, which all too few of you participated in."

She paused to let the shame sink in. We hung our heads and stared at our lab tables until she resumed speaking.

"I am pleased to announce that Valerie and Skyler are the winners of this year's science fair, for their project 'Juggle Your Way To Health-Fact Or Fiction,' as well as for winning the best three-out-of-five at roshambo." She paused again, then made a "let's go" kind of gesture. "Applaud, please."

Wc applauded, in the loosest meaning of the word.

"Before we start today's lecture on DNA and the manipulation thereof, I'd like to update you all on the chicks." She paused a third time, staring pointedly at Camacho.

He shrugged. "Eh, just go ahead."

The Yog sighed. "The eggs are getting ready to hatch. By this time next week, we should be swimming in chicks." Again, she looked to Camacho.

Again he shrugged. "That wouldn't even make sense."

"Hasn't stopped you before."

He shrugged a third time, then returned to doodling on his lab bench.

"Okay, so, for serious this time." The Yog turned to the board and drew a series of lazily curving lines all wrapped up in each other. Perhaps she had some kind of intelligent design behind her scribbles, but all we in the audience saw was an impressionistic black rope. It was fortunate that The Yog was a teacher of the sciences rather than a teacher of the arts. "Deoxyribo--"she began.

There was a knock on the door.

"Oh, come on!"

The door opened fractionally and the thin-mustached man I had seen earlier slipped his head inside. "Ms. Yogmier?"

She whirled on the newcomer, her mouth wide to spew a venomous retort. When she saw the man, though, with his slicked-back black hair and charcoal suit, her jaw snapped shut and her throat pulsed with a heavy swallow. "Hello?" she said at last.

"Yes, hi. I'm Detective Totoro."

"Is it me you're looking for?"

Detective Totoro blinked. "As a matter of fact, yes it is. Could I speak with you in the hall for a few minutes?"

The Yog--who, for the first time I could remember didn't insist on being referred to as such--looked back at her "diagram," then at us, and then at the detective. "What the hell." She capped the marker and tossed it back over her shoulder as she followed the thin-mustached detective from the room.

I expected a flurry of whispers to sweep the room then, but everyone remained morose and silent. Well, almost everyone. An exaggerated sigh came from behind me, and I turned to see Camacho slumped over the next lab bench back. His usual partner, Jesus, was gone. In an uncharacteristic fit of pity, I cleared my throat and spoke thus: "Hey, Camacho. Want to sit up here today?"

He lifted his head from the bench top, then slunk up my way. I expected him to slide past me and into Edgar's seat, but instead he leaned against my bench and turned baleful eyes upon me.

"Hey, Macho Man, how are you?" I essayed.

He blinked, long and slow. "I am empty inside."

"Wow, that's, uh, that's rather existential."

"No. Literally. I am empty." He indicated his lean belly. "My colon is a desolate wasteland where nothing lives. I can barely digest food."

"I'm... I'm sorry to hear that," I said.

"Whoever did this, I hate them."

"Ah, yes, the demi-mythical 'Mad Crapper' the news was talking about." I shook my head. "Can't say I have fond feelings for such a person either."

His lips trembled in a prelude to tears. "Why would someone do this? Why would someone... why would someone be so *cruel*?" His shoulders lurched as he fought back sobs.

In another uncharacteristic fit of pity, I patted Camacho's shoulder. Right away, the intensity of the sobs diminished, and I couldn't help but think that this show of emotion might be more than a bit fabricated. "Hey, it's fine; the police are here. I'm sure they'll find this Mad Crapper, assuming he or she actually exists."

He sniffled; there was a distinct lack of any mucosal sounds. "You really think so?"

I snorted. "Hey, maybe it's The Yog. After all, they took her away."

He shrugged. "Yeah, but it's just... it could be anyone really, couldn't it?"

I returned the shrug. "Hell, it could even be me."

He laughed and made a show of wiping his dry eyes. "Yeah, right. Well, if they come for you, I'll know why." He flashed me a sideways smile.

Despite his overtly creepy attention grab, I couldn't help but find catharsis in laughing along to his joke. "Yup, I'm sure they'll be along to arrest me any minute now."

There was a creak from the back of the class as the door opened. Camacho and I turned, expecting to see The Yog's return. Instead, the thin-mustached man stood alone in the doorway. "Excuse me," he said with patient politeness, "is there a Joanna Matheson in this class?"

Camacho and I exchanged glances, and I felt the psychic heat of a dozen sets of eyes on me.

"Oh, snap..." Camacho muttered.

I offered up the final shrug of our conversation and followed the

101

detective from the room.

***

The detective and I marched down the hallway, our shoes echoing on the yellowing linoleum.

"So, you're a freshman?" he asked, his voice friendly.

I could only nod. Words failed me when I left the classroom. Being escorted in the direction of the principal's office was never a good thing, no matter how innocent you were. Being escorted by a cop... Well, words failed me.

"Pretty nice school. I might have to move into the district when my kids get old enough." He sniffed theatrically. "Shame about the smell, though."

Sure enough, we ended up outside the principal's office. The detective opened the door. "After you."

With much trembling and trepidation, I crossed the threshold. All principal's offices should have a sign reading, "Abandon hope, all ye who enter." Even without the sign, I abandoned hope.

Behind his desk sat Principal Thumbs, looking exhausted and just a little sheepish. He had never before called me into his office: my family wasn't rolling in donation money, but my dad had clout and could discount community college programs for incoming Kelso Amboy students. And seeing as those discounts were between dad and Thumbs, well… there had been accusations that our beloved princi-*pal* might be lining his pockets.

Standing in front of the desk was The Yog, looking unfriendlier than I had ever seen her. She scanned me up and down, and then made... a face. I couldn't name it--a grimace, a sarcastic smile?-- but I knew what emotion lay behind it: disappointment.

Beside the desk sat Edgar. He gave me that kinda-sorta-yeah-definitely angry face I had seen the day I stuffed the rat down his tuba, only this time it was tempered with... what? Triumph? Smugness?

Atop the desk, crouched like a leopard ready to pounce and rip out my jugular, was my Science Fair display, festooned with phrases like "Laxative Effect," and "Intense Diarrhea."

My hypothesis thus far was that this trip represented due diligence; surely, the entire student body would be interviewed in the coming months. It seemed that hypothesis didn't hold up to empirical testing.

"Jo, please, have a seat!" Mr. Thumbs invited.

The detective slid behind me and closed the door.

I sat.

Mr. Thumbs cleared his throat. "Well, Joanna, I'd like to thank you for agreeing to speak with me. I'd like to make you aware that this is not a disciplinary matter; it is merely an inquiry to establish the... veracity of certain events." He smiled in a reassuring manner. I was not reassured. "So, if you wanted to speak to your parents, or their lawyers, you are of course allowed to, but we would rather--"

"May I?" the thin-mustached detective cut in.

Thumb's jowls waggled as he nodded, spraying thin flecks of sweat over my trifold display.

"Hi, Joanna, I'm Detective Hinson Totoro. I just have a few quick questions that I'm hoping will help us piece together exactly what happened last Saturday. Are you willing to help us out?"

I most certainly was not. I may not have known exactly what was going on here, but I could see where it was going. Newspapers posit that what happened at the Jamboree was a terrorist attack--> Popular consciousness determines that this so-called Mad Crapper was at the school to carry out the attack--> Here I was at the Jamboree with a report on crap-pills. Now the administration has a patsy for an issue obviously stemming from unsanitary cafeteria practices, and the public has their monster. Well, hell no, Detective Totoro, there is no way I am going to help you.

"Ms. Matheson?"

I nodded.

"Very good." He smiled, showing minuscule teeth, and then indicated my display with an outstretched finger. "Now Ms. Matheson, is this poster board yours?"

It most certainly is not! "Yes."

"And does the material on the board accurately demonstrate the nature and results of your science project?"

Here, the truth might set me free, though I was reluctant to issue it in The Yog's presence. Though I had a solid hypothesis and an elegant experimental protocol, the fact remained that I had a limited data pool, and may have extrapolated my conclusions further than was prudent. However, I'm pretty sure that wasn't what the Detective was asking, so I settled on a simple, "Yes."

He nodded, then reached behind the trifold to pick something up. He brought it out from hiding, and held it close to his body so I couldn't see what it was. "One last thing. Does this look at all familiar to you?"

With a flourish, he produced a piece of lined and rumpled notebook paper. Writ large upon it in multiple colors of glitter ink, in a delicate, feminine hand was a single sentence: "Dear sir, you shall taste my blistering fury."

The room fell quiet. When I wrote this letter weeks--an eternity--ago, it had seemed so simple, so nearly *fun*. All I wanted to do was put Edgar on edge, annoy him a little. And though the laxatives had given me an out when it came to Edgar's involvement in the project, I *still* hadn't come up with a good final revenge beyond the tuba rat. And now they thought this had something to do with the Crappening. What, did they think I used my laxative research to humiliate Edgar, and the consequences escaped my control and spread to the whole school?

"Ms. Matheson," Detective Totoro said, "we think you used your laxative research to humiliate Mr. Latterndale, and the consequences escaped your control and spread to the whole school."

"I--I--" I couldn't let them pin the Crappening on me. "The note was just to scare him. That rat in the tuba, I will freely admit to that. But this, all the crap--" Wait, something didn't make sense… I pointed a quavering finger at Edgar. "How is he wrapped up in all this?" I widened my eyes, trying to look hurt and innocent.

"When the going theory was some kind of biological agent," Totoro explained, "we tested all of the baked goods for signs of contamination. It turned out the entire conflagration stemmed from the marching band's brownies, which had been laced with a near-lethal dose of over-the-counter laxative." I cringed at that news.

"After a little digging, we found out about the threat Mr. Latterndale received, as well as your feud. And I have to say *this*--" he held up the note and shook it--"is pretty damning."

"I didn't do it!" I yelled, standing from my seat. "Near-lethal" was never a good phrase to hear when being accused of a crime, *especially* a crime for which you were innocent. "Please, you've got to believe me!"

Detective Totoro nodded and stroked his clean-shaven chin. "I'd certainly like to. Tell me, would you be adverse to us looking in your locker?"

Mr. Thumbs was sweating heavily now, his whole face glistening in the fluorescent light reflecting from his oily chin. "I-I'm afraid that's legally a little shaky for the school without a proper warrant--"

"Yes!" I shouted, then "No!" as I finished parsing what the detective said. Everyone in the room stared at me, each lost on their own private rabbit-trail of grammatical ambiguity. "Please, feel free to check my locker!" I clarified. With that declarative statement, it felt as though a weight tumbled from my shoulders, or a long-held pressure lessened and gushed forth--no, stopping there. They may have evidence, and I could be construed as having motive, but that was circumstantial at best. A cooperating suspect, showing that she had nothing to hide in her locker? No way they could pin this on me.

Detective Totoro stood, a dashing smile spreading across his face. I heard what sounded like The Yog swallowing and coughing. "After you, Ms. Matheson" the detective said, gesturing to the door.

Everyone save Edgar stood and followed me from the office.

I led my little party through the school, fighting back the urge to vomit any time a door opened and stirred up the spicy smell that still lingered so. We made quite the clatter as the four of us roamed the deserted halls; every once in a while, faces would peer at us through window-pierced doors, come to see what the commotion was about. Whenever we caught sight of these faces, I'd turn away in a lame attempt at preserving my anonymity. Mr. Thumbs would perforce smile and nod, and The Yog would offer a particular kind of stink-eye that screamed, "Shut up and do your work!" Detective Totoro, for his part, followed along behind me, withholding his judgment for the time being.

We made it down the hallway, up a flight of stairs, and around a corner to another hallway, lined on all sides by lockers. I approached my own little home-away-from-home, located near an intersection. I spun the lock, opened the door, and held out my backpack for inspection. "Ta-daa!" I managed to not say.

Though I stood legs apart, backpack held out, and breathing heavily before Detective Totoro, he didn't notice me. He continued rubbing his chin, then walked a few feet away where he stood stock-still, legs also spread, hands in pockets. The wall of lockers containing my own seemed more interesting to him than the locker contents he had asked to see.

I lowered the backpack and glanced at my two remaining compatriots. Both The Yog and Mr. Thumbs shrugged.

After a full minute of staring at the lockers, Totoro straightened and walked the few feet to the hall intersection. There was a trashcan at the corner, and the plastic barrel consumed all of the detective's attention. "Mr. Thumbs," he said at long, long last, "is this the trashcan where the all those Gelfelax packages were found?"

My gut churned, not unlike the reaction I might expect had I consumed the contents of those Gelfelax packages.

"Not the actual trashcan, no, that was taken as evidence," Mr. Thumbs replied. "But it was that spot, yes."

"I see. So the locker was located five feet from a trashcan containing the wrappers of over three hundred Gelfelax tablets." Detective Totoro turned back to me, his previously relaxed face now hard and uninviting. "Thank you, Ms. Matheson. I believe I have all the answers I need."

CHAPTER 11
BRANDED

I sat alone in the narthex of the principal's office. Narthex wasn't the right word. Antechamber. Foyer. Screw it, narthex was good enough. It sounds like narcotics. Narcotics officer. Narc. As in Edgar had narced on me. Which begged the question: What the hell, Ed? *He* was probably the Mad Crapper, and poisoned the school with Gelfelax so he could blame *me* as revenge the tuba-rat incident. That was cold, Ed, real cold.

If true, then Edgar and I were now honest-to-God feuding, doomed to a cycle of revenge that led to nothing save tragedy. Maybe our children would one day kill each other.

Raised voices drifted from the office beyond the narthex. Two blurry silhouettes gesticulated vigorously behind the principal's frosted office window/door.

"That's it?" my mother asked, her voice distorted with rage. "Presumptive guilt, no trial?"

"Certainly not, Luann!" Thumbs said, fear of losing a contributing member of the PTA mixed with righteous indignation in his voice. "We're doing this as a precautionary measure... until this thing goes to trial."

"You're pressing charges?!"

"People were in the hospital! They almost *died*!" Those last three words were more assumed than heard; Thumbs was on the verge of yelling himself hoarse, and his throat chose that moment to get experimental. "Your own husband, Luann! *You*! Hell, *me*!" His voice was back, but I could imagine the words leaving long claw-marks in his soft tissue.

"She's a good student!"

Thumbs issued a derisive snort. "Her science grade says otherwise."

"She's a good kid."

Thumbs issued another derisive snort. Wonderful; his counterarguments were preliterate, and he was still parrying mom's rhetorical jabs. "She confessed to stuffing a dead rat down a tuba and threatening another student."

Mom now resorted to Thumbs' tactics, issuing a weary sigh. "She's my daughter, Rick."

"Look, she's got a clean record for now. After the trial, if she proves innocent... You are still going with the innocent plea, right?"

I heard a barely audible--imaginary?--growl.

"Okay, yes, well, if she proves innocent, we'll take the suspension off her record, okay? It won't stop her getting into any colleges. Though I guess nothing would stop her getting into Telethepee Junior--"

Another growl.

I issued a sigh of my own and leaned back in the miniature plastic chair that had been my home for the last forty-five minutes. Suspension. Wow. I'd been a good kid for the last decade of school, only two write ups, no detentions, and now Bam Suspension. Ten days, the maximum allowed before it would affect my grade. Thumbs claimed it wasn't retaliation for the Crappening. After all, how could it be? What I had done was still an allegation at this point; once I was formally charged in front of a judge, well, that would be different. So this suspension was for my safety. Thumbs expected reprisals the moment it came out that I had--allegedly--spiked the marching band's brownies with a near lethal dose of Gelfelax brand stool softener. Why he didn't just, say, punish students who might violate school rules by enacting reprisals against me, well… That wasn't important right now.

A light tapping at the outer door of the narthex drew me from my embittered ruminations. I issued another sigh and drummed my fingers against the molded plastic that was designed for a butt some ten years younger than mine. *Tap! Tap! Tap! Thrump! Thrump! Thrump!* I actually had a pretty good rhythm section going here.

The tapping grew more insistent. Was no one going to answer that? I looked around the office, making eye contact with group shots of graduating classes' past before settling my gaze upon the cluttered desk where the secretary--sorry, "School Administrator"-- usually sat. Her chair was empty, and that's when I remembered that she was still out with a wicked case of the squirts. *That* was why no one was answering the door; my bad. In more ways than one, it seemed...

Taking upon myself the secretary's--excuse me--"School Administrator's" authority, I got up and opened the door. The indistinct, frosted-glass shadow in the hallway beyond resolved into Agnes. She leaped and clutched me in a bear hug.

"OhmyGodJoIheardyouwenttotheprincipal'sofficeandI--"

I wheezed and tried my damnedest to wriggle from her crushing embrace. "Hey, whoa, slow down, I can't understand you."

"Oh, Jo..." With a sobbing breath, she released me and backed out of my personal space. "Someone said the police came and got you in science class, and you missed lunch, then a bunch of people saw you in the hall with the detective with the thin mustache and Thumbs and The Yog, and... well... what's going on?"

"I did it."

"What?" Her glasses rose as she furrowed her eyebrows in confusion. "What'd you do?"

"Poisoned Edgar's brownies. Put Gelfelax in them. Gave everyone the generically-branded chocolate squirts. I am the Mad Crapper."

She looked aghast.

"That's what they're saying, anyways." I ratcheted my eyebrows up as high as they would go and stuck out my lower lip. "Please, Ag, you've got to believe me, I didn't do it. They're trying to pin the rap on me, but... I didn't do it, I swear!" *Please believe me,* I psychically projected to her, *please believe me, please believe me...*

"I believe you," Agnes said.

Ohhhh, thank God. At the rate everyone else was jumping on the bandwagon, I was concerned Agnes might as well. Yet here she was, proving once again why she deserved to be my best friend.

"And you know what?" Agnes continued. "We were together the whole night! I'm a witness! They have to let you off if I get you an alibi! I'mma march right in there and set them straight."

"Oh, Agnes, thank you. This is why you're such a better friend than Edgar."

She took a few galumphing steps towards the inner office door before turning back to me. "By the way, what are we talking here? A few weeks of detention, a suspension, maybe?"

Though the trial hadn't happened yet, I was confident they would not find in my favor. I looked down at my feet, and with great guilt let Agnes know what her con of a BFF was in for. "Suspension first, then they're pressing charges. A trial for criminal mischief, maybe more, and then hundreds of hours of community service and possibly a few months of juvie."

Her glasses almost slipped off her face as her jaw dropped. "*What?*"

"The thing everyone keeps repeating is that 'people almost died.'"

"Holy crap, Jo. I... I don't think I can..."

Seeing the fear and confusion and, yes, betrayal, writ large on her face, that was what hurt the most. It didn't matter that *I* knew I *was* innocent. In that moment, *she* knew I *wasn't* innocent. If my best friend didn't believe me, what chance did I have with twelve strangers?

"It's okay, Ag, I get it."

"I--It's just that… well, I mean, I wasn't there when you were at the science fair, and what if, well, what if they take that discrepancy and try to tie me in as a partner or something…."

I could appreciate her fear. Ever since showing off my locker had damned me, I clammed up, just in case further cooperation dug me deeper. "Go on, Agnes, be free."

She swallowed, nodded, and pushed her glasses back up her face. Then she was gone.

I slumped back into my little plastic seat, eliciting a fart of displaced air. My muscles tensed, a new reaction to that sound, but when I felt no movement deep inside my insides, I relaxed. A moment later the inner office door opened and mom slunk out. "C'mon, Jo, let's go home."

***

I followed mom out to the car. She fumed silently as we crossed the hot asphalt; I could feel the heat of her anger radiating from her, far hotter than the heat from the blacktop below. A few times, as we approached burgundy sedans that turned out not be ours, her composure would slip, and she'd hiss out a strangled swear of vile ferocity. At those times, I would edge away, putting as much space between her wrath and myself as I could manage.

Her anger began to spill out in earnest when we found our car. Mom jerked her door open and threw herself inside, slamming the door shut in her wake. She gripped the steering wheel, which by then must have been hellishly hot, and gritted her teeth. I followed into the passenger side and tried my best to appear contrite and believable. I winced as I sat down, the hot pleather burning through the seat of my pants. God, we needed to invest in a windshield cover. I was about to suggest as much to mom, but one look at her apoplectic face reminded me that this was a sub-optimal time for such a conversation. The engine turned over, mom cranked the AC and the seat coolers and... we sat there.

Her breathing was heavy, getting close to sob levels. "Why, Jo?" she asked, her voice dead neutral. "Why'd you do this?"

"I didn't," I said, matching her tone.

The horn let off an abortive beep as she slapped the steering wheel. "Don't lie to me, Jo! Really! What were you thinking? How could you be so--so *stupid*?!" She was on the verge of tears now, her eyes red and puffy.

She leaned towards me, lips twitching with contained emotion, and hissed, "Your father almost died, Jo. Give me one good reason, one good justification for what you did." Left unsaid was a desperate, "*Please*."

I turned as fully as I could in the confined space and engaged in unwavering eye contact with mom. "I didn't do it."

She let out her breath in one compulsive gasp and slumped forward onto the steering wheel, eliciting another short beep. "It was Agnes, wasn't it?"

Sudden conversation changer, that. "What?"

"She put you up to this, didn't she? Mr. Thumbs said you were at her house when you wrote that thrice-damned note. Did she push you into this? I always knew she was a bad influence."

"What? No, Mom, Agnes had nothing to do with this." Though Agnes refused to stick up for me, it was my duty to stick up for her. Even had she been my alibi, Agnes couldn't have kept me from drowning in spurious accusations. "Agnes had nothing to do with it," I repeated, putting as much sincerity and authority into the statement as I could. "And I had nothing to do with this, aside from the note."

Mom raised her head and stared across the parking lot into whatever unfathomable void lay beyond. "I really thought we raised you better..." She threw the car into gear and craned her neck to see as she backed out. "I just wished we had done something back before all this started."

I ignored her and focused on picking at the flaps of skin beside my fingernails. I wished she had done something about it, too.

CHAPTER 12
TRIUMPHAL RETURN

Knock, knock, knock… I opened my eyes, eyelashes scraping against my none-too-soft pillowcase. Someone was knocking at the door… That should have been obvious from the start; where else do people knock? I was better than halfway asleep, and having a hard time buffering events as they happened.

Hinges squealed as the door swung open and soft footsteps padded across the carpet. A presence loomed at my bedside... In my confused, pre-waking state, the presence felt like the specter of death, preparing to clutch my soul and drag me away to some stygian abyss.

"Hey, Jo, it's time to wake up," my mom said.

I woke up a bit more. "Huh?" I pushed away my pillow, exposing my face to pale grey light. Beyond mother, my room was a confluence of shadows. That was odd; noon should be brighter. Another oddity: why was mom waking me up? She should be at work by now. Had there been another containment breach? I scraped together enough brain cells to produce a halfway intelligible, "Wha timeses?"

"It's six forty-five. C'mon, get up."

Once more, I felt the presence of the terminal guest, waiting to escort me away. "Wha?" Without school on the menu for today, I had intended to sleep in as much as I wanted. Sleeping in was fun, growing more so the older I got. Still, sleeping all day was a no-no; no wonder mom was pissed. I sat up, blinking and wiping a days' worth of condensed ooze from my eyes. Mom was dressed for work, the pale light from the window glowing off of a clean lab coat and--

Hold on. This window didn't get evening light. And six forty-five should still have a fair bit of warmth to it, even this early in the year.

"Get dressed, Jo. You're going to school."

Mom reached down and yanked away my blankets, leaving me shivering on the mattress. "I don' ga szool..." I protested, sure my eloquence would drive through mom's anger and convince her of the rightness of my argument.

"Yes, you do. I don't care what that incompetent boob Thumbs says, I'm not letting you get tried and punished by the court of public opinion. The school has no grounds to take disciplinary action against you, and until and unless they get a court order to keep you out of school, you are going."

"Heh. You said, 'boob.'" I closed my eyes and curled into a tight ball to preserve what heat I could without the blanket, hoping mom would go away and leave me to my exile if only I ignored her.

After a few moments, I heard mom's footsteps retreat to the door; I was home free. Perhaps if I did this when the grim reaper came for me, I could induce a similar result. That or challenge the Dark One to a game of Risk; play long enough for the sets to be worth twenty armies or more, and the game would just go back and forth, unending, for all eternity. With that last hopeful thought, I drifted back to sleep...

Lights blasted on overhead, cutting through gloom. I yelped and curled in tighter. From below came the sound of claws cutting through carpet as the cat sprang from under my bed and disappeared towards parts unknown.

"Up, Jo! NOW!" I split one eyelid and peeked out from under a protective arm. Mom's face was skull-like, her eyes pits of darkness against the too-bright light now burning my retinas. "Downstairs in five minutes," she growled, "or believe me, things will get far worse than they currently are."

She stormed from the room, shaking the bed with the force of her footfalls. When she was gone, I levered myself out of bed. I tossed on yesterday's jeans and a baggy shirt; seeing as I was sure to be a pariah at school, I didn't much care how I looked. Scooping up my book bag--thankfully not confiscated as evidence--I followed mom downstairs.

I diverted into the kitchen to grab breakfast and a bagged lunch, and then stopped short when I spotted dad at the kitchen table. He was all done up in suit and tie, hunched over a container of probiotic yoghurt that was supposed to rebalance his microfauna. He looked up when I entered; I wished he hadn't. Radiating from him was anger beyond rage, beyond fury. It was deep and abiding hatred. His teeth ground harder and faster the longer I was in his sight. After an eternity, he looked away. In his face, I had seen rock bottom. For mother, I was a failure, a disappointment. For dad, I was his biggest mistake. As far as he was concerned, I had nearly killed him, and that was something he could not forgive.

Wolfing down the remainder of his yoghurt, he stood on shaky legs and scuttled from the room. I remained in the doorway another minute, expecting mom to come in, but she didn't. Hoping that I might eat and be on my way to school before she had another chance to vent her seething rage at me, I poured myself a bowl of bran flakes and took dad's spot at the table.

***

Edgar was missing from my morning commute; for that small mercy, I was profoundly grateful. Other kids joined me as I neared KAMH. Most were strangers: upper-class kids who couldn't swing a car, or under-class kids who were too close for the bus. Most passed me by, crossing the bridge or jumping the creek before ascending the stairs into the school.

A few recognized me, though. Based on the way they shied away and whispered behind raised folders, I knew that the story had spread, and that the whole student body knew my guilt.

At the edge of the schoolyard, I read the Kelso Amboy sign.

Yesterday, it had announced the closure, but today it read: MAD CRAPPER CAUGHT! REJOICE YE WEARY! The second "!" was an upside-down "i." A burst of dread ripped through my gut.

The sound of splashing drew my attention down to Agnes, crumpled in the creek and dripping wet. She had tried the jump, but had come up short. Old instinct sent me picking my way down the hill to help my friend. She caught sight of me as I navigated around a gnarled root; for a moment, we just stood there, basking in each other's presence. Then she turned away and started up the opposite bank, dripping chilly water in her wake.

I let her get far enough away that it was clear we weren't traveling together, then continued down to the creek and up into the school.

The next few hours were tolerable, and I managed to avoid making any waves. I got a few odd looks now and then, but people left me alone.

Then there was Science.

I tried slipping in unnoticed right before the bell rang. Edgar was already present, about halfway down the room, so I stayed near the door, taking a seat at a spare lab bench. I pulled deep into my shirt, hiding like a turtle from the outside world. Unfortunately, at five and a half feet tall, I couldn't hide by hunching, and was noticed right away by Camacho. He stood near me, radiating quiet rage.

I tried ignoring him; I could guess the gist of what he would say, and wasn't looking forward to another haranguing. Yet when he began twitching and humming a low, dangerous growl, I had to concede his presence. "Hey, Macho Man, how are you?" I essayed.

Camacho stared at me with baleful eyes. "I am empty inside."

"Wow, that's, uh, that's rather existential."

"Literally. I am empty." He leaned across the lab bench, invading my personal space with his warming intensity. "My colon is a desolate wasteland where nothing lives. I can barely digest food." He reached around to his backpack and produced a carton of yoghurt. He shook it, eliciting a wet slosh. "I have to eat this for three weeks so that my stool might once more become solid. After that I have to spend months bulking up *just so I won't die of malnutrition!*" This last part he said as a desperate hiss, the words a prelude to tears.

"I'm... I'm sorry to hear that," I said.

"*And it is all your fault.*" There was hatred in his face, the same hatred I had seen in dad's face. It wasn't any less painful coming from a relative stranger. "Why? Because I was *creepy*? Or just unlucky? Was I just some collateral damage to you?"

I opened my mouth to protest my innocence, but The Yog shuffled in then. She considered me for quite some time before placing a hand on Camacho's shoulder. "Macho, dear," she said in a deadpan, "would you go down to the office and ask Mr. Thumbs to come here?"

Camacho nodded, flashed me an evil grin, and hurried from the room.

I pulled deeper into my shirt under the weight of The Yog's glower and deeper still when her expression became suddenly jovial. She headed up to her desk and faced the assembled class. "Good morning, students. It seems we have a very special guest with us today." She gestured, and I watched in stunned horror as sixteen faces turned to look back at me. "Though she is supposed to be gone today on protective leave, our very own Joanna Matheson has returned to grace us with her presence."

The collar of my shirt was now up above my nose.

The rest of the class issued a collective sneer before turning back to face front. The Yog continued her announcement: "I'd like you all to take a chance in the coming weeks to *really* get to know Joanna. She's a very special young woman, and as I'm sure you've heard by now, starting next year she will no longer be with us. Spend some time with her today, before she is swept off to the juvenile penitentiary, and you lose your chance."

I noticed Edgar still turned around, facing me. I ground my teeth, fighting off a wave of rage. Yes, that was right, I was getting angry, too; why the hell not? Damn it, this wasn't fair. I. Was. Innocent. Even if I *were* guilty, The Yog had no place publicly shaming me like this, inciting my peers to hate me! It was cruel and unusual!

And I had no legal experience on which to base that claim.

117

Sigh.

Camacho returned sometime later, Principal Thumbs in tow. "Alright, Brunehilde," Thumbs said to The Yog, "why'd you drag me out of a budget meeting to--" That was when he noticed me. "Jiminy Cricket, Jo, what are you doing here?" Before I could answer, he held up a quieting hand. "No, not here, you can tell me in the hall."

I slid from the stool, and he and Camacho stepped aside so I could exit. As I passed, Thumbs turned to the class and cautioned, "Please, kids, don't make anything bigger out of this that it needs to be. Just go back to your work and learn, okay?"

The excited chatter that followed his words told me just how effective they had been.

The principal joined me in the hall soon after. He didn't speak for a while, just ground his fingers into his eyes and mumbled to himself. It sounded like sobbing. For my part, I used the delay to compose myself; as much as I wanted to scream and shout and let it all out, I knew a rant wouldn't help my cause.

"Jo," he said at last, his voice a hoarse whisper, "why are you here?"

"I have a passion for learning that just won't stop, sir."

"Damn it, Jo, be serious. I don't want to have to call your parents two days in a row."

"My mom wanted me here. Her reasons were long and varied, but it basically boiled down to me not being treated as a criminal until I legally was one, sir."

"Damn it." He continued grinding his eyes. "I'm... I'm not trying to treat you like a criminal, Jo. I tried to tell your mother that, but I guess she wasn't in a mood to listen."

I bit down on the thousand and one comments I had for that line.

"It's for your own protection, Jo. Really it is. I don't condone violence, nor do I expect it, but people are not... Well, they're not thinking straight. There's the possibility for reprisals. I don't want the police coming back. If you're here, the chance of them coming back rises exponentially, and I do not want police back in my school." He finished grinding and looked at me with puffy, wet eyes. "Can you appreciate that?"

I could; I didn't want to see the police any more than he did. Unfortunately, it seemed I would be seeing a lot more of them a lot more frequently.

"So why don't we just call today a fluke, and let you go home, okay?" he said.

I wanted to answer, "Okay." What self-respecting kid wouldn't? The principal himself was giving me permission to play hooky. But... but. School was now the only place where I was free from the disapproval of my parents. Sure, there was the disapproval of my peers, but in this crazy mixed-up world where no one believed my cries of innocence, what choice did I have but to pick the lesser of two evils? "Are you making it official, then? Are you charging me with a disciplinary referral to make my suspension official?"

He ground his teeth. Saying, "No," would keep me here as a disruptive influence; saying, "Yes," would send my mom off on some crusade, raising a fuss in the PTA and the local media. Thumbs released a wheezing sigh that seemed more death rattle than exhalation and gestured to the Science classroom's door. "Return to class, then, Ms. Matheson, and on your own head be it." He stumped back to his office, heavy footfalls echoing in the empty hall.

I slipped back inside the classroom, repeating my earlier entrance by slipping straight across to the unused bench. Only one person saw me enter this time. Edgar was turned around, staring at me, and stayed that way through the rest of the period. I wilted back into my shirt under the ferocity of his gaze, and tried to get through the rest of the day.

CHAPTER 13
REPRISALS

The reprisals started out innocently enough. Someone would knock into me at lunch, spilling my food a little. Someone else would knock into me in the hallway, spilling my book bag and scattering papers across the hall. Oh, they'd offer to help collect the papers, then they'd galumph around, oh-so-accidentally spreading the pile of school work farther and farther afield. Then the bell would ring and they'd hurry off to class, apologizing along the way.

The worst part was that I wasn't 100% sure these *were* reprisals. Instances of "random accidents" were up in my vicinity, but not outside the curve of a normal distribution graph. If these happenstances kept up for long enough, I could settle my paranoia and know for sure that the school really was out to get me. That's why, when more overt reprisals began, they came as a perverse relief.

While swap-grading our homework, mine came back with every answer checked wrong, even those that were blatantly right, with the words "Mad Crapper" scrawled across the top. In one case, I swapped my homework with someone and she just crumpled the paper and threw it to the ground. The teacher saw the whole thing, then ordered me to pick the paper up and gave me a zero for the assignment.

People also threw things at me; not dangerous things, but cruel notes, pieces of garbage and, worst of all, a plastic grocery bag filled with dog poo. Until then, I'd kept my head down, not let the administration know of my frustration, but a bag of dog poo? Really? I had rights.

Stinking bag still in hand, I marched down to Thumbs' office, determined to receive a modicum of justice.

"And did you see who threw it?" he asked after I'd showed him the offensive missile and plead my case.

"No, but--"

"And any of these other happenings, do you know who did them? If so, can you prove malicious intent? Maybe they just... bumped you on accident."

"Right, like I *accidentally* dumped a near-lethal dose of Gelfelax into those brownies."

The shock my statement elicited stretched most of the wrinkles out of his jowls.

"I mean, why do *I* have to prove malicious intent?" I asked.

"You do have a record."

I leaned forward and snatched the bag off his desk, then flung it with much force against the far wall. It didn't rupture, but the principal dodged away on the chance that it might spew poo. "I do *not* have a record! I have a bunch of tenuous links and presumptive guilt! What if Scott from my math class threw this bag at me, huh? He has a dog. There, that's a piece of evidence and a name chosen at random! He's friggin' guilty! Go and suspend him for his own good!"

Thumbs stared at me. I stormed from the room.

Things escalated from there.

The following Monday morning, someone vandalized my locker. Across the door was scrawled the slogan "DEAR SiR YOULL TASTE MY BLiStERiNG FURRY" in dripping brown paint. It looked to be the art teacher's handwriting. Great; somehow, news of the note had gotten out as well. Someone-- likely several someones, based on the variety of sizes present--had kicked dents into the once smooth locker door. Despite myself, I couldn't help being impressed by this particular show of hate: my locker was on the upper row, and kicking it was no mean feat.

Opening the locker brought another flurry of surprises: stuffed through the locker vents were a plethora of hate notes, small plastic rats, and the occasional fake turd. It seemed Edgar had been spreading his story, weaving his own hurt history into the tapestry of my public disgrace.

A locker opened nearby. Turning, I spied Agnes immersed in her locker, head down, glasses fogged with breath. "Hey, Ag," I ventured. She slammed her locker shut and headed off to first hour. A moment later the bell rang, and before long, I was alone in the empty hall.

I leaned against my locker and slid to the floor, hitting the stained and peeling linoleum harder than intended. My teeth rattled, my body shook, and something snapped loose deep inside. I cried.

This morning's vandalism, though no worse than what that had come before, hurt the most. It had been nearly a week since I had been branded the Mad Crapper, a weekend between the school turning against me and this very moment. I thought that, maybe, humans being statistically kind creatures, the hatred aimed my way might have diminished some.

Thanks to life-long habit, I took a deep, racking breath in through my snot-clogged nose, trying to at once clear the orifice and fill my lungs. I gagged as the horrifying stench of the school made its way past my shield of snot.

The pungent reek eking through the halls was similar to that of a public restroom. Not a nice, clean, public restroom, as could be expected in a restaurant. No, this was the earthy aroma of an old National Park restroom, sharp and sour, abandoned in the middle of the forest, left to rot forever more. But that was only a small part of the smell. If one were to scrape up all of the incipient filth in that forest-bound poo-bunker, dump it into a porta-potty to marinate for a few weeks, then take *that* and let it dissolve in an Olympic swimming pool's worth of industrial strength bleach, *then* one could start to imagine the lingering stink. There would still need to be some twenty competing fragrances of air freshener and scented candles to mask the original odor, all of which served less to smother the stench than to smother those who might smell the stench.

I gasped in another deep breath, despite the smell, this time dislodging the snot. I then began choking as the dislodged snot hit the back of my spasming throat. I coughed, tears of physical distress following tears of sadness down my cheeks.

Over the sounds of my bronchial rebellion, I heard the soft squeak of sneakers moving towards me through the empty halls. I spotted a puff of blue and gold suspended on thin white columns, then blinked away tears and recognized Clarice, the head cheerleader, glaring down at me with an expression of utter disgust.

"Are you all right?" she sneered.

I had a few responses prepped for just such a run-in: No, I'm practicing for an upcoming school play; I'm fine, I was just helping the cafeteria staff prep some onions; No, I'm reeling from the revelation that nothing in high school matters in the real world. If *I'm* this distraught, how are you as a cheerleader possibly going to survive? To my eternal regret, I was too busy trying to breathe to loose any of this wit.

Clarice crouched next to me. "Is this just something temporary, or do you need medical attention? Nod for medical attention, shake your head for something temporary."

I ignored her, instead focusing on clearing my throat and getting my breathing under control. "Yeah, no, I'm good," I said as soon as I was able. "I'm really here dying, and need the help of a chccrlcader to get through it."

"I was just trying to help." There was a sarcastic whine wound around her words.

"Look, I'm not going to be some kind of charity case for you, Clarice. You can go make yourself feel superior to someone else, alright?" I clambered to a standing position, wiping my eyes and trying to look as though my day were going according to plan. Or that I had a plan, and that my life wasn't spiraling out of control, and it was all because some coward had--

I turned back to my locker, ignoring the vandalism, and finished my business there.

"I was just trying to help," Clarice repeated.

I took my time digging through my book bag, and after another half-minute or so, Clarice walked away, her footsteps fading until I was alone again. With no further reason to delay, I sealed up the locker and headed for homeroom.

***

I survived Monday without further incident, aside from the all-encompassing disdain of my peers. Once home, I made a slime-encrusted ham sandwich and plopped down in front of the TV for a bit of mindless escapism. There was homework to do, quite a lot of it actually, but why should I care? I wasn't going to be around to attend classes next year.

I pulled up the latest episode of "The Evening Report With Lentils The Wonder Dog" fresh on streaming after last night's live premiere. I glanced sidelong at my sandwich, remembering what this show had done to my appetite last time I had tuned in, then shrugged and took a bite.

Lentils flailed about on screen, only occasionally getting his one eye into contact with the audience. He started out quoting stock-market figures--a necessity for fifteen-year-olds such as myself--before moving on to the first big story of the episode.

"In other news--" Lentils wriggled dramatically, ensuring his one extant eye faced his viewers. Behind him, the computer-generated newsroom dissolved into stylized flames. "--tragedy strikes the small town of Telethepee, Ohio."

For the second time that day, I choked. This time, I was able to expectorate the offending particle, and a chunk of even slimier ham burst from my mouth and landed smack in Lentil's good eye. I leaned forward as the ham slid down the TV screen, desperate to hear more. Telethepee was my town, the only home I had ever known. What story was big enough to get national attention? And why hadn't I heard about it yet?

"They say hell hath no fury like a woman scorned," Lentils continued in an over-serious tone. "But what hath a teenage girl? Well, she hath blistering fury."

The rest of the ham began crawling its way back up my esophagus, eager to join its compatriot in free-flying fun.

"Earlier this month Kelso Amboy High School freshman Joanna Matheson was involved in a messy break-up with long-time beau Eddie Latterndale. Rather than play hard-to-get and write depressing poetry, Joanna decided to get revenge. Rather than limit the scope of her blistering fury to the young man who jilted her, Joanna decided to get revenge... on the entire student body!

"Yes, at the yearly Kelso Amboy All-School Jamboree and Swap Meet, Matheson poisoned a batch of brownies sold by the state-championship winning school marching band, the Potoos, of which Eddie was a member. Using over-the-counter laxative Gelfelax, Matheson struck down over four hundred attendees... with extreme diarrhea!" The camera zoomed in, milking the dramatic reveal for all it was worth.

Or maybe not. Maybe that was my own vision constricting with rage, cutting out extraneous detail.

"But Matheson wasn't entirely without heart, as proven by this warning letter she left for her classmates."

And there it was, on screen, a scan of my note: "Dir sir, you shall taste my blistering fury." My handwriting, broadcast to the whole nation. Worse than that: the entire world. How had they gotten it? I assumed by now it was in police custody, logged as evidence in my impending trial. If it wasn't, that meant it was still in the hands of its rightful owner, the one to whom I had given it. If so, only one person could have given the Lentils producers access to that thrice-damned note: Edgar. I clenched my fists and let out the start of a truly epic scream. This betrayal, the second betrayal my supposed best friend Edgar Latterndale had subjected me to, was far, far worse than the first. Flaking out was one thing, but exposing me like this? Lying about our relationship? On global television? That was too much.

And then Edgar was on TV, his hair slicked back and his blinding white forehead shooting lens flares into the camera. "She just couldn't handle my band commitments. I couldn't help her out with an extra credit assignment, so she shoved a dead rat down my tuba, and then... then did all this." He paused, listening to a question from the camera operator. "Yeah, that was after the note." There was a hard edit, minutes of interview cut to get to the really juicy stuff. Ed flicked his eyes back and forth, uncomfortable with what he was about to say. "Off the record? She almost killed her dad. I don't know what she was thinking."

And then there was Camacho, face serious, though a smile kept flickering in about his lips. "Yeah, I've thought for a while she was kind of crazy. Every time she saw me she'd make these weird, crude jokes. I don't know what her problem is." He paused for several long seconds. "I offered to help her out with her project, you know, after her falling out with Edgar? She just shut me down, told me I was creepy."

And then there was Agnes. I gasped; Edgar's betrayal no longer seemed to hurt by comparison. No, not you, Agnes, you can't talk to these scumbags. You're supposed to be better than Edgar. "Well, she came over to my house, and... well, I admit that I talked her into writing the note. I just--I just thought it might distract her, you know? She'd write it and get Ed paranoid, and then leave it at that." There was an edit, some context lost forever to the void. "I don't think she did it. The Jo I know wouldn't poison the school, intentionally or not." Another edit. "No, no I have no idea who might have really done it."

And then there was the Yog. This time there was no betrayal, just a sense of confusion as to why a teacher would be taking to the media at all. "Who are you?" she demanded. "Did you check in at the office? What the hell are you doing here? Get out! Hinson!" The camera whip-panned away before returning to Lentils. Oh... well... that was a relief, at least.

I scrabbled for the remote and shut off the TV before Lentils could say any more. Having my dirty laundry aired to the world was bad enough; I didn't need some cheap summation finished with a stupid pun.

From then until my parents came home, I sat on the couch, letting my rage grow.

CHAPTER 14
BACK TO SCHOOL

I hadn't seen Edgar on my morning commute since just before the Jamboree. Perhaps he was actively avoiding me, or perhaps I was subconsciously avoiding him; either way, our interaction was limited to standoffish interactions in science class. But that Tuesday, I was determined to confront him.

I snuck downstairs while my parents still slept and made my way out of our housing development to wait in ambush by the main road to school. One tense hour later, my stakeout bore fruit: there was Edgar, trudging through the morning dew, shoulders hunched and hair freshly trimmed back to expose his eyes and ears. Nationals were a few weeks away yet, but he was already prepped for his trip to Washington.

I waited until he passed by my hiding spot behind a curving brick fence, then stepped into the street and sped up to match his gait.

"Hey," I called.

His steps faltered, but he continued his slow plod without acknowledging me.

"Saw Lentils last night," I said, careful to contain the supreme vexation boiling just under my surface. "Got me thinking. Maybe we should patch things up and start dating again, huh?"

He grunted.

It was time to let some of the venom flow. "It's nice to see *something* good came out of the Crappening. For the first two days after, I was terrified my dad was going to die. In fact, that first day, the doctors said it was likely. They said it was the worst case of dehydration they had ever seen. But knowing you managed to get on national TV with his suffering? I'm sure that'll make it all better for dad. He's always liked you; knowing he did something to boost your career will be like a balm for his wounded soul, just as it was for mine."

There was the faintest sound of brakes squealing as he came to a screeching stop; he'd probably need a new pair of sneakers after that. "Oh, I'm sorry, did you not like me talking to the press? Maybe I should have asked your permission first. After all, you were kind enough to warn me beforehand when *you* did something unconscionable. Maybe we could rectify this? Perhaps a finder's fee, say fifteen percent of the sum Lentils payed me for an exclusive story?"

Mother duckling; he got *paid?!* My paper lunch sack crinkled as I balled my hands into trembling fists.

"Of course," he continued, "I'm sure there's no way you'd accept such an offer from me. After all, taking that money would cut into the amount I've earmarked for the band to travel to nationals. I know how generous you are, and that you'd never stoop to petty chicanery to defraud the Potoos of the funds needed for this trip. And they do need it, seeing as how that unfortunate business at the Jamboree robbed them of their brownie money."

The paper sack ripped open as it impacted Edgar's face, sending sandwich parts and potato chips flying. I couldn't remember crossing the street--it must have happened during Edgar's sanctimonious speechifying. I also couldn't remember knocking him to the strip of grass beside the street, or straddling him, or repeatedly smashing my lunch sack into his smug little face, but it seemed safe to assume all that came in short order after the street crossing.

I continued plugging away at his face, the jelly of my sandwich appearing as rich arterial blood as it spread over my hand and up my arm. My knees went numb from the dew soaking through my jeans. Edgar took it for several seconds, too stunned to react, then pulled back and popped me in the jaw.

Now stunned as he had been, I rolled back and lurched to my feet before stumbling away, rubbing furiously at the warm spot where his fist had connected with my face. "You bastard!" I yelled, taking my hand away and spraying chip crumbs over the crushed grass.

Now he stood, weaving on unsteady legs, dukes up in a stylized fight stance. "What!" he yelled back. "Can't take it? Can't stand it when someone gets one over on you?"

"You profited on my suffering!"

"The whole school suffered! Because of *you*! *You*, trying to get back at *me*. So now *I'm* trying to get back at *you*. Can't you handle your own medicine?"

I rubbed my jaw again, aware I was spreading a thick layer of peanut butter and jelly over my face. "What the hell are you talking about?"

His stance shifted, his center of gravity dropping as his shoulders came up and his arms spread wider. He was no longer half-joking: the hint of malevolent playfulness that danced in his eyes during his eloquent faze was replaced by cold malice. "You think it's all about you. You were failing Science, and I was the bad guy for not bailing you out. You stuff a rat in my tuba, you damn near kill me, your dad, and half the school, and *I'm* the bastard for using that situation to save my band and get a little counter-revenge on the side. Well, I have some choice words about what you've done, but you know what? I'm going to be the bigger person and not say them." He relaxed a fractional amount, lowering his arms and stepping away, though his shoulders remained hunched, his body still primed for action. "You got revenge on me, and now I've gotten revenge on you. How did you like it? Because I didn't like it. And now we're even; I'm willing to let it go. So are you going to stop acting like a child, or are you going to continue this, make it into a full-blown feud?"

I ripped up a handful of moist grass to scrape some of the lunch-mess from my face. "Screw you, Ed. You're pissed off that I got revenge over nothing? How about you, then? I'm not the Mad Crapper; I didn't poison your damn brownies. So what? You'll just spread lies about me because everyone else is already spreading lies?" Angry tears trickled from the ends of my eyelids, oozing down my cheeks and adding their mucusy stickiness to the jelly.

"If not you, then who?"

"Screw you, Ed," I repeated.

He continued to glare at me, nervous energy radiating from him. At last he relaxed, standing straight and drooping his shoulders. "Thought not." He walked away in the direction of the school.

Once I had enough of the jelly off my face to appear normal, I followed him.

***

With my bagged lunch destroyed, I had no choice but to partake of our venerable cafeteria for sustenance. I scurried from my hiding spot when the bell rang at the end of Science class and made my way to the cafeteria. Though not the only person in the hall--it's amazing how many "bathroom breaks" are requested immediately prior to lunch--an expansive bubble of personal space surrounded me. Everyone in the school now knew me by sight, and my reputation as an unstable delinquent kept the masses well away.

The upside: I was among the first to get in line for lunch. Today this was especially good, as the suspense was killing me. When the daily menu was read over the intercom during morning announcements, I had... other things on my mind, and had missed the missive. Smelling what wafted through the halls after Science class served up no further clues, as there was, well... a smell already lingering. Being in line, shuffling my wet and "sanitized" plastic tray along the lunch-room rails, was my first chance to see what was on offer today.

What I saw was disappointing. Ranked in the steam table before me was corned beef with brown gravy, boiled black beans and cabbage, chocolate pudding, and chocolate milk. Other students weren't the only ones getting back at me; the cafeteria staff had a bit of a mean streak as well. Though why they would inflict this horror of a meal on the whole school and not just myself, I did not know.

I disengaged from the line, leaving my tray in front of the first sneeze guard, and walked empty-handed to an empty table. In retrospect, the pile of discarded trays midway down the luncheon railing and the lack of cash-register sounds should have been a clue that I would find the school's lunch unappetizing.

Sitting alone at the empty table, I traced out the whorls of the faux wood-grain tabletop and waited for the bell to ring so that I might get this thrice-damned day over with. The longer I sat there waiting, the more I reflected on Edgar's words this morning. Had I been acting childish? Well, I had taken this whole Mad Crapper business sitting down, not looking for the true culprit, not doing more to prove my innocence than cry out, "Hey, I'm innocent!"

But I don't think that's what he meant... Screw it; I *knew* that wasn't what he meant. Innocence aside, the fact that I had mustered enough chutzpah to put a rat in his tuba did hint that I wasn't doing my best thinking. If I could harvest a dead rat for revenge, maybe--just maybe--I could have done the project on my own, leaving Edgar to get on with the Potoos, free of my obligations upon him. I shuddered at this moment of self-realization. All things equal, I was still a--if not *the*--victim in all this, and wasn't about to let myself become the bad guy.

My abortive soul-searching was interrupted by a dull thud and a shifting of the table as someone heavy sat across from me. The sheer gravity of this mystery visitor pulled my attention up from the whorls of the tabletop, and I raised my head to see *two* heavy someones sitting across from me: Cal and Hez, each identically dressed in yellow hoodies and matching stocking caps.

"Hey, Jo!" Cal essayed. "What's happening? You look down."

"Yeah," Hez continued. "You don't have any food."

They stared expectantly at me.

Though I knew *of* the two, I couldn't say I *knew* the two; our interactions consisted of a round at their coconut shy last year and a rather embarrassing school-wide rendition of "Happy Birthday" over the intercom earlier this year. Their interest in me at this time indicated they only had one thing on their minds, the one thing I was most reluctant to discuss.

"I'm good," I lied. "I just forgot my lunch at home, and didn't really feel like getting anything here."

"Oh." Hez thrust one hand below the level of the table and gyrated for a moment before bringing his hand back up, holding something tan, squishy, and wrapped in plastic. "You want a Hot Pocket? I've had them going all day; they're warm by now."

Though I hadn't yet had any lunch, I could feel what I hadn't had for lunch coming up again. "No, I'm... I'm good."

He glanced at the... *thing*... then back at me. "You sure? It's no problem, really; I've got another one. You shouldn't go hungry just because you forgot your lunch."

"I'm... I'm not hungry."

Hez shrugged, then peeled away the plastic and began picking layers of bread from the... *thing*... and eating it in thin, slimy strips.

Cal rubbed his wispy-whiskered chin and studied me with suspicion. "What's wrong?"

"What do you mean?"

He too retrieved a Hot Pocket and peeled away the plastic before eating strips of bread from atop the meat pastry. He swallowed his first mouthful and said, "No one's not hungry unless something's wrong."

"Or if you've just eaten," Hez chimed in, mouth full.

"Yeah, but she hasn't just eaten, has she?"

Hez opened his mouth to reply, then closed it as he parsed out his brother's syntax.

I stared between the two, trying to take in both brothers at once. It wasn't a simple task: sitting close together as they were, they spread over a considerable length of bench. According to their logic, they must live stress-free lives.

"So," Cal continued, "What's wrong? I know we're not teachers or counselors or anything, but we like to think of this school as ours, and feel responsible for the students in it. You can tell us anything, and we won't judge."

"Unless you tell us you have a lot of friends with bathing suits, stage talents, and a strong desire for world peace," Hez supplied

"Or a selection of artisanal pies."

They tilted their heads together and stared at me, their soft, hairy faces resembling nothing quit so much as teddy bears stuffed with meat.

I sighed in defeat. "Yeah, okay. I'm a little pissed off at... well, at everyone and everything at the moment. And everyone and everything is pissed off at me. It's the Crappening, you know, and-- wait, why are you two being so nice? Why aren't you pissed?"

"Oh," Hez said, shaking his head and blinking, "we weren't affected by the so-called Crappening."

"Yeah," Cal said, a little more focused on the conversation than his brother. "It was Shy Night; we only eat coconut-based products on Shy Night."

"They were selling coconut brownies," I said.

"Were they?" Hez looked crestfallen. "Damn."

"Well anyway, I'm pissed," I asserted, getting the conversation back on track, "because everyone is accusing me of being the Mad Crapper and I. Had. *Nothing*. To do with it. I'm innocent, but no one believes me. What's worse is I have no way to prove my innocence. That's what's wrong, that's why I'm not eating. Well, that and I don't like corned beef."

They continued to stare owlishly at me for several long seconds. Their attention had reached the point of being uncomfortable when they turned their heads towards each other and performed some kind of arcane nonverbal communication consisting of twitches, exaggerated pantomime, and sundry expressions. When this interplay had played out, they nodded and returned their attention to me. Though they still appeared kindly, their faces had grown serious.

Cal spoke. "Look, we spend a lot of time hanging around the office; we pick up on a lot of things. Consequently, we had front-row seats to the whole investigation, and let me tell you, there was a lot of political pressure behind the scenes that the student body was not privy to."

Hez offered a confirming nod, and I leaned in closer, caught up in Cal's subdued oratory style.

"The superintendent wanted answers, and fast, so Thumbs was pushing for a quick and easy conclusion to the whole sordid affair.

Totoro found evidence painting you as the Mad Crapper, but he felt there were plenty more interpretations for the facts at hand. He said as much to Thumbs, but the principal shut him down; said he didn't want the detective's hunches disrupting the school any more than necessary. So now they've got a smoking gun that's secure enough to prosecute, and the whole thing gets solved, nice and easy. That's good enough for the superintendent, and that's good enough for next year's funding."

I sat straighter, my whole body on alert. "You're--you're saying there's some kind of conspiracy, and I'm the patsy?"

Cal shrugged. "Maybe. Maybe not. For all we know, you really are the Mad Crapper. Heck, you could be a criminal mastermind who's able to get her hands on thousands of dollars' worth of Gelfelax on a moment's notice. After all, your mom works at a firm that helped design Gelfelax."

I glared at him. "Yeah, but even so, how would I--wait, how did you know that?"

Cal shrugged again. "We read your permanent record."

"WHAT?"

"Relax," Hez said, "we read everyone's permanent record."

"But that is neither here nor there," Cal continued. "What's important now is that your defense didn't get the same level of scrutiny as your prosecution. A thorough examination of the facts at hand, as well as additional facts that may prove to exonerate you, has not been performed. Indeed, quite the opposite has occurred. Based on the facts at hand, you have already been tried and found guilty by the media--and by 'media' I mean the Teletheepee Weekly Times and Lentils the Wonder Dog--and that is a violation of your basic rights as an American."

He studied me for a moment, his eyes growing wider with excitement as he did so. Suddenly they snapped open fully; I could imagine a lightbulb glowing into life above his head. He stood, turning to face the flag hanging from the wall of the cafeteria, and placed his right hand over his left breast. "This is still America! You are innocent until proven guilty. This is still America! The burden of proof is such that there can be no reasonable doubt of your guilt. This is still America! You are protected by rule of law, not subject to the whims of public opinion, and we will see that the rule of law is upheld! Come, Hez!" He turned back to face us. "We must go and discover every shred of evidence, we must explore every possible chain of events, we must track down and thoroughly examine every lead, no matter how preposterous, to ascertain the truth in this matter!"

Hez stood to join his brother. Cal doffed his cap and bowed deeply to me. "Have no fear, Joanna Matheson! Cal and Hez are on the case! We will see to it that you have your day in court!" They about faced and began to march away.

"But I don't want a day in court!" I called after them.

"You know what we mean!" Cal replied.

"No, I don't!" I answered.

"And neither do we!" Hez concluded.

I watched them go until they left the cafeteria. When I turned away, I was shocked to discover everyone present staring at the afterglow of Cal's spontaneous patriotic screed.

"*Ce fut très étrange...*" I heard Genevieve say in the ensuing silence.

I stood and followed my erstwhile investigators from the room.

CHAPTER 15
COUNTING MY CHICKENS

I snuck into the Science classroom on Wednesday, flitting in like a fart upon the wind, unseen, only vaguely smelt. No one else was in yet, so I took my seat at the spare bench and disappeared within my hoodie.

I might have remained so ensconced had I not heard a plaintive "Squeep!" from the front of the classroom. A quick visual scan revealed no source for the noise. Perhaps it was the air conditioning system...

"Squeep!"

There it was again. I sat up and squinted at The Yog's desk. The sound seemed to be coming from there, not the HVAC system. My blood chilled: could it be rats? It sounded like rats.

"Squeep!"

"Squip!"

"Squeep-eep!"

There were more sounds now, high-pitched and very nearly cute. I rounded the lab bench and made my way up the room's center aisle. As the squeeping continued, I homed in on its source: the incubator, looming in the corner of the room. I interposed my head between the warm orange lights overhead and the chicken litter below, casting a wide shadow, and gasped at what I saw.

Three fluffy yellow chicks--well, two yellow and one mottled brown--stumbled about, scrabbling at the litter and staring in wild fascination. Their eggs lay a short distance away, burst asunder and dripping with ichor. Two other chicks had freshly hatched; they flopped around in puddles of meringue while the remaining eggs cracked and shivered.

I continued to stare in fascination at the little critters, unconcerned that I was now a public target for the class that would be intruding on me at any minute. Let them see me, let them judge; I was witnessing a miracle of nature.

Footsteps echoed into the classroom before stopping with a squeak. Edgar stood in the doorway, sneering at me. As he turned to leave I called out to him, unconcerned about our feud for the moment.

"Ed, come here! Look at this!"

"Squeep!"

He edged towards the door, then came to some decision and made his way down the room to join me. I stepped aside, giving him room to view the incubator. He didn't gasp aloud as I had done upon seeing the chicks, but he was fighting back a smile, and I could see a little bit of my former friend in his face.

"Okay, that's actually pretty cute," he conceded.

"Look at that one," I said, pointing to the brown-speckled chick.

Edgar snorted. "An hour into the world, and he's already spattered with shit." He prodded at the chick; it nuzzled into his finger and squeeped excitedly. "I'll call him Poopy."

"Squeep!" said Poopy.

In the far corner of the incubator, an egg was beginning to fracture and bow out. In a few moments' time, a questing bead broke through, and produced a "Squap!" of its own.

We stood watching the hatching as the room filled over the next few minutes. As each student came in and saw us, they would hesitate for a moment before peering in at the chickens transitioning from one existence to the next.

The wonder of nature's majesty continued as the final bell rang and The Yog entered the room. "Oh, good," she said, looming at the far end of incubator. "I was getting concerned; they were supposed to hatch Monday. If they kept up like that, by Friday we'd have another wonderful smell added to the school." At this juncture, she likely glowered at me, but I was too wrapped up in the chicks to notice. Poopy was scurrying to and fro, knocking into his siblings and squeeping with delight.

By this point all the eggs had hatched and fifteen healthy chicks were getting the hang of these new-fangled extremities in the litter below us. They all squawked in hunger and excitement and whatever other emotions chickens were capable of feeling.

The Yog pushed forward, interpolating herself between students and chicks. "Now class," she said once we had given her room to speak, "I'm glad you've all enjoyed that, but I'm afraid it's time to actually settle down and get to some science work today. As I'm sure you'll remember, there is a project associated with these chicks."

There was a round of disappointed groaning at the mention of work.

"Oh, come on, everyone, this will be a fun project! Each of you grab your chicken and your partner, then take it back to your table. We're going to catalog a list of traits: color patterns, height, weight, talon size, the whole thing. It'll be fun!"

She stared at us with eager open eyes, awaiting a burst of answering eagerness. We stared back in dead-eyed confusion. Watching the chicks hatch was fun, yes; recording observations, less so. Our overwhelming dearth of anything resembling her level of enthusiasm rankled The Yog. "Okay, don't everybody jump up at once."

We obliged her.

"Okay, everyone jump up at once."

Now we failed to oblige her.

"C'mon! Hiya, hiya, let's have some enthusiasm people!"

"Um, Ms. The Yog," Clarice said, raising a hand though she was only a few feet away--playing the teacher's pet, per usual--"we don't exactly know which chicks belong to which group. The markings are on the eggs, but the chickens are loose now, and we can't... um..."

The Yog closed her eyes and issued a long-suffering sigh. "Pick a chicken, and record enough data so you know which is yours tomorrow."

I pointed to Poopy. "I was in here first; I saw that one come out of the turd egg. That was mine and Edgar's." I had seen no such thing; in fact, the turd egg had been among the last to hatch. But I had grown attached to the ugly little thing, and was unwilling to part with him.

The reminder that we had been assigned as lab partners hit Edgar hard, and all the joy of witnessing the miracle of life drained from his face. He thrust up his hand, straight and insistent.

"Yes, Ed, what is it?" The Yog asked

He lowered his hand. "I would like to request permission to change my partner assignment, ma'am."

"Hm." The Yog shot a venomous glare my way, also reminded of my existence as a pariah, and unwilling to shackle Edgar with more crap than he could handle. She tugged at her lip and did a quick head-count of the class; it came up eighteen, enough for complete partnerings. "Well, as much as I understand the desire to avoid certain... *persons*... there are no spares, so I find myself disinclined to acquiesce to your request."

Edgar's shoulders slumped. Mine went a little straighter. It felt good knowing I wasn't entirely beyond the reach of proper schoolhouse ethics.

With The Yog's clarifying ruling on which chicken belonged to which group, my classmates pressed forward, arms outstretched and clutching for white meat. I was shuffled to the back of the throng, and waited as squawking little balls of fluff were scooped up and dragged away.

The throng thinned out as those with chicks backed away from the incubator. Ed and I took this chance to swoop in and clutch a chick of our own. I was relieved to see that Poopy was still there, hopping and flapping his stubby wings.

"Squeep!" said Poopy.

Edgar reached past me, hand outstretched to ensnare Poopy. The chick issued an alarmed "Squeep!" and tried to scuttle away, stumbling and rolling in his panic. He got maybe six inches before Edgar wrapped his hand around the fuzzy little body.

With our proverbial chicken in our proverbial basket, we backed away from the incubator and let the remaining students retrieve their chicks. Then, for the first time since my abortive suspension, I followed Edgar back to our shared lab bench. Though I hadn't forgiven him for kicking off our falling out, it was nice to be back at the familiar bench and pretend for a moment that we were still friends.

Edgar let Poopy loose on the tabletop, and the chick wasted no time in exploring its strange new world. I laughed as he bobbed and weaved, cheeping and scrabbling all the while, and used my arms to scoop him back to the middle of the table whenever he neared the edge and the devastating drop to the floor four feet below.

"Squeep!" said Poopy.

As this interplay between chicken and arm carried on, The Yog explained the terms of the assignment as she circulating amongst us, issuing worksheets and lengths of twine.

Once she had passed us, I picked up the twine and raised a questioning eyebrow at Edgar. "What the hell are theses for?"

"Goddammit, Jo, really? Did you hear nothing?"

"Correct. Now what is this for?"

Edgar extended one hand to grab Poopy back from the brink.

"Squeep!" said Poopy.

"I'll make this simple: not even extra credit can save your soul at this point, so just stay out of it, alright? If you want to do the project on your own, fine, but I don't want any help from you. I'll make all the observations, do the daily measurements, everything else. I just won't do it with you. Do your own work if you must, and don't talk to me." That said, he gripped the wriggling Poopy tighter and wrapped the twine around his fluffy brown body.

"Squeep!" said Poopy.

"You know," I said, letting a bit of ice into my voice, "if you hadn't left me to, quote, do brackets my close brackets own work, ellipses end quote, we wouldn't be in this mess now, would we?"

He tightened his grip on the squirming bird, eliciting another "Squeep!" "So you've chosen feud, then? You're going to keep blaming me for your problems, then getting back at me while I do my best to keep one step ahead of your stupidity?"

I would not let him make me the bad guy. "You're the one who's chosen to feud. All I did was the rat in the tuba, then I sat back and let the cookie crumble where it may. You're the one who seems so very interested in keeping this going, on *insisting* on an ultimatum from me."

"Squeep!" said Poopy.

Edgar lifted the chick higher, abandoning the twine and making up-close observations about Poopy's feather pattern distribution. "Shouldn't that be, 'let the *brownie* crumble where it may'?" he asked after some minutes.

Red flashed across my vision, and I was tempted to slug him again. My hand twitched on the tabletop, clenching and unclenching as my mouth opened and closed, trying to swear and yell and rant without my permission.

"Squeep!" said Poopy. The chick struggled in Edgar's grasp, pushing his head up and trying to fly with one little stump wing. Edgar loosened one hand to adjust his grip, and Poopy took his chance to nip at Ed's fingers, spread his wings, and hop majestically to the floor. He hit and bounced before stumbling to his feet and crowing a triumphant, "Squeep!"

"Damn it!" Edgar snapped, blowing at the red mark on his finger. He hissed at the pain of the beak-bite and glanced at me, perhaps seeking some measure of sympathy. Well, he would get none from me. That would be my contribution to the feud: silence.

The Yog floated up behind us then, her slippered feet whispering against the tiled floor. "Is everything all right over here?" she asked, shifting her gaze between us. "And where's your specimen gotten off to?"

"Yeah, we're fine, I just--just, wait." Edgar slipped from his seat and scrabbled after Poopy as the chick slalomed between lab stools.

Despite myself, I laughed at the display, breaking my stubborn silence; too many years as Edgar's friend had conditioned me to appreciate his antics. And what with the cheeping, the laughing, and the muttered swears from down around knee-level, the rest of the class soon had their attention on us. Even though I, the great pariah, was in their line of sight, they laughed as well. Even The Yog got in on the mirth.

With an "Aha!" of triumph, Edgar snagged Poopy from under Clarice's table and stood, brushing bits of floor-lint from the chick.

"Squeep!" said Poopy.

"Very good, Ed," the Yog enthused, "you've just made a very useful observation. This little guy's a fighter, a runner, a survivor. I wouldn't be surprised if he ends up being among the biggest of his brood mates."

As happened so often when The Yog complimented Edgar on his scientific prowess, he beamed.

I held out my hands as he returned to his seat. "Since you seem to have made such good headway on observations, mind if I hold him a bit?"

Edgar raised Poopy and tilted him to stare into his face. Poopy's head turned to counter the move, and he blinked. "Yeah," Edgar said, holding the chick out to me, "I guess so." Still breathing heavily from his merry chase, Edgar slid the chick into my cupped hands.

I held Poopy up to my own face, getting my first in-depth look at the thing. "Oh, you're just so cute!" I said.

"Squeep!" said Poopy. Then his belly split open, and his intestines tumbled out.

I imagine most people have a good idea of what the inside of a chicken looks like. After all, the average non-vegan is exposed to... oh, probably hundreds of thousands of chicken carcasses in their lifetime. What they fail to account for, though, is that what they see is the clean, sanitized meat portion of the chicken. There's the light bits, the dark bits, the bone, and sometimes the mysterious multicolored nugget. Even in the preparation of raw chicken, all one sees is a pearlescent pink.

Yet there is more--so much more--to a chicken. For one, there are the giblets: the organs and intestines and gizzards and such. Now, these are eaten, certainly, but almost exclusively by the elderly, the mad, or the Southern. I myself only had one previous run-in with the giblets, when I was three and my loving grandfather told me they were gummy candies. I don't remember what color they were: I've blocked out the memory and--to the eternal consternation of my mother--the grandfather. Still, the giblets, when eaten, are prepared and sanitized, cooked or fried or pickled, chemically changed and devoid of blood.

So in the moments when Poopy split and his entrails became his extrails, I thought I was prepared for what was to come. I would not enjoy it, certainly, but I was prepared.

As it turns out, I was not. What came out of poor little Poppy was a surprise to me, and I daresay would have been a surprise to most people.

Purple.

That was the color. Brilliant, deep, rich purple, nearly Tyrian in its intensity.

Media had not prepared me for purple. Zombie movies always throw blood on intestines, supernaturally bright red blood. Sometimes, depending on the audience, rating, and "realism," the blood will be a thick brownish color, and the intestines will be a deep red, with maybe some grey bits thrown in for good measure.

But this thing I held in my hands, this tiny yellow and brown tennis ball with a beak, when he was split, he was--

Purple.

"Squee..." His little eyes bulged and looked imploringly up at me.

I screamed. Blood gushed over my fingers as I spread them wide and dumped his body unceremoniously on the lab bench.

"Squee..." The little cache of purple... stuff... lay on the slick faux-marble, twitching as Poopy breathed his last.

I turned away, still screaming. That was when everyone got a good look at my wet, purple hands. They screamed, too.

I whirled on Edgar. His scream was an octave or so lower than mine, his eyes bulging, just as Poopy's had. I saw them flicker to the tabletop, and then his scream was muffled by his own clutching hands.

I followed his eyes to the bench, saw Poopy's talons feebly kicking at his--

And then my scream was muffled by my clutching hands. Mistake. Big mistake. My hands came away, hair matted and tangled in Poopy's blood.

I turned back to face the class, still screaming. They still screamed. Camacho was curled on the floor, twitching and crying.

The Yog, her glasses perched at the very end of her nose and threatening to fall off, waved an arm at the door. "Go, go!" she shouted over the screaming. "The bathroom! Run, run!"

I ran.

***

I spent the rest of the period in the bathroom, scalding water cascading over my hands, the matted blood and viscera never seeming to dilute no matter how much water passed over it. The sink was now stained rose red as the blood trailed onto it, filling the basin and not quite draining away as gallon after gallon of scalding water washed, and yet never diluted. Out, damned spot. Out, stain of Poopy, his death fresh on my hands. In the mirror above the sink I could see my face, covered in a thick purplish substance for the second time in two days, my face streaked with long-dried tears, and still the blood on my hands refused to dilute, refused to be washed away.

When Science class ended, The Yog came into the bathroom. She stood at the sink next to mine, washing away the little bit of blood sticking to her fingers. I guess Poopy had gone on to his final resting place.

Water ran for a moment then shut off, and then the Yog just stood there, her hair drooping, her glasses sliding down her sweat-slick nose. "I was ready to blame you," she said after what seemed like an eternity, her voice echoing and hollow in the porcelain-studded chamber.

I stared at the rose-colored water that sloughed off my hands.

"I thought, 'There she goes again, blaming Edgar for taking away her extra credit. She's killed a chicken to ruin his grades.' But then I heard you scream. Sure, screaming was the natural reaction; everyone did it. But you kept on screaming."

She stepped away from the sink and dispensed several yards worth of paper towels. The door opened, and there was a blast of lunchtime noise.

"For what it's worth," she said over the din, "you'll get credit for the chicken assignment."

The door closed. I blinked away a fresh set of tears. In the sink below, the purple stain on my hands seemed to be diluting.

CHAPTER 16
SEEKING SOLACE ELSEWHERE

I left the bathroom about halfway through lunch. My hands were a glistening pink, though whether scalded or stained or both I couldn't tell. I made my way to the cafeteria, in need of something to take my mind off the previous class. Poopy hadn't weighed much in my hands, but he weighed heavily on my soul.

I entered the cafeteria, mind swirling with paranoid conspiracies about what had just happened. Had this been the opening salvo in the next round of the feud? Ed had a mean streak--Lentils had proven that. But there had been ulterior--even selfless--motives at work then. I could see no gain for Edgar in exploding a chicken on me. What I could see, in the shock of Poopy's death, was that Edgar was right: this feud had to stop.

As I neared the empty lunch rail, the last student to partake of the steam tables for the day, smells wormed their way through my consciousness. There was the constant shit-stink of the school, mixed with the underlying funk of overcooked beans and slightly off vegetables that always clung to the cafeteria. Above these, though, was something new, fresh. It was tangy, a little spicy, rich and savory. For the first time this week, I dared to take in a deep breath through my nose. My mouth watered at this new smell, anticipating today's menu. I was glad it would be something good, something I could dig into and focus on so I could ignore--so I could ignore everything.

I slid my tray down the rails and stopped before the craggy visage of an elderly cafeteria lady. She smiled as she saw me, her face crinkling and a strand of snowy hair escaping from her hairnet. "Well, hello there," she said. "Running a bit late are we?"

I smiled back, hoping the expression would be enough to allay further questioning.

She lifted a lid from a tray, eliciting a gust of fragrant vapor, and rooted around behind the sneeze guard with a pair of tongs. "Can I interest you in a breast or a thigh?"

Time spent around Camacho had ingrained certain responses in me: the first thing I noticed was just how low the front of her uniform hung below her shoulders. Then my mature brain kicked into gear and I parsed out a non-perverted meaning behind her question. My mind hung up on the answer, all of my processes stalling as the cafeteria lady lifted the tongs into my field of view. Clutched in the metal claw was a brown oblong, glistening with succulent grease, thin on one end and bulging on the other. I stared at the flaky, breaded, deep-fried *thing* clutched in the tongs, remembering the savory smell I had savored moments before, and had to fight back the wave of acid clawing its way up my esophagus.

The tray went flying as I jerked away from the food line.

"Hey!" Despite her age, the lunch lady dodged the flat black projectile with spry ease, and fixed me with a withering glare. "Just because you're one of those damned filthy hippie vegans doesn't mean you have to take it out on me!"

I spun around, my shoes squeaking on the slick tile. Arrayed before me were so many people, so many Styrofoam plates covered in thick, savory chicken grease. I saw a hundred smiling mouths, a hundred mouthfuls of chicken, a hundred chins dripping with juice. There was laughter, the sounds of happiness, the "Squeep!" of Poopy as he took in this magical new world--

I stumbled away, found myself folding over the edge of a red plastic trashcan, my long-since digested breakfast jumping and leaping and trying to break free.

147

Something broke free. I'm not sure what, but it was something. I recovered in time to straighten and see five students, all carrying used trays, all staring at me as if I had gone insane. Maybe I had. I wiped my mouth and backed away from the trashcan. They looked disgusted.

I ran.

I skittered through the hall, on the verge of face-planting into the unforgiving ground, my pistoning legs somehow keeping me up and alive. Squeaks followed me, the soles of my shoes finding partial purchase before skipping to the next step, the next, the next. I had to get out of here, had to get away from this horrible shit-smelling, chicken-smelling place and find someone to talk to, someone to tell me how to get out of this situation.

Ahead of me, light streamed into the locker-lined halls. The light grew brighter as an external door opened, and I crashed into whomever it was who was coming into the school.

"Hey, whoa, hold it there, young lady! Just what the hell has you running scared?"

Hands grabbed my shoulder, held me still as my legs continued to piston. The purple of Poopy's--the purple faded from my vision, and I recognized the thin-mustached Detective Totoro. Sunlight glared from his freshly washed hair, and the musk of strong cologne hung about his body.

"Ms. Matheson, what's going on, why are you running?"

I turned the questioning back on him, hoping to distract him enough to let me go. "Why are you here? Haven't you done enough? Because of you I'm going to jail!" I writhed in his grasp, not unlike Poopy in Edgar's.

"I'm here to see Mrs. Yogmier. I've got... further questions. Now, what did you mean about--"

I twisted my shoulders and managed to break his hold. I sprinted away, out into the blinding sunlight, stumbling down the hill on this side of the building.

"Ms. Matheson!" he called after me. "You can't just leave school in the middle of the afternoon!"

I paused long enough to shout back, "I'm not even supposed to be here! I've been suspended!" then sped away, off into the world to find someone to talk to.

***

In movies, whenever a character is in need of spiritual advice, they go to their local Catholic church to speak to a priest, assuming no mentor figure has been provided. The troubled character, upon realization of their troubles, walks around for a bit, plops down in the back of an inner-city cathedral, and waits for a priest to come by and lay some time-appropriate wisdom upon them. Unfortunately, not only was I in the suburbs, I was nominally Methodist, so finding a priest might be a bit on the hard side.

Still, a bit of searching on my phone turned up Our Lady of Perpetual Gloom, a Catholic congregation located not three miles from school. I could walk there, achieve spiritual enlightenment, and be home in time for dinner. Assuming the school didn't start an uproar over my absence, and my parent's didn't escalate the situation by sending police.

I arrived at the church an hour later and stared at it from behind a chain-link fence. It was a towering Gothic structure, all points and spires and gargoyles and grimness, made of light stone stained dark by years of exposure out on the prairie. This place radiated an aura of mystery, a sacred place that held many sacred secrets. The effect was diminished somewhat by the orange-brick outbuilding grafted onto one side, which stretched around a fenced in patch of scrubby grass. This relatively modern addition dampened my faith in the place.

Putting aside my misgivings, I made my way around to the front of the building and inside through a set of colossal wooden doors, bleached grey by the sun. I arrived in a vestibule, sparsely furnished by an end table and a bulletin board. The wallpaper looked like it hadn't been updated--or cleaned--in fifty years. Continuing through the vestibule and another set of great wooden doors, I passed into the sanctuary. Now this… this was a place where I might find some answers.

The ceiling stretched at least fifty feet above me, ribbed by stone arches that descended to form buttresses on either side of the ancient pews. Light streamed through stained glass windows, shining rainbow patterns on the worn rugs adorning the floor. At the front, hanging above an altar polished smooth by decades of congregants, was a crucifix. At first glance, it looked like unvarnished wood, bleached like the front doors, but movements in the stained glass light exposed a lustrous sheen. As I took it all in, I tried to ignore the fact that sunlight came in from both sides of the building at once; I would just get my advice and get out.

Backtracking to the door, I took a seat in the very last pew, luxuriating as I ran my hand over the red velvet cushion. Already I could feel the trauma of Poopy's death fading... Knitting my fingers together, I rested them on the back of the pew in front of me, closed my eyes, and waited. In the movies, it was only a matter of moments before a humble priest noticed my supplications and inquired as to whether I had any spiritual needs to be fulfilled.

I waited.

As I waited, I reflected on what had brought me here, the thoughts coming unbidden into the forefront of my mind. Was it all my fault? Had I acted stupidly in handling Edgar's betrayal? Certainly, I had done my level best to push him away. And Agnes, oh, Agnes... Perhaps the tuba rat had been too much. It was no wonder she wouldn't talk to me following the Crappening; she knew I was capable of all manner of depravity, and so didn't believe me when I said, "This depravity is not mine!"

I wondered what her parents must think about all this. "You better stop hanging around with that Matheson girl. You see what she did? I'd better not see any reports saying you've killed half the school and half killed your father! Now get back to band practice; that punk music is keeping you out of trouble."

Ah, parents... If only my parents could be a little more understanding, or at least pretend to hear my protestations... Maybe they just needed time. They had been raw and angry at first, unwilling to hear. Maybe now that nearly two weeks had passed, an eloquent defense could sway their minds...

And Poopy... poor, poor, Poopy... I looked at my folded hands; they were nearly the same color as the seat cushion.

I waited.

And some amount of time later I was still waiting. I huffed and stood up. Spiritual guidance had proved a complete wash. Maybe next I'd try binge-eat fortune cookies; at least then I would have the solace of junk food to sooth my soul.

As I stormed out of the sanctuary and into the vestibule, I noticed a small sign on the table that I had missed when I entered: "For all weekday inquiries, please visit the office." Below that, an arrow pointed to a small door perpendicular to the main flow of traffic. So life wasn't like the movies after all. In retrospect, it seemed obvious. Of course the clergy would have offices and office hours; they couldn't spend all day in the sanctuary on the off-chance that someone might stumble in. Well, the Buddhists might, but I wouldn't be looking to them for guidance until Friday at the earliest.

I pulled open the perpendicular door and found myself in a beige hallway, decorated by children's drawings and smelling of aged paper and cleaning supplies. At the far end of the hall was another door, cracked open and filtering in faint light. I crossed the mildewed carpet and knocked at the door.

"Come in!" called a deep, lilting voice.

The door opened on a book-lined study, cluttered but not messy. Seated at a desk was a curly-bearded man wearing a black golf shirt with a high collar. He was middle aged, maybe forty, and rail thin.

"You're new here," he said. "Who are you?"

"M-my name is Joanna Matheson. I've come for… for spiritual advice." I'd made it all this way, and *now* I was getting nervous.

He stood and extended a bony hand for me to shake. "Joanna, hello. I'm Father Rabinowitz. Welcome to Our Lady of Perpetual Gloom. Please, sit down." He indicated a spindly chair across the desk from his own.

I'm not sure why people in offices indicate chairs when they invite a guest to sit. Usually the only extra chairs are right in front of the desk, and it would be just plain rude to take the host's seat. Father Rabinowitz could have invited me to sit without any further instruction, and I could have figured it out.

I sat. "Our Lady of Perpetual Gloom," I stated. "That's kind of a weird name."

He returned to his seat and shrugged at my comment. "Well, it fits the church. We're a rather un*orthodox,* congregation." He stared expectantly at me.

I waited.

"Un*orthodox*?"

I continued to wait.

"We're Catholic? Unorthodox? The three main branches of Christianity: Catholic, Protestant, Orthodox--never mind, forget it, forget it." He straightened and fixed me with a serious expression. "So, young Joanna, what can I do for you?"

"I need spiritual advice."

"Really? That's why you came to see a priest in the middle of the week?" He mimed wiping sweat off his forehead. "Load off my mind. For a minute I thought you were doing a fundraiser."

"I'm... I'm not doing a fundraiser."

"Would you like to?" He reached to the side of his desk and pulled over a flimsy cardboard box filled with chocolate bars wrapped in plain white paper.

"I'm... I'm facing jail time," I said, "for a crime I didn't commit, and... Well, I'm not accusing my best friend of the crime, but I certainly hold him responsible for all this. Beyond that, my other best friend has abandoned me, my parents have shut me out, and everyone at school hates me. Oh, and a chicken exploded in my hands."

We sat in silence for several long moments.

"I'm not hearing a question in all that..." Father Rabinowitz prompted.

I hadn't thought of a question; I just expected to state the problem and receive a koan. "What do I do?"

"About the chicken? Talk to an ornithologist, maybe. As for everything else..." Another long silence stretched between us, punctuated by a shrug. "Nothing. Suffer along in silence, and wait for everything to blow over."

"That's terrible advice."

Another shrug. "That's what you were already doing, isn't it?

That's why you're here, trying to get answers out of a stranger, rather than doing something about your problem."

Where did he get off? I wanted solace, damn it, not a guilt trip. "I'm asking questions! I'm learning! How is that not doing anything?"

He laced his fingers together and rested his chin on his hands. "Let's step back here. Is there anything you can do to clear your name? Can you give a good alibi, or any other exonerating evidence? Think about this, please."

I thought about it. Cal and Hez were launching an investigation of their own, but I put little faith in them. Agnes could provide an alibi for part of the night but... Agnes wasn't speaking to me. Besides, the crime had such a large window of opportunity that a half hour here or there made no difference. I shook my head. "No, there isn't."

"Right, so we're back to where we started. You're facing jail time. That sucks; I'm sorry to hear it. And there's nothing you can do about it. Going with Niebuhr's prayer, we've now accepted what cannot be changed. So what can be changed? You've told me you're cut off from your friends and family. If--worst case scenario here--you end up in prison, what do you want your life to look like when you get out?"

I doubted, "I want to find employment outside of the manual labor market," would be an appropriate answer so I shrugged.

"Come on, kid, give me something to work with here. I assume you want your friends and family to welcome you back with open arms?"

I took his lead and nodded.

"Great. So what you need to do is give them some reason to welcome you back. Win them over."

"But--but I didn't do anything wrong!"

He leaned back and flicked his fingers up in the air. "You didn't do anything wrong. No one does anything wrong. No one does anything. No one is responsible for the direction of their lives; they are but cogs in the great machine of society. You find where you fit, you grind along, and then you die."

"That's... that's terrible advice. Are you saying there's no point in trying anything?"

"I'm saying the big things can't be changed. Well, they *can* be, but it takes a lot of energy. Look at the world-changers throughout history. They flare bright, make a difference, and then burn out; that's all they do in their lives. Joan of Arc, there's a great example."

I frowned, baffled by this sudden sidetrack.

He leaned forward again, elbows resting on the desk. "Joan of Arc? Flared bright and then burned out? Jeez, you kids these days, with no sense of humor..."

"You were saying I alienated my friends and family."

"Right, right, right, right." He folded his arms and tilted his head, considering me. "Look, there's nothing you can do to improve your situation outside of getting a hotshot lawyer. What you *can* do, though, is tie up loose ends. You said you hold one friend responsible for all your problems? Go to him, forgive him. Maybe he really is responsible, I don't know. But maybe, after you get out of prison, you'll still have a friend left. Same with your parents. Talk to them, try to work things out, that's something in your situation you *can* change."

"I've already tried talking it out. They won't listen!"

"Have you tried talking it out, or have you just burst in on them and unloaded your problems, waiting for them to come up with a solution?"

I didn't answer.

"Here's something else to consider. What if you talk to them, try to make peace and amends, forgive your friend... and they don't listen? Wasted effort then, right? Except... then you'll know you tried to make a change. You have to have the serenity to accept what can't be changed, the strength to know what can be changed... and the wisdom to know the difference. If you try to make a change, and it doesn't work, well then: you've gained wisdom. Sure, you'll be in prison, but you'll know you've done everything you could to change your situation. Isn't that a comfort at least?"

I wanted to jump up, to grab the box of cheap chocolates and dash it across his smug face. No! That was no comfort; that was defeatist despair! I wanted to scream, and rant, and tell him how

154

wrong he was--

Except, my friends and family had already tried the same thing, hadn't they? My parents, though they hated me for what I might have done, they tried to stand up for me against Thumbs, had done their best to acknowledge my innocence even though they didn't believe it. Edgar, who still believed I had poisoned his brownies, given him crippling diarrhea, and ruined his chance at nationals, had still tried to forgive me, had given me a chance to end the feud. And Agnes, who believed I had committed a horrible crime and ruined our perfect summer trip, who could have screamed, and shouted, and railed against me and my perceived stupidity, instead chose to step away, to spare me the wrath of her disappointment.

"That was from Alcoholics Anonymous, wasn't it?" I said.

He shrugged. "I don't get much lead time, I go with practiced answers."

I pointed to the box of chocolates. "What do the proceeds go to?"

"Renovations to the K through third grade program here. We're looking at some knew playground equipment."

I stood and pulled a rumpled dollar bill from my pocket. "You can keep the candy bar; I've had enough chocolate to last me a lifetime."

***

Twilight was fading to dusk when I arrived home. As I was more than four hours late, it was safe to assume my parents would be none-too-pleased to see me skulking in. Well, more none-too-pleased than normal at least. As it was around seven-thirty, they might be in the kitchen having a late dinner. With luck I might be able to slip in, unseen, and sneak off to bed.

Throwing my future into the hands of fate, I unlocked the front door and stepped inside, only to discover my parents seated in the living room, facing me.

"Hey, guys, how are you doing?" I produced a fake smile that radiated guilt.

"Where were you?" mother asked. Her voice was ice cold, and I could see her fingers digging into the arms of her recliner.

"And what's that brown stuff all over the front of your shirt?" dad added.

I smoothed my shirt and composed myself, hoping to portray an air of competent professionalism, despite the dried chicken blood.

"Mother, Father, I apologize for my tardiness in returning home this afternoon. I realize now it was incumbent upon me to make my location and movements known to you and to seek your permission before straying from the daily schedule. However, at the time of my straying, I was suffering from a great deal of emotional distress, and did not act in a responsible manner. As I am now aware of the mistake I have made, I will do my upmost to assure that such a situation is not repeated in the future."

I took a steadying breath, pausing long enough for mom and dad to jump in with any comments before continuing. Though the priest's advice was simple--take personal responsibility for the situation and talk things out--acting on the advice was causing a deep dread to gnaw through my guts.

"As to where I have been for the past several hours, I availed myself of the time and services of Father Haim Rabinowitz, pastor at Our Lady of Perpetual Gloom Church. I sought out advice as to how best communicate with you my thoughts and feelings *vis-a-vis* the All-School Jamboree and Science Fair, and the events therein. Forthwith, I would like to elucidate, in the most basic and non-emotional manner, what my part was in the tragic event known as 'The Crappening,' and my personal opinions as to how the fallout of that event has affected me. To be blunt: I did not commit the mass poisoning of the attendees that night, nor am I the individual colloquially known as 'The Mad Crapper.' While I freely admit that the evidence gathered as to The Mad Crapper's identity does tend to describe myself, and that I have no concrete proof that can exonerate me of this charge, I do heartily maintain my innocence, and will continue to do so, no matter the opposition. Further, the backlash against myself as the putative Mad Crapper, both physical and emotional, has caused me a great deal of distress, and has eroded entirely my social and academic standing. However, I do understand that for those who were victims of the

Crappening," here I gestured to mom and dad, "the physical stresses of the attack were far greater than my emotional stresses, and acknowledge that a degree of anger and hostility is a natural response to such events. While I know this hostility is likely to extend for a great period of time, I would humbly request that my own position and self-claimed innocence is remembered once a decent interval has passed, that perhaps these issues my again be raised and discussed, so that we as a family may come to a greater peace and understanding."

I wracked my brain, looking for any further arguments that needed airing, then decided I had done all that could be done at this point. I offered up my strength to change this situation, and now all I needed was to await the wisdom that told me whether this was a situation I'd just have to accept.

I inclined my head in a miniature bow. "Thank you for your patience in this matter. I look forward to any resolution we may achieve in the future." I waited, my gut still churning, for a response.

A response seemed long in coming, however, as my parents' jaws were currently dangling slack across their chests. At last, my dad managed to get his jaw winched close enough to ask, "And what about that stain? You never explained the stain."

"Oh, this?" I gestured to my own chest. "This is chicken blood. It's a... a Science class thing."

I waited further, expecting mom to ask for elaboration on the "Science class thing," but instead it was dad who spoke. "Was... was all that rehearsed?"

"The basic arguments were prepared, but the wording was entirely extemporaneous."

"You... you know you can enroll concurrently in college debate classes next year..."

"Yes."

Mom and dad turned to each other, and commenced with some manner of telepathic communication. After several moments, they faced me once more, and mom spoke. "In the future, please be sure to inform us if you're going to be late from school... or if you plan on leaving early."

I winced--so the school *had* called.

"As for the rest, well... I think we'll probably discuss that later, after your father and I have had more time to... discuss."

I inclined my head again, the dread still gnawing at my gut, but feeling a good deal more confident than when I walked in the door. Unwilling to let the silence now between us grow awkward, I excused myself and hurried past them, up the stairs and into my room.

Collapsing onto my bed, I shuddered as tension drained from my body. That... that had been step one. It still might turn out to have been a wasted effort, they still might hate me and doubt me and continue to be angry with me, but I had done my absolute best to communicate with my parents, and now the onus of the relationship was off of my shoulders. It may not make any difference for me in the long run, but it at least made me feel better.

Sometime later, there came a rapping upon my door. "Who is it?" I called.

The door swung open with a creak, revealing my father silhouetted by the hall light. "Can I come in?" he asked in a whisper.

I shrugged.

He didn't come in. "It's... it's rather dark in there," he said after some seconds had passed. "If you were gesticulating, I didn't see it."

It seemed I had been alone up here longer than previously thought. I flicked on my bedside lamp and squinted against the sudden brightness. "Yeah, dad, sure, come in."

Dad shuffled inside and eased himself onto at the foot of the bed, groaning as he sat, the mattress groaning with him. "Jo...," he began, "this isn't really easy for me. I... I admit I haven't been very fair to you for the past two weeks or so. You have to understand, I *did* almost die, and that greatly colored my outlook and, more specifically, my treatment of you. This is by no means an excuse. Think of it... think of it more as an explanation. I almost died, and as soon as I heard evidence that you were behind it, I jumped to that conclusion, and held to it. I'm only human, and I responded in a very human way towards being hurt.

"But… well, what I forgot in all of that is that *you're* only human. If--*if*--you were the one who poisoned the brownies, you probably didn't set out specifically to kill me. You had your reasons for doing it. *That's* not an excuse either, but it is an explanation."

I opened my mouth to interject, but he raised his hand and talked over me. "On the other hand, there remains the possibility that you *didn't* do the whole brownie poisoning thing. You said you didn't, you're a good kid, and I should have believed you, or at the very least held off on judging you until I more fully understood the situation. So, for not listening to you, and for not taking what you said into account, I most humbly apologize. I'm only human. *You're* only human. And maybe we can just be human together, and learn to live with all this."

Silence stretched between us, interrupted only by the soft burbling of dad's convalescing gut. I sprang upright in bed and hugged my dad. His embrace was warm and strong, and I melted into his pillowy belly. It felt so good to be--well, not believed, exactly, but for the possibility that I might be right to be acknowledged by him. I buried my face in his armpit and cried. Not long after, his tears joined my own, filtering through my hair and down my face... We stayed like this for several minutes, father and daughter, just letting it all out.

When my emotional excess had bled off, I straightened and wiped my nose. "How does mom feel about this?" I asked through a snot-clotted throat.

"Oh, I'm the one who talked him into coming up here," said a voice from the door. Mom was silhouetted by the hall light, just as dad had been. Somehow, in the darkness of her shadowed form, there was the glint of a toothy grin. "I know we didn't respond in the best possible way to all this, but know that we still love you, and we will try our damndest to work through whatever lies ahead."

I matched her, toothy grin for toothy grin, and suppressed a chuckle. "Thanks mom, that's all I needed to hear." My response was a lie; what I really needed to hear was that they were one-hundred percent in my corner and would support me all the way. But for the time being, it was enough.

CHAPTER 17
MAKING AMENDS

The plan had been to catch Edgar walking to school Thursday morning and make an overture of peace. This time I'd stay well away from him, keeping to my side of the street and making sure I was non-threatening. I'd be the bigger person, let him say what he needed to say, and not react. I'd especially not start a fist fight, and especially not bring up poor little Poopy's death. Poopy was a sacrifice; I would not make him a martyr for my cause. The plan was scuttled, however, by the expedient of my forgetting to set an alarm the previous evening.

The first sound to greet me that morning was a rap-rap-rapping upon my door, followed by my father calling, "Jo?"

I snorted, rolled over, and went back to sleep.

Knock-knock.

Who's there? I dreamed myself asking.

"Jo, wake up, you have to go to school today."

Jowakeupyouhavetogotoschooltoday who?

"Jo!"

I snapped awake and looked at the clock: there was no way Edgar wouldn't already be walking up the front stairs by this time. Blankets swirled around me as I writhed my way out of bed and into some clothes, then smashed through the door and past my dad.

"ThanksforwakingmeupIreallyenjoyedourtalklastnightIloveyoubye
!" I shouted as I flew down the stairs, out the door, and on to Kelso
Amboy Memorial High School.

It wasn't until I was half-way there that I realized I had
forgotten not only my lunch and breakfast, but also my book bag. I
toyed with the idea of returning home, tardiness be damned, then
realized that at this point, my academic standing didn't matter. I
was likely going to prison in a few months. Grades be damned,
then.

The schoolyard was packed with students as I approached it. As
per usual since last week, a bubble of space opened around me as I
entered school property. Through this void of other students, I
gazed up to the front entrance and caught a glimpse of Agnes
passing through the front doors.

There was no choice: I had to talk to her. Our last two meetings
had gone less than stellar, but I needed to convince her that I was
not the monster she thought I was, or at the very least incite a
definitive statement from her that she no longer wanted me
hanging around. I sped up, hoping to catch Agnes at our lockers.

Unfortunately, I just missed her. As I drew close I heard a slam,
saw the back of Agnes' filthy leather jacket drifting through the
multitude, and then I was standing before my own graffiti spattered
locker, alone in the throng surrounding me. Maybe I should spend
the whole day sitting in the hall, waiting for her to come back.
Yeah, that was the answer! Stalking would make her *so* much more
responsive to my pleas for attention. I slammed my head against
the locker, producing a hollow thud.

Lifting my head away from the locker I gazed down the hall,
and who should choose that very moment to come walking my
way but Cal and Hez. Their clothing was a little more unusual
today, their hoodies replaced by calf-length tan trench coats and
their knit caps by black fedoras. They too had garnered a bubble of
personal space, and as they neared I had the horrid suspicion that
this display was intended for me.

I slid away from my locker and into a smaller cross-hall,
intending to wind my way around the floor until I could escape
down a stairwell. The increased hubbub in my wake told me that

my escape hadn't been as successful as hoped.

As I rounded another corner, my personal bubble of space betrayed me: the students before me had all spread across the breadth of the hall, leaving me alone to face whatever bizarre display Cal and Hez held in store.

Walking in perfect unison, the brothers rounded the corner. When they saw me, they raised their hands and waved. "Hello, Clarice," one of them--Cal?--called.

I straightened, realizing now I had been crouched like a cornered animal. Clarice? I looked over my shoulder to find the head cheerleader standing along one wall, shoulders-deep in her locker. She pulled out and glanced around, her vacuous cheerleader dull-eyed expression appearing more disoriented than ever.

In the confusion of the moment, I took the honorable route and slid back behind a row of lockers.

"Hey, boys, what can I help you with today?" Clarice asked, bobbing her blond ponytails. The movement got her breasts bobbing as well, sending light shimmering off the myriad buttons decorating her navy-and-gold cheerleading uniform. Each button promoted a charity-*du-jour*, something vague and trendy which made Clarice seem like a better person by proxy: Save the Whales, Stop Deforestation in the Amazon, Support Free-Range Chickens. As if she cared where the meat in her skinless grilled chicken salad came from...

Cal and Hez slunk up to Clarice, each pausing to tip their hats at the young lady. Cal rummaged around in a pocket of his coat and produced a spiral notebook and pen. "Ma'am," he said after licking the tip of the pen for some reason that must surely make sense to his twisted mind, "if you have a moment, we'd like to ask you some questions."

Clarice stared at the brothers quizzically, eyes bouncing back and forth between the rotund forms. "Um, okay, but… I have to get to class soon."

"Not a problem; this won't take long." Cal flipped the notebook open, licked the point of the pen again, gagged, and poised to write. "Do you think you could recall for us where you were on the night of the Kelso Amboy All-School Jamboree and Bake Sale?"

"Well..." she rolled her eyes up towards the ceiling and chewed her lip. "I was here, at the Kelso Amboy All-School Jamboree and Bake Sale."

"Ah-ha!" Hez clapped his hands and jammed an accusatory finger under Clarice's nose. "I knew it was only a matter of time before the truth came out! You fought long and hard, but if there's one thing I've learned in life, missy, it's that the law *always* wins!"

Clarice's eyes crossed as she tried to focus on the finger.

By now, the mass of students bisecting the hall and those that continued to back-fill behind Cal and Hez had taken notice of the odd threesome at the lockers, and were forming around them, like spectators at a fight. Sure that I would be unnoticed, I tiptoed to the rear of the crowd to get a better view of the proceedings.

After several long seconds without a response from Clarice, Hez turned to look at his brother, quirking one questioning eyebrow. Cal shook his head. Hez slumped and withdrew his finger.

"Ma'am, I am very sorry for that," Cal said. "I'm afraid my brother here got a little overexcited a little too early in the investigation. Now, to continue, based on your answer of," he flipped through several pages of the notebook, "'... Kelso Amboy All-School Jamboree and Bake Sale.' Do you think you could expand on that a little, give us some specifics on your whereabouts that evening?"

Clarice nodded, not taking her still-crossed eyes from the now-retreating finger. "Well, when I first got here, I stopped in the lobby and did the coconut shy..."

"Interesting. And how would you describe your experience with the coconut shy?"

She shrugged, unsure as to what the hell this had to do with their investigation. "Well, it was pretty fun. I actually won a coconut, on my third try."

"And the management of this coconut shy, would you say that it was well run? Competently executed?"

"I would, yes."

"Do you think you might recommend this attraction to visitors of future jamborees?"

She gave that one a bit of thought before nodding. "Yes, I most definitely would."

The brothers also nodded in response, and there was a flurry of excited murmuring from the crowd.

"Now," Cal continued, "aside from an enjoyable time had at the coconut shy, what exactly where you up to for the rest of the night?"

Clarice again looked to the ceiling. "Well, I slipped upstairs to check out the science fair, but it was pretty sparse, so I finished in maybe five minutes. Then it was down to peruse the bake sale, and that was pretty much it." She shrugged. "I hope that helps."

"Interesting…" Hez interjected. He shot a quick glance at Cal, who flipped through the notebook again. When he found the page he was looking for, he nodded and winked. Hez returned the nod and gave a thumbs up. Cal rubbed at his upper lip, clenched his hand into a fist, extended his pinky, and waggled it by his ear. Hez scratched twice at his cheek, made an exaggerated show of wiping his nose, flicked his thumb behind his ear three times and winked. Cal… just stood there.

"You lost me on the last one."

Hez sighed dramatically and snatched the notebook. He read over the showing page, his mouth moving all the while, then jerked his head up to squint at Clarice. "You say you perused the bake sale the rest of the night?"

"…Yes?"

Another flip of the pages. "Yet we have a statement from an anonymous source who placed you in a booth, selling blandies. The source says, and I quote, 'Yeah, she was selling her blandies, man. They were all like strawberry flavored. And damn was she looking good. She had her feet all out on display, and you know Macho Man knows him some sexy feet when he sees them.' End quote." He closed the notebook with a sharp click that didn't seem appropriate for the notebook's card-stock cover. "How is it, I wonder, that you were both perusing the bake sale all night long, yet also manning a booth of your own? Where you… Oh, I don't know… *Lying?*"

There was a gasp from the crowd, and Clarice flushed, her golden hair garish against her now pale skin. "No, I-I mean, I sold out pretty fast. I only brought one tray, and that was only an excuse to get in to the kitchen--" She slapped her hands over her mouth. Her eyes looked as if they were going to burst from her skull.

I took a step forward as the crowd closed in. No. Way. There was no way... Clarice? She was just a dumb cheerleader; she couldn't possibly be the Mad Crapper. Could she? Why would she frame me? And why would she slip up and tell these two idiots?

Speaking of these two idiots, they were just standing there, Hez looking as though he were still politely listening, and Cal shaking his head. He took a step forward and slapped his brother's arm. "Hey," he hissed.

"What?"

"Now, do it now."

"Oh, right." Hez stood straighter. "Ah-ha!" He clapped his hands and jammed an accusatory finger under Clarice's nose. "I knew it was only a matter of time before the truth came out! You fought long and hard, but if there's one thing I've learned in life, missy, it's that the law *always* wins!"

"It's not like that!" Clarice's head was on a swivel now, and she was casting about for some way out of this absurd predicament. She looked like a caged animal, desperate for escape, or help, or salt--no, wait, in the excitement I was taking the metaphor--no, simile--I was taking the simile too far. Clarice probably didn't want salt, although I couldn't say that with complete certainty. If her strawberry blandies were any indication of her normal diet, then yeah, she probably wanted salt. Anyway.

The crowd's murmuring grew in intensity, and certain phrases made themselves audible over the general hubbub: "Crappening." "Bitch." "Penitentiary." In a way, it was heartening. Knowing that the crowd could be so easily swayed by this partial confession helped me realize that the student body wasn't angry at me on a personal level; it was angry at the Mad Crapper. So long as I was in that role, I would be the one they hated. Once Clarice was outed as the monster she truly was, Agnes and I could be friends again, and all my problems would fade away... except for my grades.

166

Those would haunt me throughout the summer, but at this point I didn't care, so long as I was no longer the school goat.

"Okay, I was in the kitchen!" Clarice yelled. "But I'm not the Mad Crapper! Please, you have to believe me!"

Cal stepped forward, raising his eyebrows until they threatened to disappear under his fedora. "Alright, then; we'll give you the benefit of the doubt. For now. Just why *were* you in the kitchen?"

Again, the flickering eyes, again the furtive glance around the crowd of accusers, again that all-encompassing lust for salt. No. Stop that. With an effort, I smothered the rogue simile.

"I'd… I'd rather not say," she said.

Cal stepped back. "Oh, you don't want us all to know why you were in the kitchen, hanging around the very brownies that would end up putting millions of people in the hospital later that very night?"

A collective gasp rent the air.

"Oh, yes," Cal continued. "We spoke to Edgar. He told us how you sidled up to the band's corner of the kitchen, offering to help them with last minute preparations, even offering to help them divvy up the brownies and deliver them to the gymnasium."

Holy sudden revelation, Batman. She had her hands all over the brownies, Edgar knew it, and he *still* blamed me? If it wasn't for the blood of Poopy staining my hands, I would have marched right over to his locker and proceeded to kick the shit out of him until I had created the Crappening, Part II. For his sake, it's good that I'm a better person than he imagined me to be.

Clarice was on the verge of tears, and just as I thought she was finally going to give in and begin open weeping, she blurted, "I was trying to prevent nut contamination!"

Dead silence. Dead, salt-craving silence.

"I know there're people with nut allergies in this school, and it's policy for nut-based foodstuffs to be clearly labeled as such, but it was an open kitchen, and I wanted to ensure there was as little risk as possible for cross-contamination between the foodstuffs!" She still looked on the verge of tears, but now she seemed ashamed of her actions.

The crowd, for its part, just seemed confused. There was no

murmuring, no dissection of her words.

Cal cleared his throat. "If you don't mind us asking, why didn't you tell us that to begin with? A simple, 'I don't want to be nutted on,' would have sufficed."

"That's what she said!" someone shouted from the opposite side of the crowd from where I stood.

Clarice sighed and looked at her feet. "Well, it was a good deed, yeah? Or at least, looking out for the safety of my fellow human beings. When I do stuff like that, like volunteering, or donating, or ensuring nuts don't end up in brownies, I like to keep it on the DL, ya dig?"

"Ah-ha!" Hez clapped his hands and jammed an accusatory finger at the myriad buttons festooning Clarice's uniform. "Then why are you shouting your humanitarian efforts to the heavens with *these*?"

She looked down, caught up a fold of the uniform, and turned the buttons this way and that. There was a spouting whale, an Olympic runner with prosthetic legs, a smiling boy with Down syndrome, and maybe a dozen others. "Well, I'm not involved with any of these. These are causes I don't have the time or resources to contribute to, but I still think of as worthy. I try to raise awareness for them, in the hopes that even that small effort might inspire others to help in making our future a bright one."

The murmuring resumed, accompanied by many enthusiastic nods of the head, and a few subdued handclaps. Dear God; I had always pegged Clarice as the stuck-up cheerleader, yet she turned out to be the reincarnation of Mother Theresa. I wanted to hate her but... well, okay, I was still able to hate her, but at least I had the decency to feel guilty about it.

"A fine story, to be sure," Hez said. "But so far that's all it is: a fine story. Where might we find proof of your philanthropic nature, and thus corroborate your tale?"

"Well..." Clarice was back to nervous mode, though now tinged with self-effacement and piousness. "I'm afraid there's no one who can really back me up as far as the Jamboree is concerned, but you could speak to my Rabbi about everything else I do. Oh, and the local Habitat for Humanity organizer." She began naming names and phone numbers, and it was all Hez could do to confine her stream of words to his notebook.

When she had finished, Hez snapped close the notebook, again with a much sharper *snap* than flimsy cardboard should have been capable of, and nodded to Cal. Cal returned the nod, waggled one hand, and ran his forefinger under his eye and down his cheek. "Alright, ma'am, everything seems to be in order. We'll be running the names you gave us, but I think it's safe to say that you're clear in our books, and will henceforth be left out of the ongoing investigation. Thank you for your time and consideration." He tipped his hat again, and as one, the brothers strode away in the direction they had come.

Maybe ten feet on, Hez stopped short and turned back. "Just one more thing..." He flipped open the notebook and glared suspiciously at Clarice. "What are you planning on doing this Friday night, say around seven thirty?"

Clarice looked flabbergasted. "What?"

"Just following up leads, ma'am. Also, I have a hunch: do you like Chinese food?"

Flabbergastion gave way to disgust, an expression I must admit I hadn't seen on Clarice's face... ever, really. "No."

"Should I take it that you're no longer cooperating with--Ow!"

Cal punched Hez in the arm.

"Okay, fine, thank you..." Hez muttered, rubbing his biceps and allowing his brother to drag him away.

There was a clamor of excited exclamation as the group around Clarice collapsed inwards.

"Thank you so much for all you do--"

"I'm allergic to nuts--"

"That's what *she* said--"

"I can't believe those two dorks were harassing you like that--"

"*I* can't believe they were trying to shift the blame from that creepy Jo kid onto you--"

Oh, right--there was still harsh reality to contend with. Yeah, I had forgotten about that. I slipped away from the scene of the investigation unnoticed. The morning had been a complete wash. I tried telling myself that this was just one of those things I couldn't change, and that I just needed the serenity to accept that, and then I'd be fine.

Somehow, though, that thought failed to comfort me.

CHAPTER 18
A PACT SEALED WITH BLOOD

Following my abortive attempt at communicating with Agnes this morning, I didn't want to miss any chances to speak with Edgar. Since the Crappening had eliminated the gym as a viable gathering place, gym class had been nothing more than a glorified study hour. So I cut gym and headed to The Yog's Science class forty-five minutes ahead of schedule.

I felt guilty for this--after all, I was not a misbehaving child, no matter what the current consensus held. But speaking to Edgar was important, or so I told myself. As I sat cross-legged on the floor outside the lab I ignored the small voice reminding me that any action requiring justification was probably not an action I should be taking in the first place.

This period, the lab was serving as a sophomore chemistry class, taught by someone other than The Yog. From inside came the clinking of beakers and the cheeping of chicks. Only fourteen chicks today... As I sat and waited, I went over the words I would say to Edgar, trying to balance humility with a sense of strength and moral rightness.

After forty-odd minutes of waiting, the next bell rang, the door opened, and out belched a line of slightly-older teenagers. Most looked down as they noticed me; kids sitting around waiting for entrance to a classroom was *so* seventh grade. A few recognized me, giving a wide birth as they shuffled by. As the line thinned and finally ended with the teacher's exit, I climbed to my feet and slid into the room.

I bypassed the unused back bench and walked the length of the room until I stood abreast of the lab table shared by Edgar and myself. For a moment, I was possessed with the notion of sliding all the way through and taking the coveted stool by the window. It sat there, bathed in a ray of shimmering sunlight, picked out by a thousand gently drifting dust-motes, inviting me to climb up and rest my butt on the warm maroon plastic. At the end of the moment, I fought back the temptation. Though I had won access to the seat by divine right of having arrived first, giving Edgar something else to grouse about would do nothing to help my cause. Instead I pulled out the nearer of the two stool, the cold one that huddled in the shadow of the overhanging work surface, and sat down. Despite expectation and narrative momentum, it too was warm, made so by the butt of its previous occupant.

I didn't have long to wait for Edgar to arrive. Students began to drift in as the first bell for next period rang. Edgar was among the first few, and when he drew abreast of the bench, he stopped to consider me. "You've come out of hiding," he said.

I nodded.

He slid past me and took his usual seat, melting as he passed into the ray of sunlight. "What do you think The Yog has planned for us today?"

I shrugged. "Guess more of the chicken stuff."

Edgar stiffened, and right away, I regretted speaking. So far, my apology was off to a great start. There was nothing for it then but to forge ahead and hope sheer momentum would bowl him over.

"I've been thinking about what you said," I said.

"And what saying did I... said... are... Starting over: what are you talking about?"

"Tuesday morning. The ultimatum? About me not acting like a child, or else we could continue fighting?"

"Oh, that." He gingerly rubbed his nose, wincing at the first touch of his fingers. "So what did you think about, about that?"

"Well, honestly, I'm still pissed off that you so thoroughly misrepresented our relationship to the news media."

He grew even stiffer, his ears pulling back and his shoulders rising. If he had fur, I was sure the ridge just north of his tailbone would be sticking up with nervous excitement. "That was not my fault! I reported the facts as I knew them, and they misrepresented us entirely without my consent."

I took note of his defensive tone, and filed it away for later use. The conversation wasn't going the way I had planned, but I saw a way that I might be able to turn that to my advantage later on. "Okay, well, that's beside the point now," I continued, leaning away from him to show that I was not on the offensive. "I'm not here to talk about how *I'm* pissed, I'm here to talk about how *you're* pissed."

His eyes narrowed with suspicion. "I'm listening."

"Well, okay, you were pissed, and I'm willing to admit rightly so, about the way I've been treating you since our lab-partnership fell through, up to and including discounting the reasons for your departure. And though at the time I felt perfectly justified in my actions towards you, a series of events has transpired which has caused me to realize that my actions were completely out of line, and I would like to offer you my deepest and heartfeltest apologies to you." I inclined my head, ceding the floor to him on this point, to either accept or reject my apologies as he saw fit.

He didn't answer right away; I saw that as a good thing. I remember as a child, being forced to apologize immediately after some infraction had occurred, or being forced to accept an apology immediately. In either case, the apology or its acceptance felt wrong. When someone, still actively scowling and angry with you for getting them in trouble mutters, "I'm sorry," you know it's not true. And the times when it had been me muttering? Well, I *wasn't* sorry, and that was lying, and usually, lying would be seen as a worse infraction than whatever infraction I was being forced to apologize for! But that was parent's logic for you... The fact that Edgar was taking so long proved he was considering my words, judging the sincerity of my intention.

At last, he inclined his head as well. "Apology accepted. Thank you. I take it this means we're ending the feud as well?"

I extended my right hand out to him. "Friends?"

This, too, he observed for a long while. At last he shook his head. "No."

I winced, retracting my hand.

"No, not friends. You hurt me, Jo, and I'm not ready to trust you yet. Not friends. But not enemies, either." Only now did he extend his hand, grasping my own and giving it one firm shake, up and down, before releasing his grip. "I'm not averse to the possibility. Maybe someday, okay?"

I nodded, and he scooted away from the bench, leaning down to root around in his backpack.

The conversation hadn't gone exactly as hoped, but at least there had been a positive note, there at the end.

"Hey, Jo," Edgar said after several minutes had passed without The Yog's arrival, "shouldn't class have started by now?"

I checked the great round clock installed in the far wall. "I don't know; I can't read old-people clocks. Let me check." I slid my phone from a pocket and checked the time. "Yeah, it's been about five minutes. The Yog's late."

"Huh. That's a first."

"Yeah..." I had planned on holding back the rest of what I wanted to say for a later date, once emotions had cooled and Ed had more time to warm towards me, but The Yog's unprecedented tardiness seemed too much like divine intervention to not take advantage of. "Okay, so, hey, apropos of nothing here, but now that we're no longer feuding, I have a quick question for you. There remains a *slight* possibility that it might offend you, and before I ask, I want you to know that I'm not trying to offend you."

He ran a hand over his recently shorn hair. "Is it my haircut? Because I know it looks stupid, but this is nationals."

"No, no, this is like, a serious question."

Again, he paused to consider his response. I snuck a glance at the rapidly spinning second-hand of the clock, praying his delay didn't cost us this period of open discourse. "Okay, shoot."

"Poopy." I leaned in close, opening my eyes as wide as they would go in an effort to embody "sincerity." "When Poopy died, did you kill him? Was that some kind of revenge on me for the Crappening?"

Ed's jaw tightened as he blushed with anger. "Hell no! First, I wouldn't do that. I don't know how you could think that; we've been friends forever, and I would never do that. Second, that would kill my chance for extra credit. Why would I sabotage myself like that?"

"I'm just saying that exploding a chicken on me damn sure looked like some kind of feud gesture."

"Well, it damn well wasn't."

I fought to hold back a smile; just because we were no longer feuding, didn't mean I couldn't enjoy his falling into my rhetorical trap.

"So would it be fair to say that this situation bears some resemblance to your interactions with the Lentils crew? You performed some innocuous action, and it got twisted all out of control, and ended up looking like some kind of bizarre revenge?"

Again, he paused; this boy just could not issue two responses in a row without falling back to regroup. This time though, as his pale face glowed bright red, I intuited that his pause was less about considering and more about choking back anger.

When his face had settled back to a sickly desert sand, he spoke. "Yes, I could see how some might conflate the two situations and draw parallels."

"Well by damn, that's what the Crappening is. I know how the situation looks; hell, in retrospect, the Crappening *would* be the best revenge against you, assuming I could keep the consequences centered on just you. The Crappening fulfilled the terms of my threatening letter to a 'T.' But I had nothing to do with it, aside from the letter. I just performed some innocuous action, and it got twisted all out of control, and ended up looking like some kind of bizarre revenge."

This time when he paused, I could see through the pupils of his eyes and watch the machinery whirring within. There were delays as the machinery was stopped, gears were swapped out, and the whole of his mental faculty was retooled to operate with this new observation. At long, long, last, ten minutes after the technical start of class, a response came out the other end of his thought processes. "I guess I can see how that might be that way, then. I don't know if... if I can accept that interpretation, not immediately, anyway, but I will certainly ponder that assertion further. Okay?"

I inclined my head. "That consideration is all I can rightly expect from you."

And then, as our conversation came to a close and all our issues were either resolved or on their way to being so, The Yog entered the classroom.

She hurried to the front of the room, taking small, mincing steps, and whirled as she reached her destination, her ropes of tight-curled hair swinging free and her glasses askew. Her face, usually a deep chestnut, was infused with enough blood to glow a cheery sienna. "Sorry, class, sorry, sorry. Um..." She blinked and adjusted her hair. "Um, if--if this ever happens again, uh, just come up and retrieve your chicks and just... just start making measurements, alright? Jo and Ed, just... mingle I guess, or play on your phones, or whatever." She let loose with a shuddering sigh.

There was a general mutter of confusion at her words.

The Yog took in a deep breath, reinflating and recomposing herself. "Whoo, okay, again, sorry I'm late. Detective Totoro stopped by just after last hour to ask some more questions, and of course I had to do my civic duty."

The Yog's eyes played over the class before stopping on me. Here it came--despite our repartee following Poopy's death, she would take whatever she had learned from the detective and rub it in, use it to humiliate me and further alienate me from my classmates.

To my great consternation and reluctant relief, she instead flashed me a dreamy smile and an exaggerated wink before urging the class forward to begin their second day's observations. As the classroom exploded with the sounds of stools scraping on tiles and lunch-hungry students stumbling forward to collect their chicks, I remained seated, mouth agape, and put all the clues in their proper order. Oh, The Yog! Doing her civic duty indeed...

CHAPTER 19
A CONFRONTATION LONG DELAYED

Saturday afternoon found me in the living room, vacuuming the carpet. More specifically, I was on my knees before the couch, bent double with my forehead touching the carpet, stretching to get at the last few dust bunnies under the far corner of the sofa.

It was while I was in this position that mom came into the room and decided to hold a conversation with me. "Hey, Jo, could you turn that off? I need to speak with you."

That's what I assume she said, anyway. Her words are speculation on my part; what she actually said was drowned out by the sound nature abhors. It was a sound not dissimilar to what my social calendar would be doing in the near future, to say nothing of my career prospects.

"Jo, turn off the vacuum!"

Still speculation. Hell, for all I know, she might not have said anything as she entered the living room. She might have walked up behind me, gulped down a lungful of air with a force to rival my cleaning instrument, and let forth with--

"JOANNA!"

I plowed headfirst into the sturdy wooden frame of the couch while the cat went careening past me. Once the stars dancing before my eyes diminished in intensity and I returned to some manner of consciousness, I scuttled away from the couch and switched off the vacuum.

The roar of the vacuum's motor died before mom again spoke. "Yeah, so, I was out in the garage, organizing all of those pinecones knocked down during your escapades last month."

I looked down at my knees and studied the thin white scars crisscrossing my skin; the incident was still fresh in my mind.

"Anyway, I got the ladder down, all ready to put the pinecones back up, when I noticed a... smell. In fact, I've been noticing a faint unpleasantness in the air recently, but it was only when I opened the attic that I got a full whiff."

I nodded, giving the impression that I was following along. In truth, I had smelled nothing in the house, pleasant or otherwise; high school had numbed me when it came to olfactory information retrieval.

"Based on recent activities in this household, I have reason to believe there may be a colony of dead rats upstairs, slowly rotting and diminishing our quality of life."

I shuddered; the one dead rat I had come into contact with had thoroughly put me off the concept of dead rats in general.

"So," mom continued, her frustration leaking through now that she was into the fourth paragraph of her explanation and I had refused to catch her drift, "I was thinking you should take a break from this and go up there to clear out any unsanitary aberrations in the local environment."

I gritted my teeth. "Ooh, yeah, there was a lot of poison up there, and by proxy probably a lot of dead rats. Unfortunately, the experiment has been placed on indefinite hiatus, so the collection of further specimens and resulting disruption of the experimental location might be scientifically unethical. Sorry."

Mom gave me her *look*. "No one forced you to quit that project. But you did. And what's the most important step of the scientific process that is *never* taught in schools?"

I sighed, unable to argue this point. "Always clean up your experiments."

"That's right. You never want your work to contaminate your environment. Now come on, I'll be in the garage anyway. Get up there and muck it out." She started to turn and leave the room.

I jumped up, wavering somewhat as I compensated for my recent head injury. "But--but I can't! That's the reason I quit the project: I can't deal with the dead bodies!"

She turned and gave me another dose of the *look*, stronger this time. "What do you suggest, then? Getting Ed out here to do it for you?"

"We could burn the house down. Move away, start fresh somewhere else. It's a buyer's market."

"Come on."

I followed mom, delving ever deeper for an argument against doing this terrible thing, but there was none. Soon I stood beneath the spindly attic ladder, looking up at the dark portal with great fear and trepidation. Perhaps I should just dig my heels in and vehemently refuse. That might alienate my parents, but after all, did I really need them? And hey, we were getting along a little bit now, and they were almost ready to concede that just maybe I possibly might not be the Mad Crapper; surely a temper tantrum wouldn't harm that. Right?

I backed away from the ladder and approached our garage's utility corner, scooping up a flashlight, broom, and several plastic sacks. Then it was back to the ladder and up into the void.

The attic was just as spooky and downright unpleasant as I remembered. As I stared into the darkness intermittently lit by the dim yellow circle of my flashlight, I was beset by the gnawing suspicion that I was not alone up here. I knew not if rats had souls, but I could find a place in my theology that allowed for the possibility.

I picked my way across the ceiling beams, trying not to fall into the drifts of insulation filling the space. From time to time, I'd come across a little brown shape and experience a moment of panicked revulsion, only to calm down once I recognized the shape as an orphaned pinecone. Then I'd cringe as the inevitable spider crawled from betwixt the spines, bat it away with my broom, and continue on.

I'd made it to the point where the trapdoor was little more than a pleasant memory and so far there were no rats, not even dead one.

That was good; perhaps the poisoned specimen that had ended up flying over Kelso Amboy stadium had been enough to send the other rats fleeing for safer locales. What poison had I used up here? I should have kept my notes... Now that I was up here, it seemed a shame to abandon the project completely. Not that The Yog would let me turn in any extra credit at this point, unless it was a project on the human reproductive system, nudge-nudge, wink-wink.

Then there was a noise. Though little more than a scrape and a crinkle, I swung my flashlight towards it, tensed and ready for action. A clump of insulation was moving. Ready to bolt at the first sign of trouble, I observed the insulation for about a minute. It continued to tremble, gently rising and falling, but there was no more extreme movement. I relaxed; it was just a draft, fiddling with the insulation. Nothing to be afraid of.

That's when the rat poked his nose out from under the fluff.

I screamed and tumbled backwards, swinging the flashlight and broom to stave off the beast.

"Jo?" mom called, her voice muffled by the ceiling.

I righted myself and trained the flashlight back on the rat. There it was, twitchy little nose still poking up over a beam. He hadn't hidden again when I yelled... weird.

I edged forward, broom held ready for swatting. The little creature writhed, churning up the insulation and squeaking piteously. Its panicked "Squeep!" reminded me of Poopy. I reached the beam nearest the creature and looked down on it. It was trying to scrabble out of the insulation, its tail trailing back into the foam, unmoving. Poor little guy was stuck...

"Squeep!" wailed the rat.

Against my better judgment, I decided to help. "Okay, little fella, you're going to be okay..." I brought my broom around and swept aside some of the insulation. More of the tail was showing now; it looked to be tangled up in some kind of cable.

As an experiment, I brought my hands near to the rat. It shied away from me, and as I brought my hands closer, it didn't appear to want a bite of my sweet, sweet, human flesh. That was a good thing. I was close enough now that I could touch the rat's tail; I did, and though it issued another shrill, "Squeep!", it made no attempt at biting.

Alright, Poopy, I thought to myself, *this one is for you. You died so this rat might live... also, so mom wouldn't find out about this thing.* I traced the length of the rat's tail back into the figurative rat's nest of cables at the bottom of the more literal rat's nest and tried to pull the tail loose. Shaking and finagling didn't help.

Perhaps I could cut this cable, assuming it wasn't something important. I felt along its length; it was warm. Okay, that issue should be raised with the folks down below in the real world. A warm cable, underneath all that insulation? Not a good thing. To make matters worse, it appeared frayed, its surface scaly and sprouting thin fibers--

Oh.

As I pulled my hands away from the tangled mass of rat-tails, a dozen or so other heads poked up from the insulation. And so I learned where all the rats in the attic had gotten to.

Shredded foam flew as the rats surged upwards in a chittering mass, spraying me with soiled insulation and-- I'm going to leave it at soiled insulation. I didn't want to think what else might be there besides soiled insulation. In fact, soiled insulation was pushing it. Hngleugh.

Through the haze of flying foam and drifting dust, I could see the rats in their entirety, above the insulation. What I had taken moments before as a rat's nest had resolved into something far worse. I stumbled back, too terrified to scream, brandishing the broom as insufficient protection against the thing before me. In my terror, I dropped the flashlight, and in its yellow oval, I could see what I now faced: twenty rats, all tangled together by their tails, swarming and writhing, chittering and squeaking. I knew what this beast was: a Rat King.

"You're an urban legend!" I cried as I knee-walked away from the horror, hoping my questing legs would find the emptiness of the trapdoor beneath me.

"What's going on up there?" mom demanded.

The swirling, writhing form of the Rat King lurched closer, and with a piteous "Squeep!" of my own I turned away, questing for the light of the trapdoor, increasing my speed though I did not yet see it. I felt resistance as numerous minuscule jaws clamped over the tip of my slipper. I persisted, dragging the beast, crying out as it worried at my footwear, shaking my whole leg. All told, the gestalt Rat King weighed a good forty pounds. At last, my foot slipped from the slipper, and I shot forward. "You're an urban legend!" I yelled again.

There, in the distance: a rectangle of faint light, the warm glow of safety. It was too far away; already I could hear the scrabbling of four hundred tiny claws on the beam behind me. There was no choice then but to turn and face my nemesis, to take the monstrosity head-on.

I turned, broom held at the ready like a sword set to fell a beast most foul. Light from the trapdoor glinted from twenty pairs of eyes and outlined the form of the Rat King as it collected itself and leaped at me. WHAP! I struck the beast a mighty blow with the broom, sending the creature flying away like a not-specifically-branded flying disk.

"What the hell is going on up there?"

It came at me again, zig-zagging drunkenly as the twenty rats each tried to forge their own path. WHAP! It squealed monstrously--not at all in an appealing manner--and began to revolve as some of its constituent rats tried to run. WHAP! That did it. Enough rats now thought it a good idea to leave me alone that the Rat King surged into the outer darkness, two or three brave and/or deranged rats forming a butt that nipped at me as the greater conglomeration disappeared into the void.

"Jo!"

I made my way back to the trapdoor, dropping first the broom and then myself to safety.

Mom was staring at me, incredulous. "Just what in the holy hells were you doing up there? Look at you! Have you been rolling in the insulation? And where're your slippers? And what's that smell?"

"Don't worry about the smell mother. The rats are gone now. I don't think we'll have to deal with an infestation ever again."

With that, I returned to my vacuuming, my mother still staring after me. From above, I heard the muffled sound of something gigantic trying to squeeze its way out of our attic by any means possible.

CHAPTER 20
GOOD PAYOFF FROM BAD INVESTMENT

Monday's science class began with The Yog pausing near the unused bench as she entered the room. "If you see Detective Totoro around today," she whispered to me in a conspiratorial tone, "he's not here for you." She continued to the front of the class, humming a tune that I recognized as "Girl, Got Them Overalls Half-Off" by Bluker's Creek. I shuddered at the resulting mental image.

Class began, and I perforce tuned out. While other students were busy measuring chickens or learning or whatever it was they did at this time, I took the opportunity to dig into my book bag for a little light reading. I pulled out a thick legal document, festooned with brightly colored sticky-arrows, and flipped through the legal-length pages, the words of the document even more incomprehensible than those spoken by The Yog.

My parents and I had gone to visit their lawyer Friday after school, and as we three sat in the cozy, wood-paneled office, the lawyer explained that, in simple layman's terms, I was screwed. As had long been suspected, the evidence on hand was damning, and all the prosecutor had to do was lay on a bit of innuendo to sink me. However, despite my own thoughts on the matter, it seemed the prosecutor wasn't entirely without heart. Seeing as how this was my first offense and that I had not in fact killed anyone, he was willing to offer a plea bargain settlement. That settlement had passed from prosecutor to defender to parents to me, and now here I sat, squinting at the thickly-worded minutiae, trying to decide if accepting this was a sucker's bet.

The gist of it was that I plead guilty to being the Mad Crapper and headed off the whole dragged-out trial business; in exchange, the charges would be reduced from felony mischief and practicing pharmacology without a license to reckless endangerment and possession of controlled substances. The resulting sentence: six months' probation, and two semesters at the county reform school. As my parents' lawyer delighted in telling us, this meant no felony charges, and thus no life-long black marks. Further, since I was charged as a minor, all my criminal record would be expunged upon my majority. I could enter adulthood a free woman. Unless of course anyone remembered the whole global-news coverage thing, in which case I could sue for discrimination should the issue cost me a job. Great.

I'll admit, I was willing to consider signing the thing. As my parents' lawyer delighted in telling us, this was the best deal I was likely to get, and would save me a lot of heartache in the long run. The fact that he refused to acknowledge the possibility of my innocence was a bit of a bummer, but the situation *did* look dire. And really, the deal wasn't bad. Six months' probation I could handle just fine. The year at the reform school, though, that was going to be a bit more painful. Being away from my friends-- hell, being away from any sense of familiarity for eight to ten hours a day--was going to be rough. And being around the other rough kids there... Sure, *I* was an innocent sent there by a miscarriage of justice, but it seemed unwise to assume that everyone else there was in the same boat as me. Still, I could make it a year, if I had to, maybe take--shudder--summer school and still graduate on time. It was doable, it was all doable.

But.

But I was innocent, dammit. It did so irk me to throw in the towel and bargain my way to a compromised level of guilt. Not only would I be accepting the punishment for a crime I didn't commit, but the real Mad Crapper would get away, scot free. I wondered idly if the Mad Crapper was really that bastard from math class, Scott Phree, then remembered he had been at an out-of-state funeral during the Jamboree.

But.

But I had no chance of proving my innocence in a court of law, and then I would be sentenced according to the original charges. The prosecutor had been firm on that much: once the trial started, I could kiss the bargain goodbye.

But.

But did I actually have to prove my innocence? Assuming I actually understood case law, I didn't have to prove that I was innocent, merely that I was not guilty. If I could convince the jury that there was a reasonable doubt that I was the Mad Crapper, I'd be off the hook. Yes, they could prove animosity towards Edgar. Yes, I threatened him, and my locker was near to where the Gelfelax was found, and yes there was the nature of my science project, but there was no way I could have physically put the Gelfelax into the brownies. To do so would require access to the brownies, and that was only available at two possible times: in the school kitchen immediately before the bake sale, or in the kitchen of one of the band members. With revenge as a possible motive, the only band member I would directly assault would be Edgar, and thanks to our falling out, he would perforce disallow me access to his kitchen. Bam, vector one, closed. As for the school kitchen, only vendors and their helpers could access them. I was neither of those, so bam, vector two closed.

This... this was good. Why hadn't I thought of this earlier? Screw that, why hadn't my parents' lawyer thought of this earlier? I needed to arrange a meeting with him as soon as possible; maybe he could pull out a deposition or a subpoena or a *habeas corpus* or whatever and get some testimony that I wasn't in the kitchen. This was doable; this was a plan of attack. By damn, this was something I could change, and by damn, I had the strength to do so!

Someone jabbed me in the ribs. I looked up to see Edgar standing alongside me.

"What?" I hissed.

"You're whistling. 'Battle Hymn of the Republic,' I think."

"Sorry, I was just... happy about something."

"Well, everyone is staring at you."

I slammed the plea-bargain down and sat straight, noticing that, indeed, everyone was starting at me.

At the front of the class, The Yog cleared her throat. "Are we done, now, Jo?"

I swept the settlement from the bench-top; it fluttered to the ground where it landed with a tremendous thud. "Yes, ma'am."

"Excellent." The Yog gave her hands two quick claps, then folded them in front of her. "All right, now that Jo's little musical interlude is done, that concludes our lesson for today. Homework is pages 348-412, then write a paragraph about the breeding habits of chickens as opposed to other barnyard fowl, due Friday." She stood serenely, arms still folded, gazing over the classroom, cutting her eyes up to the wall clock from time to time.

We students did the same.

When enough time had passed, The Yog sighed and began again. "Homework is pages 348--" The bell rang, nearly drowning out her words, and as one the class leapt from our stools and surged to the door.

"--and a paragraph comparing barnyard fowl breeding habits!" she called after us, her voice barely discernible over the din.

Out in the hall, Edgar and I made our way to the cafeteria. I'd like to think this meant we were going "together," but my inner suspicion slipped up a note informing me that we just happened to be going in the same direction.

Edgar glanced my way and raised an eyebrow. "When did this school turn into a front for the 4H? We don't even have any farmland around here."

"Well, ever since that Mennonite fella got elected President, the overall curriculum's changed a bit."

Edgar nodded. "Ah, yes, President Zadok Janzen. 'Two chickens in every pot, and a goat, too. There's nothing you can't get out of a goat.'"

"He had a surprisingly liberal technology agenda."

"Indeed."

"How was your weekend?" I asked in an effort to keep this human contact going strong.

"Well, you know, just band practice. Saturday we spent all day doing the actual music, and Sunday was marching. I've got blister on both my feet and my tongue."

"That's what she said," interjected Camacho from somewhere behind us; we ignored him.

"I just can't believe we're going to Washington, you know? We'll be there in FedEx Field, performing for literally dozens of excited marching band fans. This is the top, Jo, this is the height of the craft."

"Isn't there an international competition?"

He shrugged. "Technically, but it's not worth trying so long as the North Koreans are out there. Now those people can march... Anyway, how was your weekend?"

"Well, I battled a Rat King."

"That's an odd thing to say to someone."

Now it was my turn to shrug. "I guess this was like the final part of the project we started together. A metaphor, perhaps, for the mistakes and regrets of the past, of things unfinished that haunt me yet. And I defeated it, just as I am defeating the things within me that hold me back, that nip at my feet and drag away my slippers."

There was a groan from behind us at the mention of "nip at my feet;" we ignored it.

"But you do know that Rat Kings are mythical, right?" Edgar said.

"It's not mythical, it's an urban legend. That means it's more likely to be real. Further, out of all the possible cryptids that supposedly exist, a bundle of rats knotted together at the tail seems the most realistic."

"Still, though..." Edgar trailed off, likely because of the anger radiating from my eyes. I would not take the mocking of my greatest accomplishment lightly. "You know that sounds crazy, right?"

"I am aware of how it sounds, yes."

He quirked an eyebrow. "I don't suppose you took any notes on whether or not poison was effective on it?"

"Unfortunately, I did not."

We were headed into the stairwell down to the cafeteria when the public address system squealed. Everyone around us clasped their hands over their ears and gasped in pain.

The squealing stopped, to be replaced with recognizable human speech. "Attention, attention everybody," said either Cal or Hez. "We have an announcement to make."

Thus, presumably, the use of the announcement apparatus.

"We have identified the identity of the miscreant colloquially known as the Mad Crapper, and will be naming him--" there was a flurry of whispers from beyond the reach of the microphone--"or *her* in ten minute's time. Those of you who are interested in learning the identity of this vile villain, or who are merely looking for a bit of midday excitement, are cordially invited to the accusing parlor. Dress is casual, and light refreshments will be served."

I felt a thrill course through me--or perhaps it was pain as the PA system squealed its sign-off. Either way, I was flabbergasted. Had those two idiots really solved the crime? They had to have done; why else announce it? I could feel the plea-bargain in my book bag, weighing me down, but in that moment, it seemed to weigh nothing at all.

Edgar grabbed my arm. "What the hell is an 'accusing parlor?'"

I shook my head. "No clue. But let's go find out."

Life was returning to the students crammed into the hall around us. Those once paralyzed by the squealing of the PA system were beginning to whisper, filling the stairwell with the sounds of a dozen frantic indoor-voice discussions. I could already feel their gazes on me, the interested looks. I could also feel the anger. The anger that had filled the student body since the Jamboree had never gone away; I had just gotten used to it. In this moment, I could fell the mother of all reprisals brewing. And despite the possibility of a new suspect... well, everyone still believed I was the bad guy.

I touched the hand Edgar had around my arm. "Run."

That's when the stampede started.

Perhaps it was a good thing that Cal and Hez had waited until lunch to drop this truth bomb. With every hall jam-packed with hungry students, Ed and I had an easy time hiding amidst the crowd. On the other hand, jam-packed halls of hungry students didn't make for the most psychically sane situations. As we dodged out of that first stairwell full of anger, we attracted more pursuers, trailing a tide of pent-up rage that soon engulfed the whole school.

As Edgar and I ran back the way we came, there were screams, shouts, the sounds of fists and feet and even heads slamming into lockers. The entire student body swirled in our wake, tearing through the halls in a state of complete chaos. I for one was shocked by this display; I hadn't realized civilized lower-middle-class suburbanites were so close to the edge.

"Where the hell are we supposed to be going?" Ed bellowed as we tried not to be bowled over and trampled in the hubbub.

A hand extended from the throng and grabbed at me. I twisted, and watched as my book bag, and the plea-bargain inside, disappeared into the stampede. "Think like the freaks! Where would Cal and Hez drop the big information about who framed me?"

Edgar thought long and hard, dodging and weaving all the while. By the time he came to a conclusion, we had pulled ahead of the most hate-filled of our--okay, really, *my*--pursuers and were picking our way through a crowd of vaguely-angry seniors. We were also right around the location of my locker, and as we passed by, I saw that someone had lit it on fire. I swallowed; those two had better have a very viable suspect on their hands.

"The cafeteria?" Edgar guessed.

"Good answer! But no, I don't think so!"

"Where, then?"

"They were the ones who kept pushing the Jamboree! And when they interrogated Clarice, they worked a review of their coconut shy out of her! They're still trying to make money off that!"

"Ah!"

We were now running past the door to The Yog's classroom, and I gestured to Ed that we should duck inside. We did, slamming the door shut moments before shouts and chants of "Get the Mad Crapper!" and "Kill the bitch!" floated into the hall. It seemed the mob had caught up with us, and we had escaped just in time.

Then came different shouts from within the classroom.

"Jo! Ed!"

"Ms. Matheson! Mr. Latterndale!"

There was a commotion from behind the incubator, and out stumbled The Yog, shaking her skirt and adjusting her glasses, followed by Detective Totoro, straightening his tie and flicking a glob of lipstick from his mustache.

"Hello, children," he dissembled. "I and Brunhilde--" he looked back at The Yog--"I mean, Ms. Yogmier, were just in the middle of a discussion about, um..." he looked back at her again; she wasn't taking her eyes off of us.

"Truancy!" The Yog interjected.

"Yes, truancy, and ways that police and educators can work together to combat this destructive social ill."

"Yes, truancy," The Yog repeated, panic welling up behind her vague smile.

Ignoring my thoroughly embarrassed teacher and focusing instead on my good fortune, I lunged forward and grabbed the detective's wrist. "C'mon, you're needed in the accusing parlor."

He stumbled after me as I dragged him to the door. "The what now?"

"Did you not here the announcement?"

"Truancy!" The Yog shouted.

Edgar stood by the door, peering out through its frosted glass window. "Okay, coast is looking clear-er-ish. I think we can make it to the lobby, but we need to hurry; it's already been five minutes."

We burst out into the hall, hot on the heels of the passing stampede.

"Seriously, where are we going?" the detective reiterated, stumbling as I pulled his arm in an odd direction.

We rushed along the hall, down a flight of stairs, through a set of double doors and--

Glass enclosed a floor made up of olive-green tiles. At the far end was another set of doors. To either side were wilting ferns. Around us was... nothing. Detective Totoro retrieved his hand, adjusted his cuff, and spoke thus, "Just what the *hell* is going on?"

"Seven minutes," Edgar said, stuffing his phone back into his pocket.

Why was no one here? Even if the no one else had figured it out, at least Cal and Hez should be here...

The inner door creaked as Totoro tried to slip away from us.

"Screw it, we're going to the teachers' lounge," I said, picking the location at random. "C'mon!"

I pushed past the detective, taking back his wrist as I went. "Hey--augh!"

Behind me, I could hear Edgar clumping along; ahead of me and all around I could hear the fading sounds of the stampede. Within me, I could hear my heart beating, along with the voice of reason that said, "You know, this isn't a one-off announcement. If they're right, the guilty party will remain guilty, and you can get answers from the grapevine in, like, an hour."

We passed the entrance to the office complex, me in the lead, Totoro, cursing and spluttering, in tow, Edgar bringing up the rear. Then Edgar was crashing into Totoro, and Totoro into me as I ground to a halt, reversed, and dragged the detective kicking and screaming back to the office.

"In here!" I let go his sleeve and, based on pure autopilot momentum, he followed me as I shot past the vacant school administrator's desk, down a cramped corridor lined with mail-nooks, and towards a dingy door marked "Lounge."

I slammed into the door full-bodied and bounced off, back into Totoro, who let out an exaggerated "Oof!" Stopping to catch my breath, I heard another "Oof!" as Edgar ran into Totoro from behind.

Shaking my head to settle my hair, I took one step forward, hesitated, and gave a polite knock. Done.

The door made no sound as it opened before us. In the gloom beyond, I saw Hez, draped in a maroon smoking jacket, a fez askew amidst his voluptuous fro.

"Ah, Johanna, the very lady herself," he enthused, chortling. "Do come in, I say do." He stood aside, extending his hand in a gesture of welcome.

fluorescents back." Next up was Camacho, looking drawn and twitchy. I guessed he hadn't been doing so well since the Jamboree. By his side was Clarice, accompanied by part of the cheerleading squad, as well as half a dozen students I knew by name, but didn't really, like, *know* know: Skyler, Anyong, Ryan, etc. Lots of people with Y's in their names. Then there was Genevieve, from my French class. "*Pensez-vous vraiment que ces idiots vont vous aider?*" she asked. If all else failed and I still had to retake Science in the summer, perhaps I should go ahead and sign up for remedial French as well...

And finally, sitting next to Principal thumbs, the first person I would have seen had I scanned the other way, was Agnes. My heart swelled. This was just too perfect. In less than ten minutes, I'd be free and clear, and then there would be Agnes, ready to work out our issues, rekindle our friendship, and make plans for the Bluker's Creek concert. Assuming this whole mess hadn't screwed up my grades too badly. I wondered if I could sue for an A in Science on grounds of wrongful incrimination. Was wrongful incrimination something I could sue for? That was something to ask next time I met with my parents' lawyer.

I snagged the seat next to Agnes. In the process of sitting, I sank into the spongy springs, tumbling backwards into a never-ending vortex of stained pleather. After an eon adrift in the weightlessness of the void, I came to a stop, my knees somewhere up above my ears, and looked over to Agnes. "What's up?"

She continued staring straight ahead. "Oh, you know, not much..." I had gotten words out of her; that was a start. In no more than ten minutes, there would be an end.

Principal Thumbs leaned around Agnes' right side to speak to me. "This isn't the normal furniture," he wheezed. "It's usually very ergonomic. They said they wanted to switch it out to create a mood."

"Too true!" Cal called, taking his place at the center of the circle and rotating to acknowledge his assembled audience. "And a mood we have created. A mood of subtle darkness, of danger lurking just beyond the range of our sight, of secrets and mysteries, soon to be revealed."

"Ladies and gentlemen and esteemed elder statesmen," Hez said, taking up the thread of introduction and inclining his head to Thumbs and Totoro. "We welcome you to this, our accusing parlor, as we throw back the veil that has lain upon our school this past fortnight, and expose the identity and motivations of the one who has caused this appalling state of affairs."

"Was it Colonel Mustard in the Great Hall with the Knife?" someone asked.

There was a rustling of pleather and a groan of weary springs as everyone in the circle leaned forward to look at Camacho.

"What?" he said. "I can make more than one joke. You think you know me? You think you know everything I'm capable of?"

"How apropos of you to ask such direct questions," Cal cut in. "For those are the ones that we shall be addressing this very instant."

Camacho flushed and sunk deeper into the couch. His face seemed to droop from his skull.

No. Way. Camacho had nearly died that night. There was *no way* he could be--*would* be--the Mad Crapper.

"Witnesses put you at the scene of the crime when the event took place. Several have also quoted you as saying, 'That's what she said.' One has to wonder, does one not, just what exactly it was that she in fact said. Could it perhaps be, 'Dear Sir, You Shall Taste My Blistering Fury'?"

An accusing finger bore down upon Camacho like lightning, followed later by a thunder of gasps and a plaintive "No!" from the accused.

"Could you have, in fact, somehow seen Ms. Matheson's missive, and used it to concoct some kind of sick act of terror upon the school?"

The question hung in the air, held aloft by the squeaks of old pleather as the circle drew inward, each of us eager to hear the answer to such a damning rhetorical question. We waited, the tension mounting. After nearly a minute of silence, someone asked, "Well, could he have?"

The accusing finger was withdrawn at the same speed with which it was issued, Cal thrusting it instead towards the ceiling.

"No, he most certainly could not have! In fact, he has no motive whatsoever! Neither did he have the means nor opportunity to perform the crime. Add in the fact that he was one of the most grievously injured victims, and he works his way right out of our suspect pool!"

"Then why bring me up at all, man?" Camacho asked, justifiably miffed.

"Purely to build suspense!" answered Hez.

"Yes," his brother continued, "Suspense as we examine our other suspects. Suspects such as Clarice--" As he swung his accusing finger towards the cheerleader, she growled. That was no metaphor for an angry grunt; had I been blindfolded, I would have sworn there was a dog in the room. The finger kept swinging, ending up pointed back to the ceiling. "--who has a rock-solid alibi, and has also been eliminated from our suspect pool!

"Now, with those two out of the way, we were at an impasse. Really, *everyone* was a suspect, and basically everyone was a victim. And we could not in good conscience single out the non-victims as the only suspects, as a truly brilliant--"

"Or truly stupid," Hez added.

"--criminal would perforce partake in the nefarious baked goods, so as to place themselves above suspicion. Thus, to give ourselves *some* kind of trail to follow, we asked ourselves, 'Who would profit most from this sudden attack of the crumbly tummies?' And as we followed the money, we realized that the person who gained the most from this tradgerious event was none other than our foremost victim."

Once more, the finger swung, ponderously, like a judgment from on high. And lo, did the finger rest on the very last person I-- or anyone else--suspected.

"Edgar Latterndale."

"*Sacre bleu...*" breathed Genevieve.

"*Me*?" Edgar demanded, his tone equal parts confused, hurt, and furious.

With a flourish, Hez produced a notebook--not the one I had seen before, but an elaborate affair with buckles and texture and... lace? Was that just a diary painted to look like faux-leather? He snapped the notebook open and rifled through the pages. "Let's see now... Bus tickets for the Kelso Amboy Potoos to attend the national Sousa-League marching band finals? $5,872. Brownie sales, before customers demanded compensation for their indignities? $649.55. Amount paid by The Evening Report with Lentils the Wonder Dog to Edgar Latterndale for the exclusive rights to his story? $10,000. Bus tickets, plus supplementary uniforms, all paid for by one E. Latterndale? $8,062. Clutching victory from the jaws of defeat and showing Zwick Technical who's been keeping up with the times? Priceless. There are some things fundraising can't pay for. For everything else, there's *crime*."

Edgar jumped up to protest but, due to the poor angle of his seating, he immediately slumped back into the couch. "What the hell is this, huh? You're really trying to blame *me*? *I* was the one specifically targeted by Jo--" he glanced at me-- "by the perpetrator, and *I* was the one who sacrificed my dignity on a national level to ensure that my team got where they needed to go. Blaming *me* for this is just wrong!"

As Edgar ranted, I felt a little part of myself die. Building up tension with Camacho, that had been almost, kinda, not-quite cute. But if the best that Cal and Hez could do in their investigation was victim blaming, well... I may as well leave with Detective Totoro right now and save everybody another awkward ten minutes.

"And another thing: how the hell did you get those numbers? Lentils' people said the deal was just between us."

"Ah, and it was dear boy," Hez said. "Between you, Lentils, and the SEC. The SEC is like God; they see all, know all. It's frankly a given that any financial shenanigans would include them. And by extension, us, who requested public records pursuant to our investigation."

"Umm..." Totoro began, "actually, I'm pretty sure that you're not authorized to see those."

"Really? Well, we have them anyway, so if you would be so kind as to allow us to continue our damning...?"

The detective sighed. "Proceed."

"Thank you. Now, Mr. Latterndale, You do raise some valid points, ones which we would like to address. One: You were targeted specifically. This naturally places you above suspicion. Which, in our eyes, makes you *highly* suspicious. Two: yes, you sacrificed greatly for your team, but for that very fact, you are now being named MVP at this year's sports music banquet, and there is talk of permanently renaming the first chair tuba position in your honor. Thanks to this tragedy, you have come up aces in everyone's books."

Edgar's lip trembled. I didn't think he was on the verge of tears, but he looked to be on the verge of tears.

"However," Cal said, taking over the narrative from his brother, "Two facts stand out that serve to lessen the impact of this admittedly unforeseen plot twist. One: Neither of your parents was affected by the Gelfelax. When we interviewed them, they admitted to eating copious amounts of your brownie batter before it was cooked and taken to the school. They provided as evidence cutesy videos of them rubbing batter on their noses and then licking it off."

Everyone else in the circle cleared their throats and tried not to make eye contact with everyone else.

"This gives credence to the theory that the brownies were impregnated by Gelfelax after the fact. Now, if someone where going to spike brownies to poison a school, why would they wait to do it *at the school*, rather than in the privacy of their own home? Two: Lentils contacted *you*, not the other way around, and you actually held off on selling your story. If your goal was to profit, why not contact multiple news programs to start a bidding war? We attempted to do so--purely for research purposes--and though the story would no longer be an exclusive, the American News Network offered us a cool fifteen thou."

Edgar winced; he had now learned the importance of having a business agent.

"The evidence instead points towards a victim making the best of a bad situation. That, in our minds, eliminates you from the suspect pool."

Edgar's face went completely, perfectly serene for a moment before reddening and distorting with rage. "*Then why the hell bring all of that up?! And don't just say it was to build suspense!*"

The brothers looked at each other, eyebrows raised, then faced Edgar. "I'm terribly sorry," Cal said. "We did not mean to upset you. We are merely building our case in a logical and consistent manner, so that our conclusions may be verified and believed."

"Yes," Hez interjected, "for we have already seen what happens when one merely looks at available evidence and jumps to conclusions without logical follow-through."

Detective Totoro threw his hands in the air and shook his head.

"Right, okay," Edgar hissed through his teeth, "follow through."

"Um," Clarice intoned, raising one hand and giving a little wave. "If you're not just going to come out and tell us, can we go?"

"No!" Edgar snapped. "You get to suffer through this with the rest of us."

"Oh." Clarice leaned back, wide-eyed, appearing hyponatremiac.

"Continue."

"Yes, well..." Hez shuffled through his painted diary. "While investigating you as a possible lead, Edgar, our investigation into the finances of the Crappening led to us uncovering some... financial irregularities, shall we say. According to last year's budget, several thousand dollars were earmarked for a comprehensive update of the Kelso Amboy facilities. This update would cover, amongst other things, a new floor for the gym, a completely new HVAC system, repair of various water damages on the ground floor... the list goes on. Despite a scheduled start this summer, these reparations never got underway. As a matter of fact, all of the earmarked money seems to have gone walkabout..."

There was a nervous giggle form Agnes' other side.

"So then the Jamboree happened. Suddenly the school was flooded by lawsuits, charity donations, insurance payouts, and another gearing up for the great big overhaul. Suddenly so much money was flowing in to and out of the school that a few small irregularities were just..." Hez held up clenched fists, then opened his hands and fluttered his fingers, "...washed away."

There was a thick, phlegmy throat clearing, followed by Principal Thumbs' rasping voice. "Now... now hold on just a minute here. Hold on. Those... those can't really be considered 'irregularities.' I mean, it's not the end of the fiscal year; nothing's been reported. So long as everything's in order when the books are gone over, then no harm, no foul, right?"

"Oh, very foul," Cal said.

"Wait." Detective Totoro struggled and, after a few false surges upwards, stood. "You're saying that you two uncovered an embezzlement scheme?"

Our beloved principal laughed. "Well, I think, I think *embezzlement* is a bit of a strong word, don't you? Really, it's more of a short-term loan, based on personal recognizance--"

"This whole thing was an insurance scam?!" I blurted

Cal nodded. "Basically, yes. Fearing that he would be unable to successfully pay back and/or fudge the books enough, Principal Richard Thumbs cooked up-- "

"Heh," snorted Hez.

"--a scheme that would not only provide the funds to cover the expected construction work, but which would cause enough of a cluster-cuss that making sense of the books would become impossible!" He raised a finger in triumph, and then brought it down to proclaim damnation upon the principal. "And you, Richard Thumbs, in order to save your worthless hide, did willfully and maliciously frame Johanna Matheson for the crime!"

Thumbs lurched forward, falling from his seat and scuttling around the nasty-ass carpet on his knees. "No! I mean, Edgar came to me with the letter, and I knew it would lead to Johanna, but I didn't--"

Totoro placed his hand on the erstwhile principal's shoulder. "Mr. Thumbs, perhaps we should repair to your office, have a private chat, one Dick to another."

"That's what she said!" Camacho crowed triumphantly.

Edgar was also standing, adding his finger to the accusation. "You bastard! Do you know how much literal crap I went through because of you?! Lentils' isn't the only money I'm getting out of this! You'll be sued so hard--"

"But you wrote the recommendation for my African well-digging trip!" Clarice cried. "I trusted your integrity!"

Thumbs shook, his jowls trembling and glistening with sweat.

"Please, kids, you have to believe me. Sure, I made some bad decisions, maybe played a bit too fast and loose with the Beijing Trading Index, but I would never scam you for insurance money!" His eyes were like those of a trapped animal, looking for escape, for salt, for mercy. He would find none of the above.

Now it was my turn to leap to my feet and castigate the man. Earlier, Edgar had been on the verge of tears. I was now openly weeping, tears of rage burning as they trickled down my cheek. Forgoing the accusing finger of shame, I got right in Thumbs' face, screaming at him from six inches away, "I was going to go to jail for you! My whole life was over! No college, no career, nothing, all because you were too stupid to get a payday loan! You bastard! You absolute bloody bastard! *Prison!* Do you get it? You were going to send me to *prison*!"

As the rage and hate and bile poured out of me, I felt better. Forget acceptance; now that the real culprit had been caught, I was able to let out all the vileness that had been building up in me for the past month. It felt so good to be on the other side of the accusing finger for a change.

As the yelling and castigation continued, I seemed to separate from my body, to reach some kind of transcendental bliss. Call it Nirvana. Behind me, I could see Cal and Hez nodding knowingly, turning to face one another, slapping high-fives. Before me, kneeling on the ground, his hands clutched in a beseeching gesture, was Principal Thumbs, drifting sideways as Hinson Totoro tried to drag him to his feet. Around me where my fellow classmates, united on my side. Camacho's face was transformed into a rictus of rage, and it seemed as if he were using all his willpower not to rip out the principal's throat. Clarice was shaking her head, a look of beatific betrayal on her face, her shoulders slumped as though there was no more use in carrying the weight of the world. And Edgar, dear, damaged Edgar, who had put aside his bitterness and anger towards the Mad Crapper and tried to become my friend again. Now he too was letting out the rage that had built over the past month. He had finally found the person who had so hurt him, and he was ready to let him have it. Only one person was missing from my trance of tranquil fury--

"It was me!"

The voice was high yet throaty, as though the speaker where fighting back tears. Despite the noise--the yelling, the blubbering, the farting sound of stressed pleather--the voice reached us, and as one, we turned to see who had spoken.

Agnes stood on a couch, sunk calf-deep in the cushions, her sparkling eyes the only detail distinguishable in the shadows above the ring of lamps.

"It was me," she repeated. "I put the Gelfelax in the brownies."

The detective released the principal's shoulder. "Oh, thank God," Thumbs breathed.

"Agnes?" I asked, my own throat thick with emotion, choking off the question until it was little more than a whisper.

"It was all me, Jo. I'm so, so, sorry."

"Holy shit," breathed Genevieve without any trace of a French accent.

I don't know what happened after that. I seemed to separate from my body, to reach some kind of transcendental melancholy. Call it... call it the opposite of Nirvana.

CHAPTER 22
IT ALL COMES OUT

I sat alone in the narthex of the principal's office. Through the frosted glass of the office door, I could see blurry silhouettes gesticulating vigorously. There were Agnes' parents, standing close together, her father pointing and jabbing, her mother swinging her arms. There was also Detective Totoro, hands held wide apart, on the defensive, trying to include everyone in an aura of calm. Agnes was in there somewhere, though I couldn't identify her silhouette. Perhaps she was seated in the far corner of the room. Perhaps she had died of embarrassment. Instead of Principal Thumbs, the final visible form was that of the district superintendent, called in to oversee the whole fracas, now that Thumbs was... indisposed.

"How can you still go through with charging her when it turns out *your* principal was using the whole mess to cover embezzlement?" Agnes' mom demanded, the muffling effect of the door mitigated by sheer volume.

"While Mr. Thumbs does certainly appear to have taken advantage of the situation to overshadow the alleged embezzlement, the fact remains that your daughter maliciously infused baked goods with a mass dose of stool softeners."

"And we have an actual confession this time," Totoro reminded everyone.

"She's a minor! Anything she says is just hearsay!" Agnes' dad bellowed.

"Actually, no," Totoro replied. "I'm afraid that, should she issue an affidavit to the effect, her confession will be upheld in court."

"My hands are tied here," the superintendent said. "She's going to be expelled for the remainder of the year, and we *will* be pressing charges."

"That's--that's--" Agnes' mom spluttered before snapping, "C'mon, Agnes, we're going home."

The door swung open, and the players filed out. Agnes trailed after her parents, eyes downcast and shoulders hunched.

The superintendent followed them as far as the door before glancing my way. "Johanna? If you're ready...?" she said, indicating Thumb's erstwhile office.

I looked to her, then back to Agnes. I hated Agnes so much in that moment... but now was as good a time as any to speak to her, especially if she was going to be expelled. "Just a minute; I have to take care of something first."

I unfolded myself from the too-small visitor's chair and caught up with Agnes just as she was leaving the office complex. "Hey, Ag, you got a minute?"

She didn't say anything, but her mom nodded. "Yeah, I guess you'd better say your goodbyes now; Aggie's grounded for life starting when we get home."

Agnes trembled and stepped away from the relative safety of her parents while they left the administrative maze.

I looked back over my shoulder to the superintendent and raised an eyebrow. She threw her hands up in exasperation and ushered Totoro back into the office before closing the door with an annoyed *click!*

Now it was just me and Agnes, alone save for the muffled grunting of Cal and Hez as they refurnished the teachers' lounge. I'd planned this confrontation so thoroughly over the past week, and now all my preparation was for naught, replaced by a million and a half new things I wanted to say to Agnes: "How could you frame me, your very best friend? Why did you hang me out to dry? All things aside, getting Edgar to crap his pants was pretty funny."

I ended up settling on a simple, "The hell, Ag?"

If I had a hard time coming up with the question, she had a harder time coming up with the answer. "I tried to tell you," she began, her voice on the verge of breaking. "When they first pulled you in here, and you told me they were pinning the rap on you, I was going to confess. I figured what, maybe a little suspension? I'm a troublemaker, I can deal with that. But then when you said... when you said they were going to make this a criminal thing, I, I..." Thick, mucousy tears rolled down her face and gunked up her glasses.

"Why, Ag? Why go through all the trouble to frame me if you were just going to confess?"

For an instant she switched from dejected to indignant. "*Frame* you? Jo, I would *never*--" She sniffled and wiped her arm under her nose. Gross. "Look, maybe I should just start from the beginning, huh? The day after you stuffed the rat in the tuba, my family had Indian for dinner. That night, as I was suffering through flaming diarrhea and thinking about your note, I came up with the perfect plan: give Edgar the unholy squirts. The only problem was, I didn't know how I'd get any laxative to him. Eventually I settled on mixing it into his brownie frosting. I didn't know how much to give him to make it work, so I went a little overboard..."

"You think?"

"Well, that's the problem. I *didn't* think. I didn't think about the other people eating the brownies, I didn't think about how slipping drugs to hundreds of people might be considered a bad thing, and I didn't think about how all of this would affect *you*. I thought Ed'd have an accident, then we'd be laughing about it the next day. I never imagined so many people would be affected, or that he'd show your note to Thumbs."

That... actually made a modicum of sense. Don't attribute to Malice what could more simply be attributed to Ignorance and all that. Assuming it had all gone according to Agnes' plan, it was actually a good prank.

"But what about all the Gelfelax packages in the trashcan by my locker? There's no way that wasn't intended to frame me."

She shrugged. "It was right by my locker, too. We're just a few feet from each other."

Oh. "How'd you get that much Gelfelax, anyway?"

Another shrug. "Made up a bunch of fake names and ordered free samples."

Oh. "Doesn't that kind of thing get you a visit from the FBI?"

She scrunched her face in thought. "It really should, yes."

"Well, I guess... I guess that wraps up all the loose ends, huh? Even why Thumbs didn't want the police around the school..."

"I'm sorry, Jo," she said. "I didn't mean to... for all this to happen. Do you think, maybe... maybe you could forgive me? Can we still be friends?"

After that, there was nothing but silence. What could I say? An hour ago, I was going to tell her that I understood why she was wary of me, but that I hoped we could be friends once all this blew over. Now... honestly, I was wary of *her*. Though there was no malice behind her actions--well, malice aimed in my direction--she had hurt me. Even with my forthcoming exoneration from the superintendent, I doubted that these events would ever be behind me. To top it all off, I *knew* she was guilty. There was no trust, no friendship, no mitigating factor to come between us. She was guilty, and quite frankly, I wanted nothing more to do with her. Was that harsh? It seemed harsh.

"Well," I said, in an attempt to force a resolution, "I guess this is goodbye, then. We're probably not going to be seeing much of each other for a while." Or ever again.

A light, a glimmer, the faintest shine of hope died in her eyes. Maybe she thought that since I had been the bad guy for so long, I'd be more understanding. Oh, Agnes... I was only the bad guy because you made me be the bad guy. She sniffed, nodded, and left to find her parents.

For my part, I knocked on the principal's door and waited for it to swing open. The superintendent's strained smile greeted me. "Johanna, what a pleasant surprise. Are you ready to talk now?"

I nodded and stepped inside.

***

The news reached home before I did. My parents rushed out, mom still dressed for work, a long white coat fluttering behind her as she ran towards me. She swept me up in a bear hug, lifted me up, spun around, gasped, put me down, rubbed her lower back. She was just *so* happy that I hadn't been the Mad Crapper. And of course, she had *always* told me that Agnes was a bad influence.

The story was much the same when dad got his turn to greet me. He smothered me in his arms, telling me over and over again that he loved me, that he was so relieved I hadn't been the one who had almost killed him.

Then there were apologies. Over and over, they told me how sorry they were that they hadn't believed me, hadn't trusted me to be the good kid I had always been and instead had gone along with the official story. Mom topped everything off by declaring me free from chores until the end of the school year. Hooray.

I should have been happy with that, should have felt free to move forward in life. Part of me was, yes. But a small part, a deep, dark, personality-defining kernel, was suspicious. Maybe suspicious isn't the right word. Paranoid? Too strong. Mistrustful? Closer. Mistrustful. No matter how much my parents sang my praises, or declared their love, I knew knew knew *knew* that I couldn't really trust them again. Them, or the school system. Them, or the school system, or my classmates. Them, or the school system, or my classmates, or my friends. That left... No one, really. I had faced just about everything life could throw at me through all this, but in the end, I had come away hurt and afraid. That just... didn't seem right, somehow. Didn't I deserve a happy ending?

I wrestled with that question through the celebratory dinner and the calls from relatives wishing me well on my innocence. My parent's lawyer showed up to tell me that the District Attorney had officially thrown out the case against me. I was scot free, and Agnes... Agnes was now in the hot seat. No matter how much I told myself that she deserved it, I felt... well, guilty somehow, in addition to mistrustful. Perhaps it was because I had never really had it out with her, had never gotten to say my piece from the other side. I never got to make amends, I never got to see if I could change the situation. Maybe I still needed to change it. To change me.

By the time I begged off to sleep at around eight-thirty, I was too wound up to sleep. I tried, for maybe half an hour, then gave up. I got out of bed and, for the very first time in my life, snuck out the window. I could appreciate the irony of acting like a petulant grounded child when I had just been declared innocent of all charges, but there was somewhere I needed to go, and I preferred that my parents not find out about my journey.

I walked the three miles to Our Lady of Perpetual Gloom Catholic Church. After a few minutes' search of the premise and some experimental doorknob rattling, I identified the pastorium and gave its door a solid knock. Though it was now past ten, Father Rabinowitz was at once at the door, dressed as I had seen him last week.

"Ah, Ms. Matheson, unless I'm very much mistaken; the local celebrity." He stepped onto the stoop of his home, closing the door behind him. "I just caught a rerun of Lentils that I'm sure you'd find interesting. What seems to be troubling you tonight?"

"I didn't do it," I said simply.

"As I recall, that was your main point last time."

"It's official now, they caught the real Mad Crapper; I'm free and clear."

His face split into a broad grin, glinting orange in the light coming through his front window. "Mazel Tov! Seems everything worked out alright for you in the end."

His joyful tone caused me to flinch. This was a positive conclusion; I shouldn't feel guilty, dammit!

"So, what is it then? Being cleared of a crime one did not commit isn't a call for mourning."

I took a deep breath before launching into the whole story. I told him about apologizing to Edgar, about Cal and Hez's dramatic reveal, about Agnes confession, and, most importantly, how I had no idea how to react to it, and how I didn't really trust my parents enough to share my issues with them, and how this whole debacle had left me feeling...empty.

He was silent for a long time. "Everything I'm about to say, take with a pinch of salt, okay?" he spake at last. "I have no kids myself, so I'm not really sure what it's like being a parent, but I do deal with enough crises of faith that there may be some cross training. Here goes: there comes a point in everyone's life when they suspect their higher power may be fallible. For most people, it's realizing their parents are not gods. Now, the manner in which you discovered this fallibility was fortunate. You didn't discover a drinking problem, or stumble upon an affair. No: you found your parents are more inclined towards believing an outside authority rather than their own daughter."

I winced as his words translated themselves in my mind: "The evidence was stacked against you kid, and your parents arguably made the right choice." Just as he had done the first time I had spoken to him, Father Rabinowitz presented me with an uncomfortable truth.

"But you're not the only one who discovered their fallibility," he continued. "They did, too. The next time something comes along that strains their trust, they're going to remember this and maybe, just maybe, they'll listen a little better.

"Now, as to your other problems... I'm glad you took my advice about making amends with your first friend. Had you gone to jail, you would have had someone there for you when you got out. Maybe, then, you should extend that same courtesy to your other friend?"

"Well, the thing with my first friend--with Edgar--doesn't really translate across to Agnes, though, does it? Agnes *confessed*."

"Joanna, I'm going to ask you to view this objectively. Edgar, the victim of a crime, was in a scenario in which the perpetrator of the crime was identified, and was asking him to forgive her, and to maintain their friendship."

"But I didn't--"

"Remember what I said about your parents being more likely to believe an outside authority? Edgar had the same statements from authoritative figures, as well as evidence pointing to you as the perpetrator. As such, he operated under the presumption that you were the perpetrator. Now you're in the same position, operating under the presumption that Agnes has wronged you, and she presumably wants to extend a conciliatory hand."

I felt like I was talking in circles. It was just like before, when I was telling people I was innocent, only now everyone believed me, but didn't seem to care that someone else was guilty. "I'm not *presuming* anything--Agnes *confessed*."

"How do you know she wasn't lying?"

"What?"

"Maybe she was acting under duress. Maybe she's a compulsive confessor. I've run into my fair share of those. Who knows? All *you* know is that an authoritative figure--Agnes, in this case-- claims responsibility for the crime, and that evidence backs up her claims. With that information, the wisest course of action is to presume her guilt, just as Edgar did to you when you ironed out your issues."

Damn. That... that kind of made sense...

"Now, you're in Edgar's position. You have a friend presumed to be the Mad Crapper, and who wants to make amends. You could decide she's not worth the effort and let your friendship lapse. Or, like Edgar, you can put your differences aside and keep trying."

I huffed in frustration and glared at the ground, invisible in the shadow of the pastorium. What had I expected when I hiked out here? A pat on the back and permission to dump Agnes on her little ratfink ass guilt free?

"Or," Father Rabinowitz said, "if you're not ready to make a decision out of hand, you can consider something else."

"Like what?"

"You said Agnes was going to confess when you were first accused. That seems like something a friend would do."

"But she didn't," I said, loading as much disgust into my voice as I could. "She chickened out, and I got stuck cleaning up her mess."

"Imagine a situation in which you were going to go to prison and have your life destroyed... unless you kept your mouth shut. We humans go to great lengths to avoid uncomfortable situations. Now, what would you do if a great amount of pain were only a few seconds of silence away?"

Huh. A variant on Hanlon's Razor, substituting fear for ignorance. "That sounds an awful lot like justifying her actions

211

after the fact."

He shrugged. "Merely pointing out that they were sane, non-malicious human reactions."

"You're guilting me into reconciling."

"What is religion other than guilting people into behaving like people? 'Love one another, or go to hell.' Look, maybe I'm trying to help you do what I suspect you already want to do, but don't feel comfortable doing. Maybe helping you realize that you're battling an equally human impulse that's been haunting you for the past month or so: revenge."

There was no answer to that.

"You told me that what hurt most when Agnes found out you'd gotten in trouble was that she turned her back on you and ignored you. What would feel better than doing the exact same thing to her now that you've switched positions?"

When I had finished considering his words, I pulled a rumpled dollar bill from my pocket. "Are you still running that fundraiser?"

***

Though it was almost dark, Agnes' mom cracked open the door after only two knocks.

She stayed in the shadows, only a strand of wispy hair betraying her presence. "Hello, Johanna. What can I do for you? And why are you all wet?"

My clothes were indeed sopping wet, and I shivered as water dripped into my shoes.

It hadn't been raining, but I made sure to walk past the community center's sprinklers in an effort to crank up my pathetic-ness. The tactic had worked in the past, and I hoped it would make me seem more approachable when Agnes opened the door. That she was grounded and her mother would answer the door had not occurred to me. "Well, um, could I talk to Agnes, please?"

"I thought you two had wrapped everything up this afternoon..." There was a slight whine to her voice, a rise in pitch at the end that seemed suspiciously like suspicion.

"Well..."

212

"She's grounded, you know. That means no visitors."

Good point. I had a good point of my own to counter, but it might be a little insensitive to say it.

The door creaked as it swung open all the way, and I could see Agnes' mom fully now. There were deep bags under her eyes, and a pinched look all around the face. I had seen that look all too recently on my own mother's face. "I can already guess what you're going to say. Go ahead; get it out of your system."

"Well, she's going to be allowed visitors in prison. Isn't it a bit... I don't know...*odd* to limit her rights now moreso than the criminal justice system will?" My hoodie squelched as I shrugged. "Just a thought."

Agnes' mom leaned towards me and whispered, "After all she's put you through, you still want to talk to her?"

I shrugged again, purposefully exaggerating the movement to squeeze out more water. Methinks I may have overdone it with the poor-sad-wet-puppy-dog routine; pneumonia seemed imminent. "I've been where she's been. And honestly, I was the one who inspired her to do it. I may no longer be guilty in the eyes of the state or the school board, but... I haven't done right by my friend."

She eyed me up and down, then stepped back into the house, leaving the doorway open to me. "Agnes is in her room. Fifteen minutes and no touching. Metal detector's in the kitchen."

I stepped inside, went up the stairs, and talked with my friend.

EPILOGUE
STARTING THE SUMMER

Thanks to Agnes' confession, her case moved forward much faster than mine had. It never got to trial, though; her lawyer reached a settlement with the prosecutor, and Agnes was summarily sentenced. Her deal wasn't near as good as mine. First, there was actual prison time. She would be placed in a juvenile correction facility from sentencing until the end of the school year--all told, about a month. Second, she had to complete two thousand hours of community service--that would likely take the entire summer. Third, she would be spending two consecutive semesters in the county reform school, followed by probation until graduation. When reached for comment, Agnes admitted that it was a fair sentence for a crime in which "people almost died."

The sentence left me with no Agnes for the summer, and no Agnes at school next year. The school didn't bother me too much; we rarely spent time together in the halls of Kelso Amboy. But not having Agnes in the months ahead? That was a disappointment. Especially since, well, Bluker's Creek. What was to become of our wondrous time seeing Bluker's Creek?

That problem was solved by Agnes' mother. Because I was the one invited to the concert, and I was arguably the one most hurt by her daughter's actions, she gave the tickets to me. As school ended and Agnes was released from prison, my mom and I drove up to Chicago to enjoy a night of shallow music, screaming teenagers, and overpriced food.

I had the time of my life at that concert. Surrounded by twenty thousand screaming fans, I was one with the crowd as we basked in the presence of five sweaty young guitarists who would have no career in a decade's time. As the stage lights strobed, as the Creek wheedled on about honky-tonks and gettin' their first truck, I was able to forget all my troubles and just be a happy kid once again.

I wasn't the only one to achieve musical release as the school year ended. Edgar, and the Potoos with him, took chartered busses east to Washington, D.C., and there performed top-tier marches for literally dozens of rapt fans. In the end, the Potoos came in fourth. A little disappointing, but when reached for comment, Ed admitted it was nice to see just how high they could really go, and were proud to be defeated by honest skill rather than cheating.

Though I agreed with Edgar's sentiment, it would be hypocritical of me to leave out the fact that I only made it out of school and to the concert thanks to the power of cheating. As it turned out, Agnes wasn't the only one to reach a settlement of some kind. What with being framed by a school official to cover up graft, as well as the numerous indignities carried out against me by school officials, the superintendent was more than willing to appease me before I had the chance to sue. My parents' lawyer was adamant that I could hold out for more, but in the end, I settled for finishing the year with a B average. The lowest grade on my report card? An unearned C- in Science. Passing through the threat of lawsuit didn't seem to be the most ethical option open to me, but it wasn't something I would be bothering Father Rabinowitz about.

ABOUT THE AUTHOR(S)

Hezekiah "Hez" Bennetts is an Oklahoman author and filmmaker. Hez attended the Los Angeles Film Studies Center, where he studied... something. Returning to Oklahoma following college, he spent a wild pool party brainstorming a story based on his brother's statement,"Dear sir, you shall taste my blistering fury."

   Hez now lives just West of the Arkansas border with his wife, three dogs, and far too many cameras.

Caleb Bennetts (the idiot brother) has a Master's degree in mechanical engineering and works as a database front-end developer at an industrial vehicles after-market equipment manufacturer.

   In his free time he creates 3D video games using 2D game-design software.